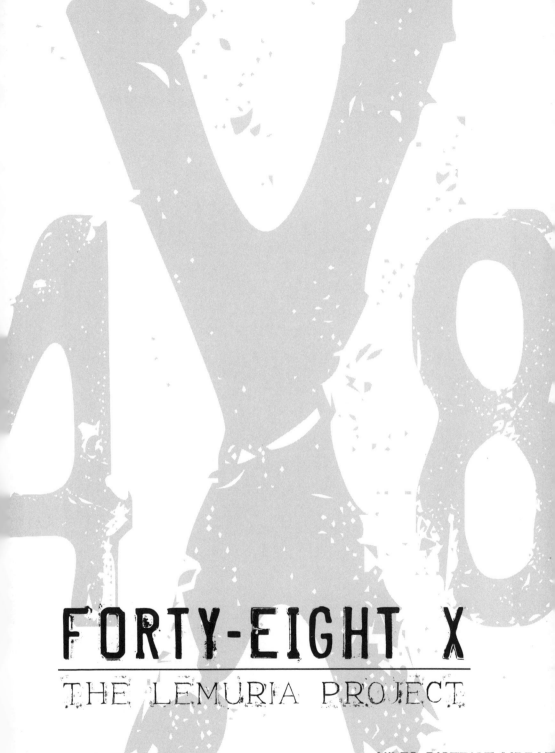

FORTY-EIGHT X

THE LEMURIA PROJECT

BARRY POLLACK

LEMURIA

BARRY POLLACK

Medallion Press, Inc.
Printed in USA

Fiction

DEDICATION:

To my wife, Margaret, who has given my tree of life roots
(and she's funny, a good cook, and a GPOA);
and my children, Emma, Joshua, and Mischa,
the branches of my life that continue to grow and give me joy
(but who still haven't cleaned out their rooms since moving out of the house)

my father, for teaching me the value of a joke and a smile
(and that sometimes you can take kibitzing to extremes)
and my mother, who taught me to endure life's struggles
(and made me at once laugh and sigh at her own)

Published 2009 by Medallion Press, Inc.

The MEDALLION PRESS LOGO
is a registered trademark of Medallion Press, Inc.

Copyright © 2009 by Barry Pollack
Cover Design by Adam Mock
Book Design by James Tampa

Printed in the United States of America
Typeset in Adobe Caslon Pro

Library of Congress Cataloging-in-Publication Data

Pollack, Barry, 1946-
  Forty-eight X : the Lemuria Project / Barry Pollack.
    p. cm.
  ISBN 978-1-934755-02-0
  1. Geneticists--Fiction. 2. Genetic engineering--Fiction. 3.
Military bases, American--British Indian Ocean Territory--Diego
Garcia--Fiction. 4. Diego Garcia (British Indian Ocean
Territory)--Fiction. I. Title.
  PS3616.O5679F67 2009
  813'.6--dc22
                            2009007476
10 9 8 7 6 5 4 3 2 1
First Edition

ACKNOWLEDGMENTS:

Helen Rosberg, for her faith and enthusiasm in a new author;
and the artistic efforts of many friends and associates
whose own turbulent struggles buoyed my own.

> *I am become Death, the destroyer of worlds.*
>
> —Robert Oppenheimer,
> watching the first atom bomb test, July 16, 1945

CHAPTER ONE

There are staccato moments that are life changing, sometimes world changing—a single step taken, a yes, a no, a signature, a nod, the swift pull of a trigger. Lawrence McGraw's life had been full of such moments. Now was to be another.

His special troops were trained to complete their assignment in eight minutes. Not a minute more. Since beginning his mission, he'd focused on time. Success was a matter of discipline, training, and precision. All had been rehearsed—a hundred, no, a thousand times. Little Boy, the first atom bomb, took less than one minute from "Bombs away" on the *Enola Gay* to its detonation over Hiroshima. One minute to change the world. Link McGraw was going to do it in eight minutes, but it would be no less momentous.

Colonel Lawrence "Link" McGraw crouched on a wooded hilltop, careful to remain unseen. Behind him, a purple hue still hung to the tops of the Hindu Kush Mountains as a setting sun buried

itself. Below him, only a few flickering kerosene lamps still illuminated a dozen mud huts in a no-man's-land village along the porous
frontier between Afghanistan and Pakistan. Smoke drifting from
the chimney of one of the houses creased the black night sky. A few
derelict vehicles lay scattered about, mechanical vegetation in a bar-
ren terrain. The night was dark, overcast, moonless. He had chosen
it that way.

McGraw wiped sweat from his brow, streaking his camouflage
paint. Thirty-six years old, he still fit the image of the steely-eyed,
ramrod-straight, invincible soldier the army liked to portray on its
recruiting posters. His forehead and cheeks were high, his nose
prominent with just a hint of an aquiline bump, and his face was
tanned and leathery but creased only at the corners of his eyes, which
made his green-eyed gaze seem ever so more piercing. He felt anxious but not fearful, though he knew the next few minutes would be
the turning point of his life. Fail here and he would die or, perhaps
worse, return to that cold ten-by-ten-foot cage at Fort Leavenworth,
Kansas, where he had been imprisoned for nearly a year. Succeed and
he would be well on the road to regaining his most prized position,
his honor. But there was far more at stake in these moments.

"We've got a chance here to change the nature of war," his commander, General Mack Shell, had admonished him. "To change the
way men have fought for millennia; to put an end to our young men
fighting and dying in war after war."

Although his troops had come to kill, they had no concept of
sin. McGraw's soldiers sat still, shoulder to shoulder in the dark confines of an M113 armored personnel carrier, gazing vacantly dead
ahead. The hot, dank air felt like a steam cooker, but there was no
grumbling, not a sound, except for their steady, almost synchronized

breathing. McGraw unlocked the rear hatch of the M113, and they quickly, silently deployed, gathering ghostlike around him, their faces swallowed in the darkness, all but the eerie glow of their eyes. He flashed four fingers on one hand and then four fingers on both hands, four and eight. *Forty-eight* was the signaled command. They obeyed immediately, readying their specially designed weapons just as he had trained them over the past several months. *Forty-eight* also stood for the unique genetic code that identified the special nature of these extraordinary troops that he was sending into battle for the first time.

An ancient stone culvert led from his position to the target, a kilometer away. One of his troops kicked at a plastic bag floating in the jetsam of the canal. Several rats scurried past, and the entire platoon gazed after them. Perhaps they just needed to be a little distracted, to feel a little calm before the storm. But McGraw still wondered if they were ready. *Forty-eight*, he signaled again, reclaiming their attention as they heard the faint snap of his fingers.

McGraw swept his palm across the head of his platoon leader as a gesture of confidence and reassurance. Then he held up one finger for a moment. With that signal, their very breath seemed to stop. He then simply pointed and his troops were gone in an instant. McGraw followed for about a hundred meters to watch their progress but, like a bomb dropped, he knew he couldn't recall them and couldn't join them, so he returned.

He illuminated his wristwatch and watched the second hand throb like his heartbeat. There was nothing left for him to do but sit and wait. He wasn't the praying type. He didn't believe in supernatural intervention, just training and more training, the right intelligence, and the right weapons. Victory in war, he knew, did not come to gods; it came to flesh-and-blood soldiers.

"The history of men at war is writ large with stories of heroes," General Shell had said before sending him off, "stories of young men who fight and often die for noble, sometimes ignoble causes. Their actions sometimes elevate them to superhuman or biblical status. They become the legend of an overmatched David defeating a Goliath; a blind and bound Samson defeating the haughty Philistines. But remember, glory is fleeting and the ends of war for survivors are most often filled with nightmares, with trinkets of ribbons and medals, and uniforms that will soon no longer fit." The general then paused fitfully. "Put an end to it, Link," he said, pressing on McGraw the firmest of handshakes.

That farewell speech reminded McGraw of his own heroes:

Sidney Coulter, Eagle Scout, valedictorian, age nineteen, died in battle, Amsar, Afghanistan.

Jaime Garza, Mexican immigrant, father of two, age twenty-four, died by RPG, Ramal.

Richard Neilson, car salesman, poker player extraordinaire, age twenty, died by IED, Baghdad.

There were plenty, too many more. Perhaps with this success, he thought, there would soon be no more.

McGraw had made one adjustment on the eve of battle that he knew his general would have frowned upon. He had given each of his troops a shot of brandy. Not enough to get drunk, but enough to slightly dull the frontal cortex that controls executive functioning, that area of the brain that breeds doubt. A little alcohol, he believed, allowed one to think more simply, to dull the noises on the periphery. He took his own swig of the red from his canteen. He, too, needed to dull his doubts.

The village he was attacking was a terrorist camp, and the men there were not novices and certainly not innocent. They were well-trained soldiers who had killed many times before. They not only professed that they were unafraid to die, but that they were eager to die for their cause.

The guard on the observation tower at the edge of the village was vigilant, but he could never have imagined an enemy so furtive. Four razor-sharp blades sliced through the back of his neck like a guillotine, severing his spinal cord just below the second vertebrae. He heard his own body loudly thump to the floor and had only a split second to be astonished at the sight of his executioner before consciousness and then life left him. The guard's death was one of the more humane that night. Others would die slower, more pain-ful mutilations from a hundred blades. Mustafa, the commander of this camp, a man who had killed dozens of men with his own hand and hundreds more by sending out "martyrs" with bombs strapped to their chests, was the last to die. A dozen of his guards would die before his quarters were breached. He patiently awaited his enemy clutching a Makarov 9mm. When the American soldier leapt into his room, Mustafa put five shots into his torso. None missed. He heard them, the wet thud of bullets impacting flesh, one after the other. His attacker was not wearing body armor, yet he kept com-ing. The bullets had penetrated both lungs, and blood was pouring into and out of his chest. But even in the throes of death, McGraw's soldier had more strength than the average man. "They have the strength of ten men," McGraw had been told more than once, and he was often surprised to discover what feats their endurance and strength could accomplish.

What kind of enemy is this? Mustafa thought in the moments before the blades sliced through him. His larynx was cut first so he couldn't scream out the last words he thought, *Allah! The children of Jews!*

McGraw heard only a little wailing, the brief rattle of gunfire, and then came the quiet. He eyed his watch again. The last few seconds of his timetable were clicking away. His heart filled, heavy like it was about to explode, and he bowed his head as if ready for the axe to fall. And then, after 480 seconds—eight minutes exactly—they all returned. Just as in practice, their timing was impeccable.

Like all American soldiers, they were trained to return with their dead and wounded. No man, no one left behind. There was but one casualty. They laid the body at McGraw's feet and eyed him. Their gaze was difficult to interpret. Did they want praise or consolation? It was not the time for either. McGraw simply pointed and his troops clambered aboard their truck as they had been trained to do. His job now was to withdraw quickly and quietly. Stealth was essential to his mission.

Of all the primates, the human being is the only one that cries. In fact, only one other land animal cries—the elephant. On this field of battle, there were no elephants around to grieve, and the only tear shed was Link McGraw's.

CHAPTER TWO

Joshua Krantz was fishing, well trolling to be exact, several hundred yards offshore from the picturesque walled city of Akko, the Hebrew name for the port city of Acre. He wasn't in search of fish but of history. He watched the monitors on deck as a metal detector hovered over the seafloor looking for a signal from the past. Just weeks before, he'd retrieved a rusted clump of metal not far from this same spot. Chemically washed free of debris, it had revealed two carved lilies, the crest of Louis VII of France, who had come to Akko in 1148 to save Christendom and battle the Arab hordes.

"*L'at, l'at.*" Slow, slow, he yelled, catching a glimpse of some promising shadow on the monitor.

Krantz's partner, Fala al-Shohada, who had been steering the forty-foot cabin cruiser slowly in ever-widening circles, surveying the seafloor, throttled back.

"*L'at, l'at. B'sedar.*" Slow, slow, all right, he hollered again in a classic undulating Israeli accent and a booming voice. If he had been wearing the nineteenth-century garb of the *shtetl*, you could imagine him belting out "Tradition! Tradition!" But today, he was shirtless, wearing only a lime-green Speedo and a chain with a gold filigree mezuzah around his neck. If you asked him, he would say the mezuzah was more a fashion statement than a religious one. Krantz considered himself one of Israel's majority, a secular Jew. It was not that he didn't believe in God; he just accepted the existence of God as the answer to how so much order had been created out of nothing. Besides, he didn't believe man was capable of understanding or describing God.

"Religion is just a man-made answer to the unanswerable," he often said. "And the Bible, well, that's just a 'good book,' a gift of the Jewish people to the world on how to view God and live a moral life. But divine revelation—no."

But inside every mezuzah rested a tiny parchment scroll, written with the words of the *shema*, the paragraph in the Bible that begins "Hear, O Israel, the LORD our God, the LORD is One." For a mezuzah to be considered "kosher," and not just jewelry, the words had to be written by a *sofrim*, a specially trained religious scribe. Krantz had paid extra to have his mezuzah "koshered." Little contradictions acted out by many secular Jews sometimes spoke more about their faith than their words.

Krantz kept his hair close cropped, a quarter-inch cut, like a marine's. He would deny it, but Fala knew it was vanity. He was balding. Nevertheless, he was still a very handsome man. In his early fifties, with chiseled features and a well-toned and tanned physique, he looked ten years younger. Only the gray hair on his chest gave away his real age. His parents had been Czech Holocaust survivors who settled in an agricultural kibbutz in Northern Galilee. He was born there in October 1956, almost seventeen years to the day from the Yom Kippur War and the momentous events that would alter his life.

His partner, in science and romance, was thirty-three-year-old Fala al-Shohada, an exotically dark and beautiful woman, once runner-up for Miss Egypt in a decade-old Miss Universe contest. She was almost as tall as Krantz, and wearing high heels she stood taller. At formal events, elegantly gowned, she never failed to turn heads. Today, she wore a flowered bikini and a baseball cap. It had a red P—for the Philadelphia Phillies—on the brim, a gift from a former professor at the University of Pennsylvania where she'd studied for her master's degree in archaeology. That's where she had met Joshua Krantz. Attracted to strong and intelligent men, he suited her perfectly. He was the man she had settled upon, and though they had some obstacles to overcome, she was comfortable that it would only be a matter of time before they would make their relationship a legal one.

Colonel Joshua Krantz, now Dr. Krantz, had received his doctorate in archaeology from the University of Pennsylvania at the same time Fala had studied there. She was his teaching assistant then, and though she was nearly twenty years his junior, they soon became lovers. In geopolitical terms, the relationship seemed doomed. She was an Egyptian, a Muslim, and a nationalist, proud of her country's ancient heritage and still on staff at the Egyptian Museum in Cairo. Krantz, on the other hand, was a *sabra*, a native-born Israeli and a former colonel in the Israeli Defense Forces, the IDF. Though they had a chemistry that seemed likely to explode, they never did. They just gave off plenty of heat.

Once a career officer, now a "scientist," Krantz had first visited Egypt on October 15, 1973, as a seventeen-year-old during the Yom

Kippur War. He followed a young major general named Ariel Sharon in Operation Stouthearted Men, the successful counterattack against the Egyptians. Israel was on the verge of defeat after the Egyptian and Syrian surprise attacks on the Yom Kippur holy day. One day Krantz was carrying a knapsack as a freshman history student at Tel Aviv University, and the next he was carrying an Uzi as part of Sharon's small force assembled to bridge a gap between the Egyptian Second and Third Armies. They ferried across the Suez Canal in inflatable boats and created a bridgehead on the Egyptian side of the canal until Israel could bring in tanks and ground troops to surround and defeat the Egyptian army. Israel's written history of the war noted that Joshua Krantz was a hero of the Chinese Farm, the irrigation project east of the canal and just north of the crossing point, where the bitterest fighting took place. In just a few weeks, Krantz went from being a fuzzy-cheeked college boy, to a sergeant in the IDF, to a captain and company commander of a hundred men, to a national hero.

But while recent history separated Joshua Krantz and Fala al-Shohada, ancient history brought them together. Besides a physical attraction, they both had an intense interest in archaeology. He was an expert on the Greek, Roman, and Byzantine empires. She fancied the Minoans, the Persians, and, of course, the dynasties of the pharaohs of Egypt. And, they were both secularists. Both disdained the fundamentalism of their countries, be it Muslim extremism, with its religious fatwas, jihads, and praise of suicidal martyrdom; or Jewish orthodoxy, with its own faithful fanatics who believed Israel's borders were mandated by the Bible and fellow Jews were deserving of stoning for violating the Sabbath. Floating beyond the breakwaters of Acre Harbor, they stayed focused on each other and the past. In the study of ancient history, the truth of past events was already known, or mostly known. Their work provided them great peace because it successfully removed them from the fury of an irrational world.

"It's a world gone mad," Joshua Krantz had said time and again, "because of beliefs in scriptures–the Torah or the Koran—written thousands of years ago by God knows who, or who knows God."

Krantz picked up his T-shirt, already soaked with sweat. He'd been using it as a towel for the last hour. They had started their work at dawn, but it was midday and the temperature was well over one hundred degrees. He wiped sweat from his brow again and listened. The engines had stopped. A problem? He looked up at the bridge to Fala for the answer. Her body glistened in the noonday sun. She was indeed beautiful. With a high forehead, thick black eyebrows, and full lips that seemed to always frame a serene smile, she bore a striking regal resemblance to those Egyptian pharaonic statues of Nefertiti—except, of course, for that damn American baseball cap. Her every movement was pleasing, Krantz thought—no, more than that, with a bikini enhancing and revealing every curve, she was seductive. How many times had they set aside their work aboard ship to enjoy each other? Was she in the mood now? Her long fingers tipped with cherry red polish were gracefully pointing toward something astern. His eyes followed.

An Israeli coastal patrol boat was fast approaching. Krantz was familiar with the boat, a U.S.-built Cyclone-class ship about 180-feet long. It had a complement of four officers and thirty enlisted crew. It was heavily armed with Stinger ground-to-air missiles, grenade launchers, four machine guns, and it was fast. It had considerable success interdicting weapons supply vessels and low-tech Palestinian terrorist attacks from the sea.

The patrol boat stood off his stern about thirty meters—standard routine—and sent a small skiff with a crew of four to board Krantz's boat. The patrol boat's .50-caliber machine guns were all manned and all pointed at him. Krantz didn't mind. They were just doing their job. The price of staying alive in Israel, a tiny island of Jews in the midst of a sea of Muslims, was persistent vigilance.

"What do they want?" Fala asked.

"Don't know," Krantz replied, stowing a bit of gear and slipping on some pants. "They probably have some intelligence that makes our boat seem suspicious. But they'll check our documents, look around a bit, and we'll get back to work. No worry."

An Israeli major, Chaim Ben-Benjamin, came aboard. The gangly, bespectacled young man, an accountant when he wasn't on active duty, was army, not navy, and, unsteady on his sea legs, wobbled a bit as the boat rolled.

"Colonel Krantz?" he queried.

"Yes."

The major saluted. Krantz lazily waved a salute back. The Israeli navy was clearly looking for something in particular—him.

"I'm not in the army, Major. I don't need a salute anymore."

"Yes, sir."

"Are we at war again?" Krantz asked, as if that was the only explanation for the Israeli military to disturb his idylls.

"No, sir."

"Would you like a drink, Major?" Fala interrupted, stepping up from belowdecks, where she'd wrapped a robe about herself and, with some residual Arab modesty with strangers, had covered her head with a scarf.

"*B'vac a shah.*" Please, the major responded.

She retrieved a bottle of water from an ice chest on deck, wiped it dry, and handed it to the officer.

"*Todah.*" Thank you, he said, and turned again to Krantz. "Colonel, you do not answer your phone. You do not listen to your radio."

"I don't have anything I want to hear. Or anyone I want to hear from."

"I've been sent to ask for your help."

"And by whom?"

The major eyed Fala with some suspicion.

"If you could come aboard, I could speak with you in private."

"I have no secrets from Fala. We're partners."

The major had orders to encourage Krantz's cooperation. If that meant being forthright, so be it.

"I am sent by *Aman*," he responded.

Krantz was taken aback. He had been a soldier, familiar with battlefield tactics and sometimes covert operations, but *Aman*—

Aman was the abbreviated name for *Agaf ha-Modi'in*, or Israeli military intelligence. It was a service independent and coequal with Israel's army, navy, and air force. It had only a few thousand personnel but provided the daily national intelligence for the prime minister and the cabinet on all Arab countries and, in fact, on all foreign risks. While Shin Bit handled domestic intelligence and the Mossad handled foreign counterterrorism, *Aman* was the service dedicated to protecting Israel from total annihilation. In the 1973 Yom Kippur War, its failures were described as key to Israel's near defeat and destruction. Since then, it had recovered its prestige and its renown.

"As to military secrets," Krantz interjected, "I have no interest and she has no interest." He made a point of emphasizing his intent to stay out of the military's business by turning his back on the major and busying himself adjusting the cables to his underwater metal detector.

"What's important is that we have an interest in you." He looked again at Fala. "Miss al-Shohada, she's an Egyptian national. Is she not?" It was a statement of fact, not a question, but Major Benjamin's tone was intimidating.

"She is," Krantz confirmed, reeled back into paying attention by the unveiled threat. "But unless we are perhaps again at war with Egypt, I believe she would do nothing to harm Israel. I would put my life on it."

But there was little need for more small talk. He knew he would go—voluntarily or involuntarily.

The patrol boat escorted them into the harbor, along the Acre seawall toward the marina.

"It must be nice," the major commented, "to live and work here. It's beautiful."

"It is," Fala agreed.

The city held meaning, as well, for their relationship. Acre was a glorious town to admire from the sea, and she'd always marveled at the majesty and history of its fortifications. It was the ancient gateway to the Holy Land—a city that had always been difficult to capture and hold. Fala smiled and wrapped her arms tightly around Joshua, a man she had captured and intended to hold.

"Did you know, Major," Fala said, easing into a teacher's role, "Akko is only mentioned once in the Old Testament?"

"Is that unusual?"

"Well," she went on, "it's such an old city, with so much history, but it's only mentioned once, in the Book of Judges."

"You know the Bible?"

"It's history, and I'm an historian," Fala replied. "In Judges," she quoted, "it says that after the death of Joshua, the children of Israel asked God: 'Who will go up for us against the Canaanites, to fight against them?' And God said, 'Judah shall go up and I will deliver the land into his hand.' But you know, Major, the Jews never drove out the inhabitants of Akko. It says that, in the Bible."

"Well, we're certainly here now," the major retorted with a serious, rebuking gaze.

"I think the point she wanted to make," Krantz cut in, "is that sometimes history is not exactly what the Bible says it is. Even with God's favor, Akko was one place where the Israelites were unable to dislodge the Canaanite inhabitants. So the Israelites and the Canaanites came to share the land together." He nodded toward the seawall they were paralleling. "That wall, while it was originally built thousands of years ago, was most recently rebuilt, after Napoleon's siege in 1800, by Pasha Al-Jezzar under the direction of his Jewish advisor Haim Farkhi. Arabs with Jewish advisors. Can any of us conceive of such a partnership today?"

"I can," Fala smiled, hugging Joshua a little tighter.

At one time the land of Israel had been peacefully shared. In their modern world gone mad, it was only their knowledge of history that allowed Joshua and Fala to hold out hope for the future.

An hour later, they found themselves sitting in the anteroom of the headquarter offices of Aman in the Hakirya district of Tel Aviv. Aman was located in one of several high-rise concrete and glass buildings that made up the Defense Ministry complex, the Kirya, Israel's equivalent of the Pentagon. Krantz had always viewed it as an eyesore because of the needle-topped sixty-story communication tower in its midst. When the new nation was first established in 1948, the Defense Ministry had located their offices in a sparsely populated area on the outskirts of Tel Aviv. Today, the heart of the city surrounded it. Although it had been nearly two decades since Krantz had occasion to enter the Kirya on "business," he walked past the walled compound frequently because it sat right across the street from the Tel Aviv Performing Arts Center and he had season tickets. While the Kirya's well-trafficked location seemed to make it a ripe target for Israel's enemies, essential business was conducted in an underground command center—"the Bor"—located six floors beneath the Defense Ministry complex in reinforced concrete offices mounted on giant springs designed to withstand a nuclear attack. The entire building could be demolished from the ground up and Israel's military would still be in business. Unfortunately, Krantz mused each time he entered the theater, while the Kirya would go on, the show would not.

Fala and Krantz had passed through three metal detectors and a hand search. Snapped to their wrists were plastic color-coded identification bands. A young receptionist wearing crisply ironed olive-green fatigues paid them no mind as she sipped on a Coke and snacked on chips between answering calls. Photos of the chain of command adorned the walls, from the prime minister to the lieutenant general currently in charge of military intelligence. An officer walked by and cast a quizzical eye at Fala. She was wearing a *hijab*, the traditional scarf-like Muslim head covering. Fala wondered if any Arab, any Egyptian, any Muslim had ever "voluntarily" set foot in this sanctum of Israeli intelligence. What secrets they must know here. Clearly it was something important they wanted from her Joshua to have consented to his demands that she be privy to any decisions he'd be asked to make. When soldiers walked by and inevitably stared at her, she lowered her head and averted her eyes and thought of a verse from the

Koran she'd memorized as a young girl.

"Believing women, they should lower their gaze and guard their modesty. They should not display their beauty. They should draw their *khumur* over their bosoms and not display their beauty except to their husbands. . . . And O ye Believers! Turn ye all together towards Allah, that ye may attain Bliss."

"We are ready," a commanding voice announced. Fala looked up. An Israeli officer was standing over them.

Krantz put his hand on Fala's arm and squeezed it reassuringly.

This is all bullshit, she thought and, as she stood up with Krantz, she flipped her *hijab* off her head and over her shoulders and marched alongside him to a nearby conference room. Modesty was for some moments. This was a moment to feel empowered.

"*Salaam Aleichem*," the *aluf*, an Israeli major general, greeted Fala as they entered.

"*Shalom*," Fala smiled in polite response.

Krantz noted the insignia on the general's uniform. He wore epaulets on his shoulders with the insignia of his rank, a fig leaf and a sword piercing an olive branch. On his sleeve he wore the symbol of the Golani Brigade, a green olive tree on a yellow background. This was the same unit in which Joshua had served, and seeing it always brought back memories of a sense of pride—and loss. As a young soldier he still remembered his indoctrination lectures.

"Green," his sergeant had explained, "symbolizes the green hills of Galilee, where our brigade first served when the nation was created. The olive tree is known for its strong roots, roots that penetrate deep and hold firm to the land. It represents how Golani will always hold firm to protect and keep this land. And the yellow background represents how far we have come. Golani took Eilat."

The Golani brigade was instrumental in capturing Israel's southernmost city, Eilat, in 1948. They were also the special forces troops responsible for the rescue of 260 hostages in the Entebbe operation in 1976. They had an unequaled reputation among the Israeli public for esprit de corps and heroism.

"Colonel—" the general began, nodding a welcome to Krantz.

Joshua Krantz was quick to interrupt. "Dr. Krantz, please. I'm no longer a soldier." He was not about to let any cameraderie he was feeling usurp his control of the moment.

Aluf Daniel "Danny" Echod, vice-commander of Aman, was not upset at being interrupted. While he was a general, he was also an Israeli and a Jew. He was used to a life of insubordination. Privates in the Israeli army had opinions and let them be known. An American general would be court-martialing soldiers right and left for what Danny Echod tolerated on a daily basis. Danny was nearly a decade younger than Krantz but came from the same mold—independent, determined, always ready with "no" as a first response, but then just as ready to accomplish the impossible.

"Doctor, do not think that your demands are met because you are so mighty. We would not have consented to your lady being here if we did not believe she could be of help in this mission we have for you."

"I have no interest in military missions."

"We have not called you here to be a soldier—but an archaeologist. You are, it seems, the most scholarly person we have in the field of military archaeology. And"—General Echod smiled toward Fala—"this is something in which I am told you, too, are expert. We want to also hire you."

"You want to hire us . . . both?" Fala responded, somewhat surprised. She was just imagining the string of curses her family would conjure if they knew she'd been offered a job by Israeli military intelligence.

"Sir, you can't afford me," Krantz responded immediately and firmly.

"Ah, your services are priceless? We are the government. We have plenty of money."

"My time is priceless. For my entire life I did what others would have me do. Now, I do only what I want."

"Five thousand shekels per day. That is quite more than your usual rate."

"As I said, my time is priceless."

"So, you want to bargain?" The general smiled toward Fala. "Six thousand."

Krantz stood up and walked to the window. It was dusk, and traffic in Tel Aviv was thickening as jobs ended and people headed home. Soon it would slow to the kind of crawl experienced during rush hour in large American cities. He remembered this land in his youth, when the roads were filled with dust and donkey carts, when it was less green but also less paved over with concrete. The skies over Israel were once ethereal blue. Now even the Holy Land had smog.

"This day is done, General. How much is my time worth, you ask? Is there a price you can pay to give me back my today and my yesterday?"

"Please. Sit." The general gestured toward a chair.

Colonel Krantz instead took Fala by the hand, raised her from her seat, and turned toward the door.

"I have no desire to sit. I have no desire to listen. I just want to go."

"I know you. The hero of the Chinese Farm. They tell stories about you."

"That was a long time ago."

"I love stories. I come from a rabbinical family, you know. But I am the first—the first of the sons in my family not to go to *yeshiva*. Instead, I spent my youth inside Megachs, Nakpadons, and Merkavas."

Krantz knew he was referring to a progression of Israeli tanks since the 1980s.

"I love stories," the former tank commander went on. "Somewhere inside me is that rabbi.

"Dr. Krantz," he began his story, paraphasing a nineteenth-century Jewish fable, "somewhere, somewhere on this earth, a Jew has died—an ordinary man, with a life of virtues and sins. After he was laid to rest and Kaddish said, he was taken to stand before the heavenly seat of judgment. There he saw the scales on which all his earthly deeds, the good and the bad, were to be weighed. His righteous advocate came with a bag of good deeds as white as snow, more fragrant than the finest perfume, and began pouring them upon the right pan of the scales. Then, his evil adversary came with a bag of sins as black as coal, as foul as offal, and began pouring them on the left pan of the scales. The scales of judgment tipped up and down until finally they stopped. A heavenly judge studied the scales carefully and announced his decision. There could be no decision. The scales were perfectly balanced. No judgment could be made. The soul could neither pass through the gates of heaven nor of hell."

The general stopped his tale, perhaps to give more meaning to its moral conclusion.

"You should know, General," Krantz interjected. "I am not a religious man. Heaven and hell and the Big Bad Wolf are all fairy tales to me."

"It is not so much a story about heaven and hell," the general responded. "Yes, it may be useful to imagine the torment of being in limbo—not being able to be chosen for your good works or your evil ones. But the horror you must imagine today is simply not even taking the time to choose. You must at least listen; then you can make your choice. After all, it takes so little to tip the scales."

The general put his hand in his pocket and retrieved something white. He sprinkled it on the table for effect. Krantz pursed his lips, then smiled and conceded to rabbinical wit. And he and Fala sat down again at the conference table.

The general nodded to his adjutant, who handed him an envelope. He opened it and pushed a photograph toward Krantz. It was a poor quality photo, clearly something taken surreptitiously in the field, possibly at great risk to the photographer. It was a photo of an unusual weapon—a small leather glove with leather laces at the wrist and, for fingers, four sharpened and curved finger scythes. Krantz perused the photo carefully. He had never seen the complete weapon before, only rusted remnants of the hammered iron finger scythes and hypothetical sketches of what it must have looked like intact. It was a remarkable find and apparently in perfect condition.

"You recognize this?" the general asked, clearly anxious for the answer.

"Yes. It's a hand scythe, a weapon believed to be used in the third century BC."

"BC? Before the Second Temple was destroyed?"

Joshua Krantz smiled. "A few hundred years before." He passed the photo to Fala, who also seemed excited to see the weapon.

"You found this in Israel?" she asked.

The general said nothing.

"This was a weapon of Iskander," she commented to Krantz, who nodded affirmatively.

"And who is Iskander?" General Echod asked.

"Iskander," Krantz explained, "is what the Arabs called Alexander—Alexander the Great. He inherited the kingdom of Macedonia when he was twenty years old," Krantz went on, giving the general a little history lesson. "With his talent for military tactics and strategy, he nearly conquered the known world in his time. But he was schooled in the arts of war by a master, a Greek teacher . . . a name you'll recognize—Aristotle. And legend has it that Aristotle designed many of the weapons Alexander used in his battles. This 'hand scythe' was one of them."

"How was it used?" the general asked.

"We can only guess."

Fala unhesitantly added her opinion. "Alexander developed the phalanx, a box formation of soldiers—a formidable military innovation at the time. The men in front carried heavy eighteen-foot spears. When they held them vertically, the wall of spears hid what was happening in the rear of the formation. When they held them forward, enemy soldiers could be killed well before they reached the body of the formation. But the spears were too heavy for the frontline soldiers to hold any other weapon. If the spear broke or was dropped, well, those soldiers were defenseless."

"Except for this," Krantz added, tapping on the photograph. "They could still fight with this hand weapon, slashing it with great effect into the bodies of their enemies."

The general sighed. He had some answers, but he had a lot more questions.

"I need to know more about this weapon, about how it was and can be used. Will you take the job?"

Krantz was still unsure he wanted to be in bed with Aman. He turned to Fala to tip his scales.

"It's not the Dead Sea Scrolls," she volunteered her opinion. "But, for a military historian and archaeologist, the battle scythe of Iskander comes close."

"I'll take the job," Krantz announced abruptly, and quickly got down to business. "Is the site secured? Because I would want to get right to this dig."

The general was now the quiet one.

"Is it in Israeli territory?" Krantz asked.

Still no answer.

"Occupied territories?" Fala asked.

Danny Echod bristled a bit. Palestinians and Arabs referred to any territory that Jews had settled as "occupied territories." He wondered what her meaning was. But he had already had this woman thoroughly screened. Of course she was an Arab and a Muslim but so were many loyal Israeli citizens. But, most importantly, he knew she was not a zealot and that satisfied him.

Almost as soon as she said it—"occupied territories"—Fala knew she had misspoke. Especially here. Surprisingly, the general patted the top of her hand reassuringly. Both she and Krantz noticed then, for the first time, that General Echod was missing two fingers on each hand. While it was just surprising to Fala, it jogged Krantz's memory.

Danny Echod—this was the man who had been captured by Hezbollah, tortured and mutilated. He was famous, not for that fact, but because he had escaped. Although the Israelis always balked at making prisoner exchanges with Arab terrorist organizations, they'd made several such trades. It was always an uneven one—hundreds of living Arab prisoners for one or two dead Israeli soldiers. The enemy had never returned an Israeli soldier alive. In fact, the only one who had ever returned alive from Hezbollah captivity was Danny Echod, and only because of a miraculous escape.

General Echod then passed several other photographs to his archaeologists. These were photos of a bloody massacre with dozens of men lying sprawled about what appeared to be a poor village. Their clothing looked Indian or Pakistani. Scattered on the ground were Kalishnakov rifles and curved swords. In the background there was a target range, with dummies dressed as American soldiers, some draped with images of the American president. This was clearly a terrorist camp.

"This weapon and the dead were all found in Peshawar Province, northwestern Pakistan," the general explained. "It appears to be a modern weapon."

"No, it's not." Krantz shook his head. "That's absurd."

"Do you have it?" Fala asked.

"The Pakistanis have it."

"It's ridiculous. Who would remake an antique weapon?" Krantz argued. "People fight with automatic weapons nowadays for godssake."

"No one here was killed by a gun. The wounds, the deaths, are all consistent with your Alexander weapon."

"Who do you suspect, then?" Krantz pressed the general. "The Americans?"

"No," Danny Echod was quick to respond. "I don't think this is their doing. As you say, they use automatic weapons. They use smart bombs. The Taliban, they're more primitive and brutal. We think this may be Taliban. But we don't know."

"Why would they kill their own?" Krantz asked, shaking his head doubtfully.

"Well," Fala ruminated, "Alexander was there. In Afghanistan.

He got as far as the borders of India. Maybe the Taliban found an archaeological site and—"

The general interrupted. "I want to know more about this business, about who can fight with such stealth and decisiveness. You and Miss al-Shohada, find me this modern Iksander." He rose to leave. His business with them was done. "I am very pleased you have chosen to be with us, Colonel."

Krantz sneered. The general had called him "Colonel" again. Clearly, he was meant to serve in the army, with a chain of command.

The general's aide whispered into his ear.

"Ah," the general nodded. "Yes. Five thousand shekels a day for the services of you . . . both."

"Six," Fala corrected.

"Yes, of course," the general smiled. And we will need receipts."

Aluf Echod extended his hand to Joshua. "We are agreed?"

Krantz looked at Fala. She nodded her final assent, and Krantz shook on it. Three fingers were enough to make a firm grip and seal the deal. When the general left, Krantz looked at his palm. It was covered in white powder, perhaps enough to tip the scales.

> *The world of reality has its limits;*
> *the world of imagination is boundless.*
> —Rousseau

CHAPTER
THREE

T he events that prompted the re-creation of Alexander the
Great's battle scythe and subsequently set in motion the quest
of Joshua Krantz and Fala al-Shohada occurred years earlier, in September 2001, just weeks after the infamous 9/11.

While it seemed that military decisions and final orders came
from within mahogany-lined conference rooms at the Pentagon, the
most momentous decision of 2001 was perhaps made at a Starbucks
on Pentagon Row. Gulping on coffees, munching on muffins, four
generals in civilian golf garb had stopped there, on their way to tee
off at the Army Navy Country Club.

General Maximillian "Mack" Shell, one of the foursome, sat at
an outdoor table at Starbucks and looked up the road. He had a clear,
though distant view of the Pentagon. There was a plume of dust over
the building. It was not leftover debris from the recent terrorist plane
crash. This time it was due to bulldozers in a rush to rebuild—to

bury the past and mask a defeat. Shell had brought along the Sunday *Washington Post*. He had read an editorial in the newspaper that morning that referenced an interesting recent event. It had caught his attention because it wasn't another rehash of the consequences of terrorism and where blame lay. It was about an African hunter, a bunch of apes, and much, much more.

The article began by describing the hunter's quarry. They were Pan troglodytes, the primate species known as chimpanzees. The hunter sought them in the Mahale Mountain Game Preserve, the most remote of Tanzania's national parks. Mahale and nearby Gombe Stream National Park were the best places in the world to get up close to Pan troglodytes—an estimated three to five thousand chimpanzees roamed there. Although both preserves were declared protected and off-limits to developers and hunters, Mahale was painfully difficult to get to. That made it perfect for the hunter because it was just as difficult to police.

Deep in the forest, the hunter would listen and follow a whooping call rippling through the air as if pausing at each tree for a different listener. As he came closer, dozens more would holler until the entire forest erupted into a crescendo of shrieks. He did not approach his prey stealthily. He didn't need to. The males scampered off as he advanced, a blur of black fur disappearing into a labyrinth of green. The females, however, lagged behind with their young, whom they carried or who held fast to their backs. They were easy targets. The hunter shot the adult females, butchered them for bush meat, and grabbed and bagged the orphaned animals that huddled by their mothers' corpses to sell on the black market as exotic pets. They were endangered and becoming more so because men like him were killing off the female population. But hunting chimpanzees was his job. It was how he fed his family. He lived in a one-room mud brick house with a corrugated metal roof in Ujiji, about ten kilometers south of Kigoma in Tanzania. This was home, too, for his wife, five small children, and a menagerie of guinea pigs and fowl that were a crawling larder.

In the week after September 11, the Ujiji man went to work again, catching his usual southbound steamer from Kigoma and disembarking at Mugambo. There he rented a small *dhow* from a fisherman friend and sailed along the shores of Lake Tanganyika four more hours to Mahale. He made his way along a familiar forest trail, an old road once gouged out by a multinational logging company, mostly overgrown now. Then the whooping began—but fiercer than he had ever heard it before. And just as suddenly, the bleating holler of chimpanzees quieted while the forest continued to boil with animal chatter and the skies clouded with flocks of starlings, sunbirds, bulbuls, and fisheagles exploding from the trees. The hunter slowed his trek. He was near his prey but something seemed amiss. He tightened a sweaty grip on his .30-06. He smelled it first, that foul, fecal odor of death. He was ever so familiar with it. When an animal dies and its anal sphincter relaxes, it lets loose its bowels. But this pungent stench embraced him and subsumed every breath he took. And then he saw—a forest floor strewn with the mutilated bodies of dozens of chimps. Standing over them, in rivulets of blood, were four adult male chimps, each about five feet tall. Their black fur glistened. Stained red with blood, they seemed to glow blue in the noonday sun. Remnants of stringy flesh hung from their mouths, stuck in their teeth. The chimps raised their heads to look at him. Their eyes were unblinking and, with lower jaws thrust out, they showed off lots of teeth. The hunter saw a viciousness he had never seen in this animal before. The sight and odor of death and the fear within him made him nauseated. He suppressed the urge to vomit but still erupted with a malodorous belch. Two more bloodied chimps came out of the bush, and they all began moving toward him. He did not raise his rifle. He just ran. But on this day, the hunted were the better hunters.

No one much mourned the death of a poacher. The local news more or less overlooked him and focused on the unusual slaughter of so many animals by their own. Game wardens had found the jungle floor littered with ears and eyes, toes and testicles. The newspapers in the largest city, Dar es Salaam, grabbed a few quotes from the local news and focused their reporting on the billion-dollar global illegal trade in wildlife, second only to narcotics in dollar value. Then, the wire services picked up the story and an editorial writer at the *Washington Post* used it to make an entirely different point. His article was entitled "Gender Politics in the Developing World." The author glanced over the hunter's death and the violence among male chimps at the African nature preserve and used the event to make a point, not about chimpanzees or animal brutality, but about how gender power would eventually alter world power. It was this commentary that sparked General Mack Shell's interest.

———————

Golf was not just a game; it was a setting for negotiations, deal making, and, for generals, laying out a plan of battle. General Shell passed the article around for his golf buddies to read.

Maximillian Shell was a poster boy of a general—square jawed, broad shouldered, with a bristly crew cut of silver hair and matinee idol good looks, tainted only by a port wine birthmark on his left cheek. As a plebe at West Point, upperclassmen had teased him and named it Sicily because it resembled the triangular-shaped island. While many called him Mack, his oldest and closest friends still incongruously called him Sissy, for Sicily. The nickname was certainly a misnomer, because among his peers, he was held in the highest respect.

Shell had begun his life as a soldier in the midst of defeat. During one week, from April 23, 1973, when Nixon declared the end of the Vietnam War, until April 30, when the last American was evacuated from the U.S. embassy in Saigon, he was a new second lieutenant in charge of covering the withdrawal. He was the last army officer on the last helicopter.

On October 23, 1983, suicide bombers exploded trucks into a Beirut high-rise barracks building. Hundreds of mostly American soldiers, members of a multinational peacekeeping force, were killed. Two days later, Lieutenant Colonel Mack Shell arrived, in the midst of Lebanon's civil war, charged with organizing a quick withdrawal.

In October 1993, an assault team of Delta Force, SEAL, and Army Rangers was ordered by President Clinton to capture a Somali warlord. In the Battle of Mogadishu, they were cut off and being slaughtered on an urban battlefield. Brigadier General Shell took charge of rescuing those men and safely evacuating all U.S. troops.

While General Shell had seen his share of victory in battle, he had seen far too many young American soldiers bloodied or maimed or shipped home in body bags, and felt mostly disappointment that the highlights of his career seemed consumed with retreats.

Shell had a deep Southern drawl and his obvious intelligence demanded respect. He had battlefield experience. He was a former commandant of the U.S. Military Academy and the current CINCPAC,

Commander-in-Chief Pacific Command. Among his peers, he was considered the most likely to succeed to chairman of the joint chiefs. When he spoke, presidents, as well as his colleagues, listened.

"This guy makes some powerful points," Shell began the discussion. "In the democratic and developed Western world, women are gaining more and more socioeconomic and political power. Women have gone beyond simple equality and now far surpass men in attending and graduating college in this country. More women than men are becoming doctors and lawyers."

"They're running for office and winning, Sissy," the general sipping the mocha latte added.

"And they're becoming a larger, more influential demographic factor in our army," General Shell went on.

There was a collective grumble.

"We're getting soft," Shell summed up the mood. "Women in politics are more loath to use military power as a political instrument. And we have to count our women in uniform as part of the whole when we measure the 'manpower' of a division. We all know that can make for a thin force."

"And there's still machismo on the battlefield," the double espresso general said. "I've seen men, sometimes at the cost of their own lives or the mission, intent on protecting their female partners."

The rest nodded their assent.

"And there are more fags we have to tolerate in the ranks, too," he added.

Shell bristled at that remark. He didn't like been bundled among bigots. While in his speech, no one would ever doubt Mack Shell's machismo, among his peers, he was perhaps the most tolerant. He had nothing against gays or women and valued their service. The only thing he couldn't tolerate was failure.

"The most important thing that's come about in the last few years," Mack continued, "is the feminization of our society and the military. This nation can no longer emotionally bear having its soldiers bloodied as in wars past. On the other hand, in the developing world, particularly with this rise of Islamic theocracies, the power of women is retreating. They're kept behind veils and mostly restrained from achieving economic, social, or political power. Men, either dictators or mullahs, rule those countries with an iron hand."

"There are places in this world, Sissy, where parents, when they discover they're having a girl, abort the fetus or outright commit infanticide," Mocha Latte injected.

"I know, I know," Shell agreed.

"And you've heard about honor killings?" Mocha Latte continued. "I've seen it. In Pakistan, I'm coming out of a meeting with my counterpart, General Jilani, and across the street, right in front of their courthouse, two men douse this woman with kerosene and set her on fire. Turns out they're her father and brother, who try to kill her because she's shamed them by marrying somebody they didn't approve of."

"In the Middle East, in Pakistan, Somalia, Indonesia, much of the Muslim world, women are viewed like commodities. They're property," Double Espresso added. "The women there, they stone them, shoot them, hack them to pieces with axes, or set them on fire, because they've brought some perceived shame on the family. A woman gets raped, it shames the family. So they kill her. A woman wants to marry somebody for love. They kill her. Wants a divorce—dead."

"The populations in those countries are becoming majority male, as well," Shell pressed his point. "And, since males are innately more aggressive, they're more malleable in becoming suicide bombers or determined soldiers."

"We've called them crazy when we've fought them," Coffee, Black No Cream, entered the conversation. "But if they were our boys, we'd be calling them heroic."

"I won't call people that are nuts 'heroic,'" Double Espresso countered. "But what's scary is that while most of these people still live with a tribal culture from the Middle Ages, they've got AKs, missiles, and fighter jets."

Shell enjoyed golf, but he was playing today, just days after September 11, to urge a momentous change.

"Boys, with fewer females to moderate their social climate," Mack Shell summed up the article, "the politics of these third-world nations is becoming more aggressive. Yet, as a society, we're becoming more feminine, soft. Their nations are crammed full of testosterone, more inclined to seek glory in victory than sanity in compromise. American men change diapers while men in the third world shoot off guns in the air for kicks. Our young boys play video games of war while kids in the Middle East play with real guns, are taught to prefer death, and are transformed into car-driving kamikazes. For godssake, we're afraid to use 'the bomb.' They're intent on getting it. And does anybody doubt they'd use it? America's character is clearly becoming more feminine. The third world, these theocracies, and most of the rest of our enemies, are becoming more masculine. What this newspaper story is asking us is this—if the nations of the world were a bunch of wild chimpanzees, how would America's more feminine chimps prevail? I think we all know the answer.

"What we need, gentlemen, is a new defense against a new enemy. America's survival can't just depend on better and better technological weapons or bigger numbers like troop strength, tanks, planes, missiles, and ships. Our destiny is ultimately gonna be shaped by biology and demographics."

Topped off with caffeine, the generals came to agree with Mack Shell's conclusions.

As the generals got ready to tee off, Mack used the Sunday newspaper to wipe some mud off his golf shoes and noticed another article he had read in the morning paper. The second article was about the latest winners of Sweden's Nobel Prizes. As usual, many were Americans. The most prominent was a geneticist from Stanford, Dr. Julius Wagner. Mack Shell had filed the name away in his head. He rarely bothered remembering trivia. But Dr. Wagner would not be trivia. The coincidence of reading these two stories was the catalyst for his grand plan.

Standing over his ball, he revealed what he had in mind all along.

"What the American army needs," General Shell said, almost preaching, "are better soldiers—soldiers bred for the battles ahead."

The others nodded their assent.

"What America needs," Shell went on, "is an army of soldiers like that bunch of crazy chimps. An army not afraid of biting the nuts off our enemies."

A few brief guffaws from his fellow generals quieted quickly. Lieutenant General Maximillian Shell wasn't smiling. He was serious. It was there, on the par-five first hole, that the plan for the Lemuria Project was first hatched with Mocha Latte, Double Espresso, and Black No Cream. Mack Shell hit his first shot straight down the fairway. Sissy would eagle this one.

> And God said, "Behold, the man has become like
> one of us, knowing good and evil. Now, lest he put
> forth his hand, and also take of the tree of life, and
> eat, and live forever. . . ." God sent him forth from
> the Garden of Eden. . . . He drove out the man.
> —Genesis 3:22–24

CHAPTER FOUR

Julius Wagner, professor of genetics with an emeritus chair at the Stanford School of Medicine, scurried out of his house in his robe and bare feet to retrieve his newspaper. His morning paper was buried in the bushes in front of his home and, as usual, it was soaked from the sprinklers. How many times had he called his delivery people and asked them to toss it on the driveway? How hard could it be to hit a wide concrete driveway? He felt a twinge of pain in his lower back as he bent over to retrieve the paper. This was just another annoyance to make his life miserable—as was arthritis, dyspepsia, and most recently, well-wishers. His seventieth birthday was approaching, and every time someone called to wish him a "Happy Birthday," he imagined them topping off their greeting with "Didn't know you were still alive." Why should he blame them? He wasn't much for keeping up with acquaintances.

There were only a handful of people in the world who he believed actually cared about him—not his fame or the influence he could wield, but him. Yet more importantly, he couldn't think of a handful of people he really cared about. There was his wife. But she was gone, having passed away from ovarian cancer earlier. That time had seen the greatest glory in his career, a Nobel Prize, and the greatest sorrow of his life. There was his daughter, Margaret, of course. He owed her a call. He didn't call her enough. She was studying for her doctorate at that "other" school on the East Coast, Princeton.

He could have arranged her acceptance into a "better" program at Stanford, but she chose Princeton to distance herself from him. It was her choice, not his. It was that distance that made them distant. But that was just a lame excuse. He was smart enough to know when he was lying, especially to himself. Even when his daughter was a child and had lived at home, they were distant. His work, not his family, had always come first. Nevertheless, he thought again, he owed her a call. There was one other person Julius Wagner cared about. It was perhaps the most honest of his relationships, but it was also the most private. He cringed when he dwelled on emotions. He hated having them. Love and hate, joy and sadness, pride and shame, they were things he couldn't measure on a graph or enter on a spreadsheet, annoying because he couldn't quantify them, study them, or control them. That's why he preferred to focus his attention on his work and why he was lazy in maintaining relationships.

Julius Wagner had a deep receding hairline with Einsteinian tufts of wild gray hair erupting from the back of his head and quite a few from his ears. He had a perpetual scowl and supposed he looked and acted like a loud, grumpy old man, even though inside he felt like a limp, seemingly spineless tabby cat. But that was okay. He still had important work to do. And the well-wishers—he'd just as soon toss most of them down a well.

The professor spread his newspaper out to dry on the rear lanai of his craftsman-style home in Palo Alto. He lived only a few blocks from his campus office. He sat down with a cup of tea, gnawed on a bagel and cream cheese, and sifted through the dry sections. He wondered why he bothered with this antiquated method of getting the news when he could easily click through the pages on his laptop. But it was Sunday morning, the skies were crystal blue, there was a cool coastal breeze, and he was surrounded by bright red bougainvillea and the sweet fragrance of oleander. The Sunday morning paper was a comforting habit, hard to undo.

Aside from the comics, the obituaries were his favorite part of the paper. The front page was always about wars, disasters, and corruption. The business section was also always the same—the market was up, the market was down—with arbitrary hypotheses as to why, written just to fill the page. The obituaries, however, were wonderful. They were full of history lessons, morality tales, and enlightenments about everything in life. A former secretary of state had passed away. He had lied for his president. An old Nigerian dictator died in exile. Decades after raping his country, he was still worth billions. And someone he knew had passed—Robert Graham. He had met the old gentleman just a few years ago at a meeting of the American Association for the Advancement of Science, an organization that Graham had founded several decades earlier.

Graham had a prominent obit, a quarter page. The photo of him, however, was one taken at least thirty years earlier; he was ninety when he died. The old man was found dead in a bathtub in a Seattle hotel room, apparently having slipped in the tub, hitting his head. *What an ignominious way for a great man to go*, Wagner thought.

Robert Graham had been a multimillionaire. He had made his fortune by inventing the first plastic eyeglass lenses in the 1950s and selling his company, Armorlite, in 1978 to 3M for $70 million. Many considered him a genius. He could have continued inventing great things, parlaying a fortune into a bigger one, or just living a good life full of comforts and opulent toys. Instead, Graham went through most of his wealth trying to bring an old idea back into favor, the science of eugenics.

Eugenics is the theory that our preeminent traits are almost entirely due to heredity. The name was coined by a multifaceted nineteenth-century British aristocrat named Francis Galton from a Greek word meaning "well born." Galton was the first to describe the distinction between "nature versus nurture." But his beliefs were shunned in his time: the fashion at the height of nineteenth-century "enlightenment" was a belief in egalitarianism, where everyone was born with equal abilities, where elegant breeding and intelligence was something that could be taught—just as poor Eliza was taught by Dr. Doolittle in George Bernard Shaw's *Pygmalion*.

Galton's belief in eugenics was fostered by his half-cousin, Charles Darwin. Darwin, whose book *The Origin of the Species* was a best seller at the time and established the new science of evolution, also wrote another book, *The Descent of Man*. It was that book that really influenced Galton. In it, Darwin wrote:

"Our medical men exert their utmost skill to save the life of everyone to the last moment. . . . Thus the weak members of civilized societies propagate their kind. No one who has attended to the breeding of domestic animals will doubt that this must be highly injurious to the race of man."

With that in mind, Galton wrote his own book in 1869 called

Hereditary Genius, which claimed that "intelligence and character" were determined by heredity and not, as was popularly believed at the time, by "environmental factors." His book was not as well received as his cousin's "evolutionary" tale. It was one thing to suggest that primitive animals could "evolve." It was entirely another to intimate that the world's masses of impoverished peasants were likely to be forever relegated to that role.

Eugenics remained an out-of-favor theory until it became popular in the United States in the early twentieth century. "Enlightened" people advocated restricting "undesirables" from immigrating to the United States and preventing the inferior members of society from tainting the "gene pool" by limiting their reproduction. The policy was given a stamp of approval by the United States Supreme Court in *Buck v. Bell* in 1927. The case involved the compulsory sterilization of Carrie Buck, a "feebleminded" woman institutionalized in Virginia, whose mother and daughter were also "feebleminded." Justice Oliver Wendell Holmes wrote the majority opinion:

"We have seen more than once that the public welfare may call upon the best citizens for their lives. It would be strange if it could not call upon those who already sap the strength of the state for these lesser sacrifices—cutting the Fallopian tubes. . . ."

This American practice ended in 1950, after states had forcibly sterilized over sixty thousand people. It ended not because of some newfound American moral propriety, but because someone else had became overly enamored with the American practice of eugenics— Adolf Hitler. Eugenics was, therefore, a theory thoroughly shunned when Robert Graham came to advocate it. But he had other ideas.

"Eugenics," Graham posed to Julius Wagner and anyone else who would listen, "has gotten a bad rap. It remains a good idea that has been carried out poorly. You should not think of eugenics as a scientific plan to rid the world of inferior people. God forbid. What a modern civilization needs is a plan to breed better people."

In 1970, Robert Graham used his wealth to create his "Repository for Germinal Choice," a sperm bank that set about collecting the specimens of geniuses for use in breeding "superior" human beings. Graham was not so arrogant as to say he could decide who was a genius. He elected to allow the Nobel Prize committee to indirectly make that choice and set about soliciting Nobel Prize winners for his "Repository."

Professor Wagner found considerable merit in Graham's plan, but the political correctness of the late twentieth century doomed it. The newspaper obituary noted that Robert Graham was bankrupt when he died. Julius Wagner wondered what would happen to Graham's sperm bank. He had a personal interest in the matter. Wagner had won the Nobel Prize in Medicine for his research on gene splicing. As a member of that elite group, he had his own "genes" stored in Graham's "Repository for Germinal Choice." But more importantly, Wagner believed in what he and Robert Graham had come to call "benevolent eugenics." He believed, as did all eugenicists, that "nature" was more important than "nurture." But that didn't mean that people had to be blessed or doomed by their genes— just that adjustments needed to be made. Dr. Wagner, like Graham, wanted to breed better humans.

Professor Wagner spent the next day on the phone making inquiries. A medical waste company had been contracted to incinerate the "genius" specimens. In a back-door transaction, Wagner purchased them. It seemed like the perfect deal. The seller was saved the expense of destroying the material and made a few thousand extra bucks in the bargain, and the buyer was someone who had a reputation to lose and could be expected to be discreet.

Dr. Wagner's purchase was handed over to him surreptitiously in a darkened movie theater in Palo Alto. When he exited into daylight, Wagner was surprised to find himself holding an old children's Winnie-the-Pooh lunch pail filled with dry ice containing sixteen tubes with less than one hundred milliliters of fluid and a few billion sperm. No one took notice. He was just another eccentric professor walking about town. The specimens were then stored in the cryogenic vaults of Stanford University's genetic research department under the nondescript acronym NOBPRIS. Only Professor Wagner needed to know it was Nobel Prize sperm. It was unusually propitious, he thought, for these unique specimens to fall into his hands at this time. After all, he was, perhaps, the only person in the world who had a truly good use for them.

In the next few days, there were other calls he would make—to his daughter and to his closest friend. They were good-byes, although neither knew it. All his usual relationships were about to end. Professor Julius Wagner had made a bargain that Robert Graham, Francis Galton, and Charles Darwin would have envied. He was about to play God. His bargain, however, was not with the red-horned, pitchfork-wielding devil. It was with the United States government, the devil we all know.

> *From time to time, the tree of liberty must be*
> *watered with the blood of tyrants and patriots.*
> —Thomas Jefferson

CHAPTER

FIVE

It was not until the morning after that first test of his special forces that Colonel McGraw realized one of their weapons had been left behind. Like other seemingly inconsequential events, this one would prove to have far-reaching consequences. And Link McGraw was all too familiar with unintended consequences.

Two years earlier he had led a convoy down the streets of Mosul. The lead vehicle was an HMMWV (M1025) or High Mobility Multipurpose Wheeled Vehicle, the colloquial Humvee. The M1025 was equipped with armor and mounted with an M2 .50-caliber machine gun. The crew was trained to scan the terrain before them. The driver kept to the middle of the road and slowly pumped the gas pedal, speeding up and slowing down as if the road was a roller coaster of hills rather than to infinity flat. Two others peered out from an open hatch in the rear.

On the side of the road, Iraqi men were doing "make work"

jobs—raking a nonexistent garden on a dirt median strip. With the recorded chant of a muezzin from the ubiquitous minarets, the "gardeners" would stop their work and take time out to lay out their carpets for afternoon prayers. The convoy watched them carefully as they rolled past, fingers on the triggers. Most of the women they passed wore black *chadors* and carried sacks of household food or supplies atop their heads. The children, caked in dust, made play with rocks and dirt, or sticks they pretended were guns. Every once in a while a collection of emaciated dogs would bark and give the convoy a brief token chase.

There was plenty of garbage on the side of the road. But small stuff, household garbage that seemed to perpetually blow in the wind. No one watching seemed concerned about the larger carcass of a dead dog lying not unexpectedly more in the middle of the road. Leave dead dogs where they lay. The sky was pale blue, without a wisp of a cloud. There was not even a hope of rain to dispel the sauna-like climate. The desert air smelled faintly of eucalyptus and lime, but nothing was in bloom. It was just a desert farmer's burn. And then in an instant, that sweet smell changed to the tearful odor of cordite.

A roadside bomb was embedded in the carcass of the dead dog. The "improvised explosive device," or IED, contained one pound of C-4, a case of nails, a corroded old 155-mm artillery shell, and a cell phone detonator. It exploded alongside the fourth truck in the convoy of two dozen vehicles and tossed it into the air like a child's toy. The truck behind it caught fire and was shredded with shrapnel. Amazingly no one was killed. Give credit to truck and body armor. Many limbs would be lost, and several of these soldiers, who with the aid of modern battlefield medicine survived horrific wounds, would die just a few decades later, still relatively young men, bound to wheelchairs, succumbing to the scars of war.

"Make time! Dismount! Dammit, make time," Lieutenant Colonel McGraw yelled as he scrambled out of his armored vehicle with the rest of his troops. "Take cover. Take cover!" The order came with crackling static over the radios of the remaining vehicles punctuated with explosions and gunfire. There was no panic in his voice. McGraw was certainly anxious, but clearly decisive and in control under fire.

Two hundred men scattered out of the remaining trucks, taking cover behind buildings and concrete dividers on either side of the road.

"We're taking mortars," his sergeant major yelled. "And . . . AKs at ten and five o'clock. We have multiple, shit . . . multiple casualties."

The decisions to make war and if so, how to make war were ultimately made by elegantly suited and beribboned uniformed men sitting in antiseptic offices in Washington. They were men with power, men with money, men who fancied themselves as "honorable" and their actions as "noble," but who were sometimes blinded by their zealotry and patriotism. Time passed. Billions were spent. Thousands died. Tens of thousands were maimed. And though the original war had come to an end, new ones were ready to be fought. And the decision makers would always need soldiers.

One such soldier was Lieutenant Colonel Lawrence (Link) McGraw, who came to sit in a ten-foot prison cell, staring at its stark walls for over a year. A fourth-generation South Carolinian, McGraw was a graduate of the Citadel, the West Point of the South, and a career soldier like his father and his father's father. He supposed that his twelve-year-old son would have chosen to become a soldier as well if he hadn't died a year earlier in a boating accident. McGraw had been on a tour of duty in Iraq. He mourned his only son but didn't return to attend the funeral. The boy was dead, and he had a responsibility to his living "brothers." In a way, his son's passing might have been a strange blessing. How hurtful it would have been for his son to discover the misfortune that had befallen his father, to hear others besmirch his most valuable possession, his honor. In just a few months, the Fates had brought him as low as any man could go. He had suffered the loss of his only son. His wife suffered that grief alone and didn't understand his explanations about "duty." What she understood was that she had married a callous, heartless bastard whose only use for an embrace was to choke the life out of an enemy. She buried her son and filed for divorce. And now, Link McGraw sat alone in a military brig—a place he had no doubt he would remain until his brown hair grew gray, his rippled belly became a paunch, his keen mind became Jell-O, or he simply became dust.

McGraw's home now was in Fort Leavenworth, Kansas, headquarters for the U.S. army's Combined Arms Center (CAC). CAC's mission was to prepare the army's leaders for war—with today's war being the "global war on terrorism." Leavenworth, however, was better known to most as the place where the army held its prisoners, those soldiers who had committed grievous crimes in the eyes of the military—thieves, murderers, rapists. Interestingly, there were no cowards held in Leavenworth. The military could not advertise that there were cowards in its ranks. Combat fatigue, shell shock, post-traumatic stress disorder, call it what you may, but there were no cowards. Such "illnesses" were crimes worthy of discharge, not prison. The men held here were, by and large, adept at killing, just sometimes the wrong people.

In his fifteen years in the army, Link McGraw had seen bullets fly in Somalia, in Bosnia, in the first Gulf War, in Afghanistan, and in Iraq. He had risen rapidly to the rank of lieutenant colonel in command of a battalion. He led mostly brave men, and he led by example. While the army advertised that it taught leadership, there was no classroom that could teach judgment under fire, decisiveness, or courage. That was something that came either with hard-fought experience or naturally. Link McGraw felt it was in his genes. He had been a colonel and had felt confident that someday he would make general. But now he had no rank. He was just prisoner #697042K.

Ironically, his father, a retired army colonel, never wanted his son to become a military man. He felt that the sense of honor the U.S. military had maintained for centuries had been betrayed in Vietnam. His father took up ministering, that other family tradition, after his military service. That role, too, probably tempered his taste for the military life and prompted his decision to keep his son out of it. So, after a conservative upbringing and education at a seminary high school in Charleston, Link's father unexpectedly sent his only son to the godless north to college, as opposed to where Link had wanted to go, the military academies of the Citadel or West Point. For two years McGraw attended the most liberal of educational palaces in America, NYU, where no rational student or professor would ever even think of becoming a soldier. Link did well there. He was orderly and disciplined, lessons learned from a military family. While the dorm rooms of his peers were covered with posters of rock stars and athletes, his wall was draped with an American flag. He was a misfit. At the end of his sophomore year, he protested a protest.

The furor of that day was called "Irangate." A civil war was raging in Nicaragua. Guerillas were trying to overthrow the Sandinistas, the Communist regime that had just come to power. The Reagan administration opposed the Communists and supported the rebels, the Contras. Congress, however, decided it didn't want to get involved in a Central American war and passed a law, the Boland Amendment, making it a crime to aid the Contras.

"While Communist governments can support Communist rebel groups around the world," McGraw lectured his peers, "we're forbidden by our own laws to support pro-American dissent. It doesn't make any sense."

Meanwhile, on the other side of the world, the United States had more woes. Americans were being held hostage in Lebanon by Islamic terrorists. Colonel Oliver North, who had links to the CIA, conjured up a scheme to solve both problems. The Israelis would supply American-made missiles to Iran. In exchange, Iran would mediate the release of American hostages held in Lebanon, and money from the sale of arms would be laundered and funneled to the Contras. The people who were involved in this intricate plan to bypass Congress—Reagan, George Bush, the Ayatollah, the Israeli prime minister, and of course Oliver North—all lied about it. The president and vice-president claimed ignorance. Only Oliver North was found guilty of lying to Congress. Link McGraw, however, respected North and what he had tried to achieve. In the midst of all the acrimony against Irangate on NYU's campus, he ardently defended the man. It didn't matter that he'd lied to Congress. McGraw made it a point to quote one statement North made to Congress that he felt was absolutely true. And with that truth, nothing else mattered to him at all.

"I haven't," Oliver North had testified, "in the twenty-three years I have been in the uniformed services of the United States of America, ever violated an order—not one."

"A soldier obeys orders," McGraw argued to his classmates. "If any blame is to be dealt out, it ought to go to the politicians who gave those orders and who make illogical and fickle foreign policy."

McGraw's peers shunned him for his views, and his professors spoke openly of him as "a bit Neanderthal." But after his sophomore year, McGraw established the decisiveness and independence he would exhibit for the rest of his life. He became his own man, not the man his father wanted him to be. He applied for a transfer. In a matter of a few weeks, he went from the towers of Manhattan to the hallowed halls of the Citadel and altered his persona overnight from a ne'er-do-well to a respected and lauded leader. What a difference a little geography makes.

His career was upward bound from the moment he swore allegiance to the Constitution of the United States and became an officer in the United States army at graduation. He knew how to carry out an order, how to accomplish a task, and more importantly, when to give credit to superiors for work he had done well. He rose more rapidly than even some West Point grads.

Lawrence McGraw's fall came three years after President George W. Bush had announced victory in Iraq. It was on the streets of Mosul in northern Iraq where he was confronted by his life-changing challenge. He was given a mission to encircle an enclave of about fifty homes suspected of harboring leftover loyalists of Saddam Hussein and sectarian religious terrorists. A "high-priority" target it was called. He knew security had been breached when his command of nearly twenty armored personnel carriers, two tanks, and 250 men was hit by two IEDs. He left a team to secure that area and handle the casualties and then moved on to carry out his primary mission. Then his troops began taking mortar and machine-gun fire from nearby rooftops.

"Stand fast," Colonel McGraw yelled into his radio. Then turning to a captain, "Lay fifty caliber into that house and bring up three platoons to take cover over there."

By rote, he quickly consolidated his command to a defensive position. The situation was improving as his troops began to lay down counterfire. Then suddenly, a dozen of his frontline men began to run. He ordered them to halt, to take cover, to return fire, to resume their positions. With those dozen men fleeing, another twenty seemed unsteady and began to retreat farther. With their backs to the enemy, more ran, and more became casualties. He again shouted orders for the leads of this retreat to take cover, but they just kept running. Then, fearless himself in the face of enemy fire, McGraw rose, stood alone in the middle of the street, a stationary target with bullets splashing at his feet, and he yelled again.

"Halt! Take cover!"

He thought they had to hear him, but fear is a deafening voice. His command was fast falling apart. McGraw carried a short-barreled M249 Para light machine gun. His finger suppressed the trigger for two seconds, and his life changed. In that time, he fired thirty rounds, the retreat halted, and two of his men lay dead by his own hand.

There was a faint and brief defense as to whether his actions had prevented a rout by hardening his men to stand and fight and had actually saved more lives. But the families of the men killed would not have their sons called cowards. And the army, as well, was loath to label any of its soldiers as cowards. So, McGraw's act was called fratricide. His leadership was described as inept. He was tried and convicted of murder, not heroism. Murder, under the Uniform Code of Military Justice, Section 918, Article 118, required a sentence of "confinement for life without eligibility for parole."

His defense attorneys performed the routine appeals, but McGraw had no hopes of clemency. Military courts, judge and jury, are appointed by the highest-ranking officer in the field. The military commander of the U.S. forces in Iraq had enough political woes on his plate. Officers permitted to go free after shooting enlisted men, regardless of the circumstances, would not play well in the media. After his court martial, McGraw's conviction underwent an automatic appeal to an intermediate court of review. That court also served on orders of the commander. He was then entitled to appeal to the U.S. Court of Appeals for the Armed Forces (CAAF), the equivalent of a federal circuit court of appeals. That court, set up by Congress, followed a more civilian rule of law. But if a military court couldn't find mitigating circumstances for an officer to shoot his own troops, was it likely a civilian court would?

While other men might have gone mad in a cell so small, with concrete walls decorated with nothing but moisture and the autographs of former residents, McGraw found solace there. He was allowed only two books at a time in his cell. No photographs. No pornography. When dusk came and with it "lights out," he closed his eyes and felt the cracks in the cement walls as if they were letters and words and poetry. Reading those cracks in the concrete walls, he believed the words came from a higher spirit than himself. Of course, he wondered, too, if this mental poetry was preserving his sanity or actually a sign of insanity.

McGraw did not cling to any false hopes for freedom. His only hope was to remain sane—for as long as possible. Then one day, he was told he would be receiving a special visitor, a superior officer, not another JAG attorney. He knew something unusual was happening when he was handed a dress uniform to put on instead of his usual orange prison coveralls. The uniform had no insignia of rank, no name on the breast, and was bare of the emblems of his achievements— his gold parachute jumper wings, his collection of marksmanship awards, and a bevy of campaign ribbons he had once proudly worn. Nevertheless, he eyed the uniform with hope and was pleased. It was a soldier's uniform, not a prisoner's.

Though he sat in that Fort Leavenworth prison box day after day, he still thought himself an infantryman, a soldier still prepared to do his duty, to die for his country. McGraw knew that wars were fought and won by infantrymen—not naval or air power, not by someone lobbing artillery over a hill or dropping bombs from miles high—but by men on the ground. And he preferred it that way.

"It's you, the individual infantryman," he had preached to his men, building their esprit de corps, "that has turned the tide in every war America fought—from Revolutionary War colonial farmer soldiers at Yorktown, to citizen soldiers in the Battle of the Bulge in World War II, to volunteer soldiers in the deserts of Afghanistan and Iraq."

McGraw dressed, set his jacket aside, and then lay in bed, waiting. He wondered if he should stay sitting on his bed when the officers entered. Did he owe them any honor, any allegiance? After all, he was, in fact, forbidden to salute. When he heard footsteps, he sat up. He slipped on the uniform jacket and eyed something he had never taken much notice of before—the buttons. The buttons on United States Army uniforms bear an eagle holding arrows and an olive branch. McGraw remembered his lessons as a cadet. The eagle faces to the right because, according to the rules of ancient heraldry, right was the side of honor. Honor . . . he was about to get it back.

> *So nigh is grandeur to our dust, so near is God to man, when*
> *Duty whispers low, "Thou must," the youth replies, "I can."*
> —Emerson

CHAPTER SIX

There were 250,000 officers in the United States military services. Lieutenant General Maximillian Shell could have chosen any of them for the special duty he had in mind. He narrowed his search to a dozen men and finally, despite the consternation of several of his associates, he chose a soldier in custody at Fort Leavenworth, Kansas, Lieutenant Colonel Lawrence McGraw, a man being held for the crime of murder.

As General Shell reviewed McGraw's record and studied his photograph, he felt he was choosing the right man—someone who had nothing to lose, but everything to gain; someone who had an allegiance to God, country, and honor that fit the fairy tale. McGraw was also a Southern boy. And that counted, too. But still Shell had a speck of doubt. That doubt would dissolve when he cast his gaze upon the man and sensed his aura. The general placed great faith on things unseen, and he had a knack for assessing character.

As a member of a select hierarchy of the army's general staff, Shell also felt some collective guilt about McGraw's situation. The man was clearly a decisive leader, and sometimes decisions in war get men killed. In another war, at another time, McGraw's actions would have drawn no punishment, and perhaps even quiet praise. To lead the troops that Shell planned to put under his command, McGraw would indeed have to be an unusual and decisive leader, someone exactly willing to put a bullet into his own men, if that's what it took to get the job done.

———————

McGraw was escorted by armed military police to an area out of the main prison compound. He was shackled, chains dangling from his wrists and ankles. Hobbling down several corridors, his metal chains clanged and echoed in the halls like effects in a horror film. He finally arrived at a conference room where two colonels awaited him.

"Take them off," one colonel ordered.

The escorts removed McGraw's shackles. The other colonel pointed for him to sit in a chair at the side of a long wood laminate table. Several moisture-beaded pitchers of ice water were set on the table. The walls were mostly bare, lined only with the standard issue photographs of the chain of command—the president, secretary of defense, secretary of the army, and chief of staff of the army. The colonels stared at him with curiosity and a bit of derision. They said nothing but wondered what their general wanted with a murderer.

When three-star Lieutenant General Mack Shell entered the room, the colonels popped to attention. And right along with them, perhaps with even more pomp, Link McGraw stood to attention as well. The general was exactly what he expected—spit and polish with a chest full of medals.

"At ease, gentlemen," General Shell ordered with a Southern accent as thick as the humidity of Fort Benning, Georgia, where he once commanded the 82nd Airborne Division. And, as he took his own seat, he looked to McGraw, who remained standing. "Be seated, Colonel."

With barely a nod, he dismissed the two other officers from the room. McGraw watched them leave like puppy dogs. A lieutenant general rated two colonels as gofers. McGraw knew General Shell by reputation. He was well respected by soldiers and politicians alike. His peers, and his men—when he was not within earshot—respectfully referred to him as Mack.

The general let his head fall to his chest, sighed heavily, closed his eyes, and set his arms out and palms up. Shell knew he was embarking on a task that would change the way of warfare and the role of warriors forever, and it weighed heavily upon him. McGraw felt a little uneasy. The general seemed to be praying—or meditating.

McGraw eyed the folder the general had in front of him. It had McGraw's name on it. However, what was most interesting about the folder was that it had red-and-white striped tape on its edges. Those markings indicated that the file was top secret. What about a convicted murderer could anyone consider top secret? Then, slowly General Shell lowered his arms, lifted his head, and turned to McGraw.

"Colonel, my name is Maximillian Shell."

He stared at McGraw. It was a bit unsettling, as if he was trying to look into his soul. Then he got to the point.

"Any excuses, son, for your actions?"

"No, sir," McGraw replied unhesitantly. "I stand by my account as before."

"This was not your first combat action."

"No, sir."

"What was different, then?"

"It's always different, sir. I've smelled blood and fire many times, and each time the smell is different."

The general was fishing, McGraw thought. But what was he fishing for?

"Any lessons learned?"

"Can't say for sure. I could have put my men a few meters off more or less, here or there. Moving faster. Maybe it would have made a difference. But retreat wasn't the right thing to do. That I knew. And I had to put a stop to that."

"And so what was the final score?" the general asked. It was a rhetorical question. He had the answer. "Five dead grunts, ten wounded; a dozen dead A-rabs; and one jailed notorious colonel."

McGraw knew he was bordering on being a wiseass but had one more thing to say. "Sir, it rained that night, too. It hadn't rained in Baghdad in two months. The rain bogged down convoys in the mud and made a few of them easy targets. I'll take the blame for that, too, if it helps us get any closer to victory."

"I believe"—the general took a moment to level his thoughts—"that you have been royally screwed. Having said that, I want you to know that there is absolutely nothing I can do to alter your sentence. But I can alter how you spend your time serving it, and I'm hoping that you are still a soldier willing to serve his country."

"You ought not have any doubts about that, sir."

The general was convinced that McGraw had the military chops to do the job. He wanted to be sure the man had the character, as well.

"How do you fill your time?" he asked.

"I read."

"Anything in particular?"

"I used to like humor—Woody Allen, Steve Martin. Now it's mysteries and historical novels. Anything that makes me think."

"*Playboy*? *Penthouse*?" the general smiled slyly.

"No, sir. They don't allow porn. But if you can get it to me, I'll read it. I still have a libido and a good hand. I may die here, but I'm not dead yet."

Where was all this going? Link wondered.

"It wouldn't have taken much lying on your part to lay this business off on the enemy."

"It would have been a lie nevertheless," McGraw quickly replied and smiled. "It would have ruined my perfect record."

"Are you religious?"

From porn to religion—what did the general have in mind?

"I believe in God but not religion. I've seen too many men die in the name of it to believe in any organized religion. And you, sir?" McGraw parried back. It was time to have a two-way conversation.

"I fake Southern Baptist," the general responded frankly. "To honor my mother. But I believe in God. I believe he gave us more potential than we've yet lived up to."

The general sat forward, quiet, intense, his fist supporting his head like Rodin's *The Thinker*. And Link sat there quietly, as well—but just for a moment before he opened up a little more. He hadn't held an intelligent conversation with anyone for nearly a year and wasn't about to let the time pass in silence. He had things worth saying.

"I do believe in reincarnation."

"Oh?" the general replied, sitting more upright, interested. "I'm disappointed."

"Why?" McGraw parried back, hoping he hadn't gone one word too far.

"Too George Patton. Old Blood and Guts had the same beliefs. Excuse me for being a skeptic, but everyone I've ever met or read about who believed in reincarnation was once someone famous—Napoleon, Caesar, Genghis Khan. Nobody was ever a garbage man."

"I don't know about that. Maybe all men don't get reincarnated. Or, maybe a former life collecting garbage is just full of memories, and odors, worth suppressing. I just know who I was."

"So, who were you?" Mack asked.

McGraw pulled off a medallion he wore around his neck. He handed it to the general, who studied it carefully. It was an ancient coin with a raised image that looked like a Roman emperor.

"Who's this? Caesar?"

"No. That's me. Ptolemy, one of Alexander the Great's generals."

"But not one of his slaves. See, nobody is ever reincarnated as a nobody."

"That may be true. But," Link began to make his point, "why would I imagine being reincarnated as a subordinate of Alexander the Great? Why not just imagine being Alexander the Great?"

"Lack of imagination, maybe."

"No, it was just who I was."

The general looked over McGraw's file again. "Says here you're Irish Catholic."

"That's who I am now."

"And did this revelation come to you after two or three bottles of Cuervo Gold?" the general quizzed cynically.

Link smiled. "It's nonsensical, I know. But some things you just know, and I know I have an attachment to this soul. I was a childhood friend of Alexander; one of his generals in the campaigns of India and Afghanistan; governor of Cyrenaica; and later, pharaoh of Egypt."

"And you believe that?"

"I do, sir."

"And, as Ptolemy, what would you say was your best attribute?"

McGraw didn't hesitate. "I was loyal."

And with that, General Shell knew he had the right man—even if he was all bullshit.

"Have you ever heard of the Manhattan Project, Colonel?" the general asked.

"The old World War II code name for the development of the atomic bomb?" McGraw quickly replied.

"Exactly."

The general went on to explain why he had come and why he had chosen McGraw. He needed a soldier who had proven leadership ability but no baggage—no lust for rank, no political connections, no family attachments, no fear, and nothing to lose. When General Shell finished explaining the duty he required of him, Colonel McGraw, the prisoner, stood, came to attention, and said simply, "Sir, I serve at your pleasure."

There was but one thing about the general's proposal that bothered McGraw, or at least his ego. Strangely, for a man who had no rank, it was the fact that he was being asked to command merely a platoon of what the general described as "very special forces." A platoon consisted of just two to four squads, perhaps twenty to forty men, and was usually commanded by a lieutenant with a senior sergeant as second in command. McGraw had been a lieutenant colonel in charge of a battalion, made up of four to six companies, with each company having three to five platoons. A battalion was the army's main combat tactical unit, with enough manpower, supplies, and administrative self-sufficiency to conduct its own independent maneuvers. A little army, if you will.

Link summoned up the courage to boost his capabilities. "Sir, I can handle the command of more than just a platoon, even if they are special forces."

"And I expect you will," the general answered. "But your command will have to evolve. First we'll crawl on all fours. Later we'll stand upright."

As soon as he had decided on McGraw as his choice, Shell thought about introducing him to Quilty, a man who had become the general's spiritual guide—his guru, sage, counselor, if you will. But that would have to take place at a later time. For now he would speak to him of Lemuria—a past and present place.

"We humans were once, eons ago, very different creatures," Mack began, speaking of the same things Quilty had spoken of to him years before. "Most scientists believe we've evolved. But there are others, like myself, who believe we once had attributes far beyond what we exhibit today. I intend to rediscover those talents and restore what we've lost."

Shell stared hard at McGraw, as if his gaze alone would convince him. "I know you will find it hard to believe," Shell went on. "But do you want to believe?"

Link McGraw was unsure of what the general meant, but he nodded his assent. Mack Shell was throwing open his prison doors. He was not about to refuse anything his angel asked.

Twenty-four hours later, McGraw found himself at a place the general had code-named Lemuria. After Leavenworth, anyplace would have seemed like paradise, but McGraw found Lemuria to be a real paradise indeed, a place where soldierly dreams come true.

> *The tragedy of scientific man is that he has found no way*
> *to guide his own discoveries to a constructive end. He*
> *has devised no weapon so terrible that he has not used*
> *it. He has guarded none so carefully that his enemies*
> *have not eventually obtained it and turned it against*
> *him. His security today and tomorrow seems to depend*
> *on building weapons which will destroy him tomorrow.*
> —Charles A. Lindbergh

CHAPTER
SEVEN

Using a Leica confocal electron microsope with resolution to one hundred nanometers, Dr. Joshua Jaymes carefully studied the dendrites of mouse neurons that had successfully morphed across a barrier of transected spinal cord tissue. This was a project he had worked on since completing his doctorate training in cellular engineering at MIT. The growth of new neurons and the regeneration of dormant neurons was his specialty. The conundrum remained to get them to perform and regenerate in special ways as opposed to haphazard ones, and in specially designated areas such as those damaged in brain or spinal cord injuries. Simple growth was not enough. What was needed was directed growth. His research had involved consideration of different triggering mechanisms—cellular pH, growth factors, enzymatic prompts, chemical and radiation stimulation—all had been tried at one time or another. His latest research, however, was bearing greater fruit as spinal cord tissue of mice whose cords had been transected was stimulated to regrow and reconnect, giving the animals some renewed ability to move paralyzed extremities. Excluding monies going for AIDS research, his was the hot project of the new century, and only a half dozen other researchers in the nation received as much NIH grant money as Jaymes. If there was a paper published on neurophysiology, his name was likely on it somewhere, as a contributor to the project or a resource to be quoted. In the tight-knit world of genetic research, he was a player. But like other researchers in his field, he held his cards close. His techniques, his results, even his missteps were kept secure until he was ready to publish. Too much was at stake. He survived on grant money, and that funding only came with results and a track record of success. He had seen too many of his peers with great potential reveal too much, too soon about their research, only to have it dismissed before it reached fruition, or stolen by better funded associates. All too often, he saw that the reward for "openness" was a job teaching undergrads in a junior college.

Joshua Jaymes was six-foot-three and morbidly obese. He had no time for exercise. His complexion matched the vanilla white walls in his windowless laboratory. His idea of recreation with his family was a movie and dinner. And most of the time he would call ahead to say he had to skip the movie and settle for dinner.

His phone rang. He had long-standing orders that none but the most urgent calls be put through during his research period. Over the years he had realized he could accomplish little if he spent his days handling mundane calls from everyone—including his wife, his children, friends, colleagues, and sycophants. His assistant had orders never to put through a call unless it was a dire emergency. As he reached for the phone, his mind raced with how to admonish her for what was likely to be a wasteful diversion.

The call was indeed to prove a diversion—one that would quickly take him away from his current work and his entire family far away from home. The call was from Dr. Julius Wagner. They had met at a conference a year earlier and chatted about the professor's break-through work on gene splicing. How does one not take a call from a Nobel Laureate? Thirty minutes later, Dr. Jaymes was sitting in the front seat of an F-15C. He had to be shoehorned into the aircraft. The pilot had clear orders to transport him, and his size wasn't going to be a good enough excuse. About an hour later, after traveling at Mach 2.5 plus, and throwing up only once, Dr. Jaymes was across the country and sitting across a table from Dr. Wagner and several uni-formed military men at a nondescript military base in the middle of a desert. His destination had not been disclosed, but by the direction and time of flight he figured the base was probably in the Arizona or Nevada desert somewhere. He mused that he was in Area 51, that infamous and secret military installation that hid top secret aircraft and maybe even the remnants of alien spaceships and spacemen.

On the same day that Professor Wagner met with Joshua Jaymes, he met five other world-renowned scientists. All were transported to him with the utmost secrecy. Employers, colleagues, family were all provided plausible but untrue stories for their departure.

Dr. Wagner's interviews were conducted like stealth attacks, quick and quiet. Should anyone refuse the offer he presented, they would be returned immediately to their homes. They were sworn to secrecy with the severest of threats and, having had their routines dis-rupted for just a few hours, they induced little suspicion from others. Over the last several months, Dr. Wagner had had several meetings like this. He was providing men who lived for science an opportunity to have unlimited resources at their disposal in a project likely to advance their careers and the knowledge of mankind in months rather than decades. Few refused.

Joshua Jaymes had just spent the last six months preparing his latest application for National Institute of Health funding. He spent as much time, if not more, preparing proposals as doing research. His current proposal for a research grant would complete an initial peer review in about a month. Another six to eight weeks would pass as the proposal was sent around the country for external peer review comments. Then, if there was consensus and if funding was still available, the application moved to a second level for review by a main advisory council. Another two months would pass. If the project was then approved, the grant funds would be awarded and checks would arrive about a year and a half after the initial process began. However, most of the time, the council would ask for revisions and the process would begin anew. Dr. Wagner was offering him a blank check for his research, a home for him and his family on an island paradise, and a hefty salary, tax free.

Every question that Jaymes had anticipated was answered affirmatively. These people had done their homework well. It all seemed too perfect. There had to be something he could ask for that would elicit a "no" response. Was there something he was missing?

"Do they have Ben and Jerry's ice cream in the stores there?" Dr. Jaymes asked. As soon as the question flew out of his mouth, he wondered how he could reel it back in. What foolishness.

But Professor Wagner pondered the question seriously and then turned to whisper to one of the army officers by his side. The officer pushed a paper and pen to Dr. Jaymes.

"What flavors would you like, Doctor?" the officer asked.

Jaymes smiled and scribbled his favorites on the paper. He was committed. Wagner smiled, too. He had another member of his team, another exquisitely trained mind, who would be exuberantly dedicated to the tasks ahead. How bizarre, Dr. Wagner thought, that the fate of an entire nation could depend on Cherry Garcia.

> *A politician — one that would circumvent God.*
> —William Shakespeare

CHAPTER
EIGHT

W e're going to move five from Commerce to Homeland," Leland Bruce offhandedly told his legislative aide, whose job was to make his boss's decisions known to the rest of Bruce's committee.

U.S. Senator Leland Bruce of Maine had been head of the Senate Appropriations Committee for five years. Bruce wrote personal checks at home for dollars and cents, but at work in his offices in the Senate's Hart Building, when he spoke in the numbers one through hundreds, everyone knew he meant billions.

Nearly three decades earlier Bruce had been a wealthy contributor to the Republican Party. He began his rise as a wiry, ugly duckling teenage computer geek with a reedy voice and the standard techie wardrobe of button-down shirts, a pocket protector full of pens, and a cheap digital Casio watch. He started out making simple gadgets in his garage and went on to create a Fortune 500 telecommunications conglomerate. He acquired a beautiful wife, celebrity friends, the requisite professional sports team, and with age and a chin implant, he actually became somewhat handsome. When the Democratic senator from his state died in a plane crash with less than one year left in his term, the Republican governor was urged by his party to appoint a Republican politician to the vacant seat. The press and the public pressured him to appoint a Democratic politician to the seat that had been held by a Democrat. To avoid the quandary, he appointed Bruce, a Republican contributor who announced that he had no political ambitions and wouldn't run for reelection. Career politicians spent millions jockeying for position in the months before the senatorial election. Political power, however, was as addictive as a narcotic. Two weeks before the filing deadline, Leland Bruce announced that he'd sold his company for nearly twenty billion dollars because he felt he could do more for the nation continuing as a U.S. senator than as an entrepreneur. Then he made several personal calls to his most likely opponents from both parties. Matter-of-factly, he told them the dirty truths he'd uncovered about their lives and the untruths he was prepared to tell as well.

"I'm prepared to spend half my fortune—ten billion dollars—to win this office," he told them.

That was more than all the campaigns had cost for every contested seat in the U.S. Senate and House of Representatives in the previous election. That was the stick he proffered. He also offered a carrot.

"Support me now," he said, "and instead of spending my fortune on ruining your good name, I'll either make you wealthy or put you in power once I'm in office—perhaps a congressional seat, a governorship, an ambassadorship. But I promise you one thing," he added. "You'll either have a loyal friend forever, or the worst of enemies."

Leland Bruce won his first election for the U.S. Senate virtually unopposed. It was the least expensive campaign run in his state in a decade. Bruce well knew that strange paradox—having obscene amounts of money often means you don't have to spend it to get what you want. In getting people to capitulate, it was like having a gun pointed at someone's head. Having the capability of pulling the trigger, most often meant you never had to.

The senator often met with administrative aides, fellow congressmen, petitioners, and foreign statesmen in his offices at the Capitol or the Hart Senate Office Building. But when he had something important to say, nay secret, he preferred talking on the run. He'd been in political life too long to trust the ears of his sycophants or the walls of his offices. His task now included funding the Lemuria Project. None of his staff and only a few of his peers knew that such a thing existed. It was a secret scientific endeavor that could change the face of war, the balance of power of nations, and do as much to preserve the United States as the preeminent world power as the atom bomb did to make it one. The costs of the project, cheap compared to most military research efforts, were buried in obtuse descriptions among the vast resources of the military's research and development budget. Only the president, a handful of congressmen, and the military elite knew of its nature. The president would keep it secret even from his most ardent and loyal supporters because he knew many would oppose it on moral grounds. And, should word of the project leak and adverse public opinion come to bear, Bruce imagined the president would be prepared to distance himself and disown it as well. Was it legal? Well, he was a U.S. senator after all. He made the laws. And anyway, he couldn't think of any senators who had actually spent any time in jail. He knew that he and his partners in this endeavor were pressing the limits of their power. He knew he was being arrogant. But sometimes, decisions to benefit your country had to be made despite the law and public opinion. Presidents were said to rule by the power of persuasion. But some of the most momentous decisions in U.S. history were accomplished by power without persuasion. Jefferson made the Louisiana Purchase unlawfully. No Congress gave Lincoln the right to free the slaves with the Emancipation Proclamation. Roosevelt put Japanese Americans in internment camps in World War II. Kennedy simply announced the creation of a Peace Corps. No Congress approved Clinton putting millions of acres of public land off-limits. Bush created an entirely new cabinet post, Homeland Security, created a separate justice system to deal with suspected terrorists, and promoted a preemptive war. So, while Leland Bruce knew he stood on shaky ground, he knew other great men had stood there before him. And most importantly, he believed Lemuria could succeed.

General Shell stood in the lobby of the Hart Building studying the centerpiece of the ninety-foot-high white marble atrium, Alexander Calder's monumental sculpture *Mountains and Clouds*. Fifty-foot-high black steel plates set on the floor represented five mountain peaks. Four huge overlapping curved aluminum plates above the "mountains" represented clouds. They were the "mobile" part of the Calder sculpture and "usually" moved in random patterns. But not today.

Mack Shell was staring up at motionless "clouds" when Senator Bruce stepped out of the elevator and approached him.

"It's broken again, Mack," the senator said.

Alexander Calder had arrived in Washington to finish the installation of this, his last work, on November 10, 1976. He had yet to make his final adjustments when he died later that evening. The mobile sculpture had since been intermittently dysfunctional.

"There had to have been some magic to the art that just wasn't finished," the senator said reflectively. "God, I think we've spent more money on electricians and engineers to fix it since Calder installed it, than the piece actually cost."

The general followed the senator into another elevator as they headed for the tunnel and the congressional subway that would shuttle them in a private car from the Hart to Dirksen Building and on to the Capitol. Each subway train consisted of three cars, one reserved exclusively for senators. Though the underground system was crowded with staffers, once in his private senatorial subway car with the automated train rumbling to its stops, Leland Bruce felt comfortable enough to speak freely.

"Well, Mack, will the ends justify the means?"

"You don't go into any fight without believing you can win," the general answered. "Sometimes you don't. But like anything, if you don't try . . ."

"You know, you can always spend more money. No one wants to see this fail. Do you need more?"

"It's not just money, Leland; it's science. They go at their own pace. No matter how much money you give these guys with PhD's, they still have to wait for stuff to grow in a dish."

"Well," the senator ruminated, "they say if you have a million monkeys clanging at typewriters for a thousand years, one of 'em would write Shakespeare."

"We don't have a million monkeys or a thousand years."

"But you've got a few billion bucks," Senator Bruce piped back in. "I'm trusting you to make this happen, Mack. You've got to manage this as not only a war against international terrorism, but a war where a fragile and volatile public opinion can be just as much an enemy. If we lose, it'll be because we lose there."

The subway stopped at the Dirksen Building and the conversation quieted a moment. General Shell knew that Senator Bruce had doubts. Everyone had doubts. But the senator was his beachhead on the Hill and he had to keep that well reinforced.

"I hear your last venture was a success," Leland commented.

"We met our goals. But there were some glitches."

"Anything I should know about?"

"We lost a weapon."

"And?"

"And I expect to recover it," Mack replied.

As they walked on, Mack spoke again. "We're going into the field again soon."

"Will there be collateral damage?"

"There always is. But it's just PR after that, and we know how to do that."

Mack took the senator's hand, holding it firmly between both of his. Taking another "soldier's" hand in his was almost his trademark. He had used it to great effect in invigorating the spirit of his troops. Words could be powerful, but there was nothing more powerful than human touch to put an emphasis on one's sincerity.

"You know when my father fought in World War II," Mack began, "more men died on a single ship on a single day then in the entire Iraq War. Every family in America bore the burden. Men were cheap. Tanks cost money. Now the costliest part of fighting a war is men. You know what it costs to train them, move them, clothe them, feed them, treat them, retire them"—the general paused for effect—"and bury them. Leland, no one knows better than you. The more losses we sustain, the more money it costs to recruit and hold. We are a country now with too many creature comforts, with all the decadence of a modern Rome before the fall. The people will let us wage war against our enemies as long as they don't suffer for it. There's no patience for victory. No tolerance for blood and casualties. No realization that wars are ultimately immoral and you can't really fight and win one without playing dirty."

Arriving at the Capitol, they found their aides awaiting them in the rotunda.

"I expect to see Calder's clouds moving when we meet again," the general said.

"I'll make it happen. You make it happen," the senator replied.

The general's aide proffered a small bag.

"Oh, I have something for you, Senator."

The general handed Leland Bruce a small package.

"Nothing sensitive I could lose here," the senator commented warily.

"A little gift. I heard you're a grandfather. I thought it was the perfect gift for a boy or a girl and since I didn't know—"

The senator opened the bag and, looking inside, smiled. Perfect indeed, a stuffed animal—Curious George.

> *On the Day of Judgment everyone will stand before Allah to be judged. They will be given a Book of Deeds. If the book is given to a person in his right hand, he will go to paradise. But if the book is placed in his left hand, it means he will be sent to hell for eternal torment.*
> —Commentary on The Qur'an

CHAPTER NINE

Joshua Krantz and Fala departed from Amman on a Royal Jordanian Airlines flight to Islamabad. There was only a single subterfuge. He carried a British passport. Pakistan, like thirty-two other predominantly Muslim countries, did not recognize Israel or Israeli passports. Fala entered as who she was, an Egyptian archaeologist. It was a long flight, twelve hours with layovers in Kuwait and Bahrain. They were tired. A Pakistani driver, holding up a sign with Fala's name, was waiting for them just outside of customs.

Islamabad, the capital of the Islamic Republic of Pakistan, was nothing like the polluted, overcrowded, deteriorating, and oftentimes dangerous capitals of most other Islamic countries. Unlike Cairo, Amman, Baghdad, or Damascus, Islamabad was a master planned city with four well-designed sectors, separated by glorious parks and open spaces. It had only become the capital in 1967, and the drive into its center was along wide thoroughfares lined with stately palms, past grand modern government buildings and mosques built of marble, limestone, and glass.

"*Shalom*," their driver said, as they drove, greeting them in Hebrew matter-of-factly.

"*Salem aleichem*," Krantz curtly responded.

Krantz took his measure of the driver. He had a long coarse beard, and wore traditional Pakistani garb—a *salwar kameez*, a long white shirt with loose-fitting pants; a colorful embroidered velvet vest; and a *kufi*, a velvet embroidered skullcap. With his beard and skullcap, he could pass just as well for a Chasidic Jew in Jerusalem. Krantz knew they were to be met by someone from Mossad, but he would not be taken in by such a subtle ploy as being greeted with a "*shalom*." He'd need more evidence to feel comfortable. Pakistan had a powerful secret service, the ISI that had ties to both Western intelligence at the same time it held hands with Islamic fundamentalist groups, including Al-Queda. Then the driver responded with the words Krantz was waiting to hear.

"You are my '*shnai hamal-ah-cheem*.'"

"*Cain*," yes, Krantz confirmed promptly, pleased that he was in safe hands.

"My name is Suleiman," the driver said. "I am Mossad, but I was born in Karachi." He eyed his passengers in his rearview mirror. The "*shnai hamal-ah-cheem*" were the "two angels" of the Bible that had come, one to destroy the evil city of Sodom, the other to save Lot and its righteous inhabitants. Were his "two angels" on a mission to destroy or save? No matter. He was a Jew and knew that whatever mission they were on had something to do with Jewish survival—and ultimately his own. A Jew in Pakistani clothing was ultimately still a Jew.

"There are still Jews in Pakistan?" Fala asked.

The driver laughed. "There are Jews everywhere. Remember, until the Temple is rebuilt, we shall be in diaspora. And not all Jews are Eastern European Ashkenazi or Spanish Sephardim. I am a Punjabi. My family name is Solomon. But it is better here to be a Suleiman."

"Are there synagogues here?" Fala wondered aloud.

"No, no," the driver snickered. "The government says they love Jews here. But if any Pakistani Jews would gather to pray, an illiterate mob would quickly kill them, and the government would do nothing. Hitler's minister of propaganda, Joseph Goebbels, was also fond of saying he loved the Jews. He loved to kill them. No, here we Jews must remain anonymous. We gather in private homes for prayer. Like in Israel, we are mostly secular Jews. But here, if anyone asks, we pretend to be secular Muslims."

Then he got down to the serious mission at hand.

"This weapon you want to inspect, it must be very important. The Americans want to buy it, too."

"And they didn't?" Colonel Krantz said, somewhat surprised.

"Not yet. But they will. We have made an offer, but if the Americans are bidding, it will be too pricey for us. Israelis? They are just poor Jews. But we will see it first. And more."

"How did you manage that?"

"The Americans, they have money, but they also have to play by moral rules. Jews, to survive, sometimes can't afford to play by those same rules. We have compromising pictures of an Urdu MI general." Urdu MI was Pakistani military intelligence.

"You blackmailed him with a prostitute?" Krantz asked.

"No, everyone sleeps with prostitutes here. No crime. No sin. But little boys? Not even Islam tolerates pedophiles. We are giving this general great rewards. He will get money from the Americans. And from us, we will give him freedom from prison or a stoning."

⎯⎯⎯⎯⎯⎯⎯◞

The next morning, they drove north, over rutted, boulder-strewn roads, built a century before by a British army that once called this land part of their empire. They drove through the ancient Khyber Pass to Peshawar and then north again to the mountainous region called Hunza. Hunza was the setting for John Hilton's novel *Lost Horizon* and indeed as they drove through this land of lush, green terraced valleys, snowcapped peaks, and the windingly beautiful Indus River, it seemed like Shangri-la. In the distance, just across the western mountains were the deserts of Afghanistan and the turmoil of war. Here, in Hunza, the people peacefully tended their fields. They were charming and friendly, greeting passersby with vigorous waves and, if you stopped, with a small offering. They seemed ageless, and perhaps they were. The Hunzakuts were also famous for their longevity. They survived on a natural diet in an unpolluted yet primitive world.

Suleiman had arranged to meet the general at the Baltit Fort, the home of the ancient Mirs, or kings of Hunza. Until the twentieth century and the coming of the modern nation of Pakistan, the people of this land located astride the Silk Road had maintained their autonomy for six hundred years. Ancient Hunzakuts kept a sword, a shield, and a loaf of bread with them at all times; and upon hearing the drumbeat warning of approaching invaders, they would run to the fort to defend their kingdom. Until the British conquered India and Pakistan in the late nineteenth century, Hunza had been free.

Set atop a peak in the Himalayas, the Baltit Fort had limited

tourist hours and little tourist traffic in any case. In the late afternoon, it would be a private and very out-of-the-way place to meet.
The Pakistani general was already waiting when Joshua, Fala, and
Suleiman arrived. He offered no greeting, no word. He simply ushered them into a room where a canvas bag sat on a solitary table and
closed the door. He knew no one would steal this treasure. The
room had a single door and one window that opened to a spectacular
view of the steep gorge below.

Inside the bag was the weapon that Israeli intelligence had pho-
tographed—Alexander the Great's battle scythe. It was basically a
leather glove mounted with four ten-inch razor-sharp scythes, curved
finger knives, not unlike the weapon Freddy Krueger used in horror
movies. It was still stained with blood.

"This is no ancient weapon," Fala commented almost immediately.
"But it's a good copy. Other than new leather and stainless steel instead of iron, it's an exact replica." She tried to put on the glove. It
didn't fit. "A little small," she muttered curiously. "Even for me."

"It's a perfect size," Joshua remarked. "Appropriate for the era.
Soldiers in Alexander's army were less than five feet tall. Men have
grown in stature nearly a foot in two thousand years. This weapon
would have fit the hand of a soldier in Alexander's army."

"But we know it's a modern weapon. Used just a few weeks ago."

Krantz played with the weapon for a moment and pondered the
dilemma.

"Well, who are soldiers nowadays?" he asked rhetorically and
continued with what seemed like the obvious conclusion. "Children.
Child soldiers are plentiful in lots of war zones. They wield machine
guns and machetes. Why not a battle scythe?"

"Yes, but those places have been mostly in Africa, not the

Middle East."

"Oh?" Krantz responded, somewhat condescendingly to his Egyptian and Muslim lover. "Islamic extremists don't recruit children for their dirty work?"

"The people killed were Al-Queda," Fala reiterated.

"They were Shiites. This could be sectarian war."

Someone knocked on the door. It was Suleiman. He motioned for them to put the weapon back in the sack. Then he picked it up and returned it to the general, who abruptly left. Nothing was exchanged. Nothing was said. But the Pakistani general was now in the lifetime employ of Mossad.

"I have bought you one more gift," Suleiman said. "I have brought you here because there is a clinic in the village below, and there we will meet the only survivor of the massacre at Takhar."

⸻

There was a small clinic in the town with broken-tiled, almost dirt floors, a dozen beds, one doctor, and a few nurses. Unlike the antiseptic odors of most medical facilities, this one reeked of urine and feces. The doctor had little to offer, some basic antibiotics, bandages, and most importantly, the gift of pain relief: intravenous narcotics, in the form of the local homegrown heroin. If you survived the place, you likely left addicted. In a corner bed there was a man, or they assumed he was a man, wrapped like a mummy, head to toe, in bloodied bandages. His body had been serrated, from the top of his head to his feet. Krantz immediately had doubts about his theory. Could a child soldier wielding a battle scythe have done this? The man had been blinded. His lips, tongue, and mouth were shredded. He was fed through a feeding tube in his abdomen and was in great pain, even with the heavy doses of narcotics they were giving him.

"Can he describe who attacked them?" Krantz asked.

Suleiman leaned over and whispered the question into the hole where the man's ear had been. The man did not move. He did not speak.

"Maybe he speaks Arabic?" Fala asked Suleiman.

"They speak Farsi here in Northern Pakistan. Arabic and Urdu are not native languages."

"Maybe he's not a native," Krantz added. "A lot of foreigners must train in terrorist camps here."

Suleiman tried the question in Arabic, then Urdu, even English. No response.

"You know," Krantz suggested, "when you can't hear by air conduction, when your ears are blocked, or, if you have no ears, you can still hear by bone conduction."

He looked about the room and found a plastic cup. Taking a penknife from his pocket, he cut out the bottom of the cup, and handed the creation to his Pakistani guide.

Suleiman put the cup to the patient's skull and repeated the question in Farsi. Still no response.

"Tell him," Krantz said, "that we will take care of his family."

Speaking into the "amplifying" cup, Suleiman made the offer. A moment later the survivor spoke a single muffled word, "Maimun." He repeated it, but they didn't understand. With a single bloodied finger, the dying man wrote the word on his sheet: MAIMUN.

———————

Back in their Islamabad hotel room, Fala and Joshua showered for a long time to wash away the dirt of the road and the horror of what they'd seen. They were staying at the Islamabad Serena Hotel. Surrounded by exotic gardens and a serene lake, the hotel was the most luxurious and most secure in the country because it hosted officials from governments around the world. Sitting outside on their balcony, they cuddled together, naked, on a cushioned chaise lounge, cradled in privacy by stone walls and a latticework of bougainvillea. It was a dark, moonless night with the murmur of distant traffic and the scent of warm jasmine breezes. There were no neighboring high-rises with curious eyes. Only the stars peered down upon them as they caressed each other. Neither had yet discussed the one-word clue they were left with and where it would lead them.

"Maimun," Fala was first to speak and break their idyll. "That is my sister's name."

Krantz sat up in some surprise.

"It's a popular girl's name among Muslims because it also means 'auspicious and good luck.'"

"Not such good luck for our Taliban in Shangri-la," Krantz added. "And I doubt your sister has anything to do with this?"

"*Maimun*? It is also the root of the word for 'right hand.'"

Krantz took his right hand and gently cupped her breast.

"Right hand," he said. And after cupping her left breast with his left hand, "Left hand." He circled her nipples with his index finger until they stood erect.

Fala pulled his hands away and sat up abruptly. "Stop! I'm making a point. I think I know what *Maimun* means."

"What's that?" Krantz asked loudly, quieting his libido.

This was exactly Fala al-Shohada's field of expertise—the military history and archaeology of the Islamic world.

"In the eleventh century," she began to explain, "the elite troops of Salah al-Din were called the 'Maimun al-Allah'— the 'Right Hand of God.'"

"Don't tell me they butchered the crusaders using Alexander's battle scythe."

"No. The Maimun did not butcher the crusaders. That's another distortion of history. The early Muslims were not butchers. When the Christian crusaders took Jerusalem in 1099, they were the ones who butchered virtually everyone there and boasted that the city was knee-high in blood. But when Salah al-Din retook the city a hundred years later, he told his Maimun al-Allah to spare those who surrendered and give them safe passage home. The knights of the crusades became famous for their chivalry, but it was the Maimun, not the early crusaders, who were chivalrous warriors. Chivalry, you see, was a custom that the crusaders adopted from their Muslim foes."

How could a woman so beautiful be so brilliant? Krantz thought. And how could it be that a poor Jewish boy bred in *kibbutz* in the Galilee could have her?

"And so all we need to do now," Krantz said, as he rolled atop her, "is find out who the new Right Hand of God is."

And then he snaked his right hand along her inner thigh until it was finally inside her. She sighed as he massaged her and whispered wetly into her ear, "This is the right hand of God." And then just as quickly, she rolled atop him. He was already erect and she took control, taking his member in hand and putting it inside her. Their lovemaking was fierce, almost vicious—just as you would imagine it would be between Arab and Jew, both relishing the battle, both exhausted from the feat.

CHAPTER
TEN

Secrets are difficult to keep. If a fool knows a secret, he tells it. But even a wise man may tell—for love, for vanity, for money. Professor Julius Wagner had a secret he feared to tell and feared he would tell. Who could guarantee that in the banter of cocktail parties and salons, among the intelligencia and nouveau riche of Palo Alto, Atherton, and Menlo Park, that the mix of bravado and wine wouldn't loose the secret that would change the method of war forever and, like the A-bomb, the balance of power for generations? Also, the time he was spending away from his offices at Stanford was creating a buzz in the university community and the scientific world. What was this Nobel Laureate now pondering? It was as if Einstein had disappeared from Princeton for weeks at a time without a hint of his activies. What rumors would abound?

It was on his last visit to the high-tech military research facility, obstensibly built just for him halfway around the world, that he agreed to return and stay for the "duration."

General Shell didn't believe in creating from scratch a plan that had already been proven. He read about and adapted all the security and scientific essentials that had been the hallmark of the development of the first A-bomb during World War II. That effort was code-named the Manhattan Project, with research being performed at "Site Y," a secret center built in the hills of Los Alamos, New Mexico. Shell gave his new top-secret project a code name as well. He called it the "Lemuria Project," with research conducted at another secret site he called "BIOT." Besides the scientists directly involved in the project, and the military who would secure it and help carry out his vision, no one was privy to the Lemuria Project except the highest officials of the government and military. Just as former General Leslie Groves had set up the resources for the Manhattan Project, General Maximillian Shell had set up the infrastructure for Lemuria. And just as Robert Oppenheimer was the guiding force in bringing the scientists and resources together for the A-bomb project in Los Alamos, Dr. Wagner was the guiding force bringing talent together at BIOT.

The central facility for conducting this experimental work had to be in a secret and isolated area. There had to be a large pool of researchers who could conduct research according to standard scientific protocols with enough freedom of expression to allow for a vigorous exchange of ideas. Dr. Wagner accepted General Shell's recommendation that the research be conducted at the British-U.S. military base on the Island of Diego Garcia. It already had sufficient infrastructure and was already one of the most secure and secret sites in the world, in the middle of the Indian Ocean.

Wagner had originally preferred being closer to home and suggested that research could take place at the military's secret base in a remote area of the Nevada desert. But this base, Area 51, also sometimes called Dreamland, The Farm, The Box, Groom Lake, and Paradise Ranch, was never perfectly free of the prying eyes of the curious who would trek through the desert or overfly the site to try to catch a glimpse of the latest military aircraft or the aliens that some believed were kept there. In the twenty-first century, how could he keep his collection of young researchers imprisoned at such a site without their clamoring for visits to the nearby oasis, Las Vegas? No, Diego Garcia was the perfect site. The most difficult part of the project was convincing top scientists to join his team. In uprooting individuals and sometimes whole families to a remote area with no options for escape, Lemuria, for some, would seem like a scientific Devil's Island. But Julius Wagner had impressive scientific credentials and great persuasive powers. Just as Oppenheimer had collected the greatest physicists of his time at Los Alamos—Enrico Fermi, Richard Feynman, Edward Teller, Hans Bethe, and many more—so, too, did Julius Wagner collect his superstars from major universities across the country, from the Universities of California, Chicago, Princeton, Stanford, and every ivory tower that had biotech research projects on genetics, gene manipulation, embryology, stem cells, neurophysiology, and neuropsychology. He had collected the most remarkable contingent of scientific talent on the remotest outpost in the world since the stars of the Manhattan Project resided in the middle of the New Mexico desert.

Now, just as he had demanded of his team, he would return to stay, for a year or five, whatever it took to achieve the result. He would just one day suddenly depart from his duties at Stanford. He left the details of how his departure would be revealed to General Shell.

General Shell set a "mythological" plan in motion and tapped Colonel McGraw to carry it out. A Nobel Prize winner would soon disappear from the world stage. The Lemuria Project was more important than one man.

"I want the world to see Dr. Wagner's Achilles' heel," was how he explained his plan to McGraw, "and we'll do it with a Trojan horse."

> *The battle, sir, is not to the strong alone; it is
> to the vigilant, the active, the brave.*
> —Patrick Henry

CHAPTER
ELEVEN

Margaret Wagner was a student at Princeton working on her PhD in genetics. She was following in her father's footsteps, studying the biochemical activators of cells. That gave her several burdens to bear. She had the impossible task of competing with her father's reputation as a Nobel Laureate. She also had to overcome everyone's perception that any success she had was due to nepotism. That's why she had chosen to study at an institution far from her father's sphere of influence. Unfortunately, the perceptions remained.

Maggie Wagner—she had always gone by Maggie—had puffy round cheeks that still looked like baby fat, deep set brown eyes, and big ears. She thought she looked more like her father than her mother. Maggie had considered her mother a stunningly beautiful woman. She considered herself plain. But she was young and knew how to make the most of her attributes. She wore makeup well and had an attractive figure. She would not have been called a beautiful woman, but nevertheless she could be eye-catching. She wasn't in the business at this time in her life of luring a husband, but she was still a young woman who enjoyed attention now and then. So, she often showed off an attractive figure in tight jeans and cashmere sweaters and favored wearing sandals and open-toed shoes. She felt her feet were her best feature, with toes always perfectly pedicured and adorned with bright cherry red polish. Her dirty blond hair was cut in a short flip, and her glasses most often sat atop her head rather than on her nose, because she spent so much of her time peering into microscopes.

Maggie bent over her microscope and intently adjusted the illuminator to shine blue light upon the slide of brain tissue she was studying. She was looking for the illumination of scientific discovery. The twenty-five-year-old researcher was looking for fluorescence. She had tagged a virus that attacked the motor centers of the brain with a fluorescent gene culled from primitive jellyfish and had injected it into mice. Now and again, she retreated from the microscope to rest her eyes. Through a window of her laboratory, she glimpsed a group of fellow graduate students taking a break, sipping coffee, watching television in the lounge. She returned her gaze to her microscope, seeking out an object just a few microns long. Exactly where in this brain, where on the dendritic cell that carried messages across a chain of millions of cells, would this virus attach itself? Her eyes ached and her mind went elsewhere.

———————

"Hold on tight," her father yelled as he held onto her bicycle and ran frantically alongside her. She was afraid to be let go. Her father, in his late forties with a gut, was panting and just as afraid for his precious little girl.

Then the little girl yelled out, "Let go, Daddy!" Her voice said both "keep me safe" and "let me go" at the same moment. It was a life ritual repeated in some form at some time in every human life, when a child demands some independence and a parent first fearfully lets go.

"Keep pedaling, Maggie. Keep pedaling," her father hollered, and he let go.

She wobbled a moment and then the bike steadied. There are some moments, just seconds in a life, that last a lifetime. She turned her head to look back. Her eyes said it all: "Look, Dad, I can ride!"

Julius Wagner was beaming. Maggie was six years old, and he had just taught his daughter to ride a two-wheeler. With all their subsequent mutual scientific and academic achievements—father and daughter—if you could ask them to retrieve a memory of the best of times, this was perhaps it.

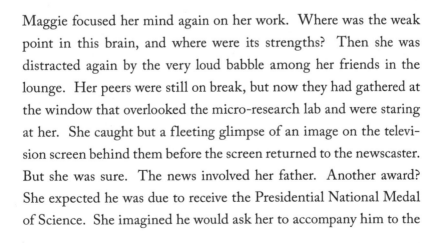

Maggie focused her mind again on her work. Where was the weak point in this brain, and where were its strengths? Then she was distracted again by the very loud babble among her friends in the lounge. Her peers were still on break, but now they had gathered at the window that overlooked the micro-research lab and were staring at her. She caught but a fleeting glimpse of an image on the television screen behind them before the screen returned to the newscaster. But she was sure. The news involved her father. Another award? She expected he was due to receive the Presidential National Medal of Science. She imagined he would ask her to accompany him to the ceremony. Her mother had stood at her father's side in Stockholm when he accepted his Nobel Prize. She was ill then, and frail. But she put on a wig and summoned the last of her strength to be with her husband for his greatest achievement. Florence Wagner would die just two weeks later. Since her mother's death, Maggie Wagner had been called upon to be her father's feminine companion. It was another one of those burdens she bore for being the daughter of a famous father.

> *Reputation is an idle and most false imposition, oft*
> *got without merit, and lost without deserving.*
> —Shakespeare

CHAPTER TWELVE

Maggie Wagner watched the television newscast replay over and over again. Another knife was slicing through her soul. Her mother had died of ovarian cancer just a few years before. She and her father had both suffered then, watching the malignancy and the poisonous chemotherapeutic agents slowly but persistently peel her mother's strength away, one painful layer at a time, until death came. She knew her father was still mourning, and perhaps lonely, but she had always assumed it was his obsession with work that prevented him from taking any time out for a social life. His life, like his speech patterns, seemed monotone. He often spoke of "colleagues" but rarely of "friends," and she had never heard him speak of female friends.

"My colleague, Dr. Adler, took a position in Nigeria, of all places. He got a great title but what does he expect to accomplish there?" Dr. Wagner would say. Or: "The Lubers invited me for dinner again.

I'm just not up to being that social yet."

But her father was also a relatively healthy man. She shivered to imagine it, but it was not unreasonable to think that her father still had a libido and that he might frequent prostitutes. But his death, this death, was an unimaginable scandal.

"Dr. Julius Wagner, Nobel Prize winner and founder and director of the Stanford Genetic Research Institute," the network news anchor began, "was found dead in a hotel room this morning. The body of a woman, an alleged prostitute, was with him, shot and killed according to police ballistic experts, with the same weapon that Dr. Wagner then used to kill himself. The room had been set afire. The bodies severely burned. But police and forensic experts have pieced a timeline and evidence together and speculate that Dr. Wagner may have murdered the prostitute after some altercation, and then, after setting the room afire to destroy the evidence, became despondent and shot himself in an apparent murder-suicide."

The story was headline news for two days and quickly subsided after the funeral. Except for the brief bio introduction of her father as a Nobel Prize winner, his scientific accomplishments were forgotten in the rush to glorify the tawdry details of his death. Scandal was entertaining and made news. Celebrity dishonor and murder trumped old war news and floods every time. But in less than one week, after the blindingly bright flame of public shame, Julius Wagner's name had disappeared from public consciousness. More copy was written in a single day about prostitution, male depression, the sexual appetites of septuagenarians, the current generation of male libido stimulants, and other lurid hypotheses of her father's sex life, than had been written in his entire lifetime about his scientific accomplishments. One misstep was all it took to destroy a reputation and the good works of a lifetime. It was for that that Maggie Wagner mourned as well.

———————

"I have to admit I was skeptical that we could carry this off," General Shell said over a private dinner at his home halfway around the world, in SOCOM, the Special Operations Center, Pacific Command, headquartered at Camp Butler in Okinawa.

Colonel McGraw and the general sat on a veranda, sipping on icy blended margaritas made by the tubful by the general's Japanese houseboy. Together they listened to satellite radio as the story Shell had written and McGraw had directed unfolded around the world.

"Having the professor simply disappear would have set off a worldwide search. Having him killed, there'd be a lengthy search for his killer. But dying in flames with lurid contexts, the business was over in days. If this all comes to a good end, Link, I think one of these will be yours someday." And the general tapped one of the stars on his shoulder.

McGraw never wallowed in successes or failures. His thoughts were analytical—what went well, what didn't. He had accomplished the mission he was given but was most happy to be back in command of his troops and was ready to take the field again in a new action.

McGraw recalled a line from Shakespeare: "Some are born great; some achieve greatness; and some have greatness thrust upon them." He was wise enough not to let a few successes go to his head, but deep inside he knew he was destined to achieve great things. He was just lagging. At his age, in his former life, he had already become the pharaoh of Egypt, Ptolemy I. What a difference a few millennia make.

> *It is easier to perceive error than to find truth, for the former lies on the surface and is easily seen, while the latter lies in the depth, where few are willing to search for it.*
> —Goethe

CHAPTER THIRTEEN

Maggie hadn't been back to California since her mother had passed away. She was too busy at Princeton working on her PhD. And in those few years, she had only seen her father three times, and briefly: once when he passed through Boston to headline a conference on DNA extraction and purification techniques and twice as his partner at award ceremonies. It wasn't that they were estranged. They were just both too occupied with their careers to bother with much more than the requisite birthday or Father's Day gifts and the occasional "what have you been up to lately" phone call. She would have gladly made efforts to accompany him at his behest for special events, but in the last several years he had been spending more and more time abroad and she had rarely been called to fulfill her role as his female escort.

In the furor of publicity over her father's scandalous passing, she had refused to be interviewed by any press. She would not feed any public frenzy of curiosity. She mourned privately, and in quiet moments alone, she reminisced about the best of times, when she was a happy child growing up in Palo Alto. More than the honors of publishing or the approval of her professors and peers, she realized now that it was her father's praise that was most important in her life. It was something she would never have again. She didn't need to provide an apology or a glorious epitaph for her father's life. His foibles would be buried with time, she hoped. His accomplishments would survive forever.

Margaret Wagner's plane landed in San Jose, California. She rented a car and drove directly to the Santa Clara Coroner's Office. She would check into a hotel later. She wanted to see her father first and deal with putting him to rest. She picked at her cuticles nervously and wanted to boost her courage with something artificial. She pictured the movie solution to ease the stress—a shot of vodka or a cigarette. But she wasn't much of a drinker, and she didn't smoke. She imagined seeing her father's burnt body pulled from one of those vaults she had seen dozens of times on television crime dramas. But government bureaucracy, which has a track record of compounding everyone's life stressors, this time set her anxieties free.

"We don't have the personnel or facilities to allow viewing here," the clerk in the medical examiner's office said. She barely looked at Maggie as she stamped, signed, and folded the appropriate documents. Clearly it was her ad nauseum routine.

"You don't want me to identify the body?"

"No, no. That's not necessary. The coroner made a positive ID.

Just sign here and we can release the body to a mortuary of your choice. You can view the body there—either before or after preparation—whatever you prefer. And . . . we are very sorry for your loss."

That was it—quick, cold, efficient, with a touch of coached condolence. Maggie signed a receipt and was handed an envelope. It contained the coroner's autopsy report. Although the body was described as extensively burned, death was noted as due to "exsanguination with gunshot wound to the chest." The envelope also contained her father's possessions. There was a frayed and burned wallet with melted credit cards and some burnt photos with only shadow images left that she was sure were once photos of her mother and her, as a toddler; a cheap digital watch her father favored because it had all the electronic gizmos he liked—stopwatch, calculator, world times, memo and alarm settings; and a bent, blackened gold wedding band that had been cut from his burnt and swollen finger.

This was the beginning, she thought, of the tedious and lonely job of packing up her father's life, his possessions at work and at his home. But she was his only child, and there was no one else to carry the weight of death and scandal—not friends, not colleagues.

After making arrangements at a local mortuary, her next surprise was that there was not much to collect at her father's Stanford University office.

"I've only been here a few weeks," his administrative assistant explained apologetically. She was a buxom black woman in her early thirties who clearly seemed overwhelmed by events. "I was only hired as a temp for the professor until he settled on someone permanent. I liked working for him. He was very nice and—I'm terribly sorry."

"Where's Sarah?"

Sarah Zito, her father's previous administrative assistant, had been with him for twenty years. She was almost like family.

"Oh, they told me she quit just a few weeks before I came. I think she got another job."

Maggie glanced at a few pieces of recent correspondence on her father's desk.

"They're letters I typed for him, replies for requests for speaking engagements. He turned them all down."

This woman was indeed new to the job. Maggie noted that she couldn't even spell *genomics*, the field in which her father won his Nobel Prize.

"He cleaned out most of his office about a week ago," the assistant explained. "He wanted to take it all home to organize his work better, he said."

His drawers were empty. His computer was virtually wiped clean—full of desktop shortcut logos with nothing inside.

"I rarely saw him," she said apologetically. "He spent most of his time these past few weeks traveling or interviewing."

"Do you know what he was working on?"

She shrugged. "I just made phone calls for him. Made appointments. Scheduled flights. I only heard him mention it once."

"What was that?"

"The Lemuria Project. I think that's what his grant was called. But I don't know if it was a grant. He seemed embarrassed he even mentioned it. But I don't know—I don't know what it was."

"He never mentioned working on anything like that to me."

"Well, maybe it wasn't important. Like I said, I've only been here a few weeks."

Maggie inquired about a forwarding address for Sarah Zito. There was none, nor any "contact" information either.

While she never knew her father to have much of a social life, he had a vigorous professional one. His enthusiasm for his research always percolated through their conversations. And since she had begun pursuing the same field of work as her father, he enjoyed keeping her apprised of his projects. But he had never mentioned anything called Lemuria.

Maggie spoke to a few of her father's graduate students. None worked on anything called Lemuria. And several of the PhD students were unhesitant in grumbling that the research they'd been assigned or encouraged to undertake for their theses were just repetitions and fine-tuning of the breakthrough genetic research her father had done nearly two decades earlier, research that had won him his Nobel Prize. Julius Wagner had worked on identifying and manipulating genes that controlled development—limb growth, organogenesis, brain growth. Professor Wagner had been the first to make the leap from using the genes of the rapidly developing *drosophila*, or fruit flies—that his peers used for research—to using identical genes in higher organisms, particularly mammals. And his work over the years since had progressed by discovering the enzymatic "triggers" that could speed gene activation. The shortcoming in his research, however, was that speeding up gene activation often caused *homeosis*, a Greek word that described the malformations and mutations caused by genes behaving inappropriately. In the fruit fly, these mutations might lead to an extra set of wings; in a rhesus monkey, a fusion of the eyes or a *cyclops*. That's why most direct human research was still taboo.

University professors often used their graduate students to assist with and become partners in publishing new research. Professor Wagner, however, in the last several years, seemed to neglect most of his doctoral students as if he had other, more important, and—with his travels—more distant projects on the fire.

One of his graduate students, Jordan Parry, a frail-looking kid with curly black hair and a goatee, did remember an unusual event.

"Barry Wilde," he recalled, "one of your father's favorites, finished his doctoral thesis last year. We were celebrating, and he asked me if I would be joining the team. I didn't know what he was talking about, and he just shut up after that. I should have asked more questions then. I don't know." Clearly Jordan was second-guessing himself.

"You know," he went on, "if your father had a new project, he could at least have given his grads a shot. I know he's dead and all—but I've lost three years of my life now. I've got to start all over again."

"Where can I find Mr. Wilde?" Maggie askéd.

"I don't know. He just disappeared off the face of the earth. We were friends. I send him e-mail. He doesn't reply."

"What about his family?"

"Oh, I spoke to his mother. She says he's traveling with friends. They get e-mails from him from all around the world."

"That doesn't sound very unusual. He's taking some time off." After completing the rigors of their academic years, graduate students often took prolonged time off to travel.

But Jordan Parry made one more telling point. "As far as I know, Wilde never had any friends. In my four years here, I was the closest friend he had. So what friends is he traveling with? And anyway, he's in a wheelchair."

Obscure research projects, affairs with prostitutes, disappearing assistants and graduate students—did her father have another life of which he kept her totally in the dark?

Julius Wagner's home was a two-bedroom Spanish-style bungalow in Palo Alto just off University Avenue, within walking distance of his office. Everything in her father's home spoke of a man who was meticulous and well organized. Unlike the disarray she had seen in the offices of many of her professors, with papers and books piled high as if they were spewed from some academic volcano, her father's home library was painstakingly alphabetized to topic and author. The sliced bread in the kitchen had its own container, labeled "sliced bread." The shelves inside cabinets were labeled with headings like "cleaners," "polish," "insecticides." Even the toilet paper in the guest bathroom had its ends folded hotel-fashion. She found a smattering of drafts of old research papers and some receipts for travel expenses, but nothing that referred to a Lemuria Project. Interestingly, Julius Wagner had kept a file—perhaps a father's scrapbook—labeled "Maggie." Inside were multiple folders, categorizing every aspect of his daughter's life. There was an academic section with everything from her grade-school report cards to college transcripts. A sports section held certificates of completion for her black belt in karate and awards for soccer and dance competitions. Most interesting was the collection of documents in her medical file. The requisite vaccination records were there. But there were also receipts and letters from doctors before she was born, mostly fertility specialists. Her mother had difficulty getting pregnant and had taken Clomid, the first-line drug used to induce ovulation in patients with fertility disorders. She had two miscarriages before getting pregnant with Maggie. Clomid was a new drug when her mother had taken it, and long-term side effects were unknown, particularly congenital defects or long-term predispositions to diseases. There was another receipt in her medical file. It was a receipt for the cryogenic storage of Maggie Wagner's umbilical cord blood. Cord blood stem cells are used to treat life-threatening illnesses such as leukemia, cancer, and immune deficiencies. But twenty-five years ago, no one stored cord blood or talked about stem cells. Decades before the science had become practical, her father had realized its potential and saved her cord blood as a source of future stem cells—the building blocks of life. Her father had loved her very much. He had even kept her cord blood as insurance. Then she came upon another receipt in the file that was baffling. Her father had withdrawn her cord blood from storage five years ago. Stored for nearly twenty years; removed five years ago. Why? Did she have an identical twin who was ill? Absurd. Lots of things were not making sense.

The movers would pack up most of the house, but Maggie personally packed a few boxes—mostly family photographs that she would keep, and her father's awards. She hefted his Nobel Prize. The medal was made of eighteen-carat gold and weighed 193 grams, worth about $4,000. Tears finally came to her. His life was worth so much more. The questions she had about her father's life were painfully twisted with the shock and grief she was feeling. After the funeral, she would return home. There, she thought, her confusion and emotions would unknot as she resumed her work.

Professor Wagner's funeral was held at the Memorial Church of Stanford University. The nineteenth-century Romanesque church sat in the most historic section of the college campus by the main student quadrangle. Campus security prevented anyone but invited guests from entering. The crowds outside were a mixture of frustrated press and uninterested students busily walking or biking to their next class. There were a dozen Nobel Prize winners at Stanford. And in this campus of twenty thousand students, perhaps two hundred had ever come into contact with any of them. And of those, perhaps only twenty or thirty knew Dr. Wagner and his work. The few dozen guests—mostly professors and graduate students—listened quietly as the minister lauded a great man's achievements, noted a daughter following in his footsteps, and mentioned nothing at all about the circumstances of his death.

As guests filed out and offered polite condolences, one man stayed behind—a lithe, handsome man in his early fifties. Crew-cut, pale, with thick-rimmed black glasses and a tweed blazer, he looked stereotypically like the physics professor he was.

"Miss Wagner, my name is Ryan Petersdorf. I was a friend of your father. I knew him well. Do you have a moment?"

No one, other than the minister, had said a good word about her father, and she needed to hear from someone that he was not loathed.

"I was your father's friend," Professor Peterdorf began. "His best friend, I think." His speech was clipped, and almost whispered, as if he had rehearsed what he wanted to say but was hesitant to say it. "My wife died about the same time as your mother, and we spent a lot of time together, often burying our grief in drink, but talking a lot, too, about campus politics, politics in general, and of course, our work, which was totally different but intellectually stimulating for both of us. But—let me, let me get to the point."

Professor Petersdorf sighed and looked about him. Photographers were snapping photos of them. He took her arm and moved with Maggie behind a sandstone pillar. "I don't believe," he said, "that your father was a murderer or committed suicide. I think he was murdered."

"What?!" Maggie was startled; crackpots and conspiracy theorists were everywhere. "Mr. Petersdorf, I don't need this." And she tried to move away.

He held her tightly. "Wait."

"I've talked to the police. I have no reason to doubt their investigation. He wasn't murdered. He got involved with a prostitute and I guess—" Maggie again tried to pull away.

"He wouldn't have gone to a prostitute."

"Why not? He was lonely."

"He wasn't lonely. He was with me."

Maggie stared at him. What did he mean?

And then Dr. Petersdorf said it more clearly. "He was . . . *with* . . . me." His tone, his meaning was now unmistakable.

She knew what he meant. More horrors, she thought. She did not want to conceive of this horror, too.

"Are you saying my father was gay?"

"Is that what you want to think? No. We were friends. You know women have close women friends all the time. When men do, people think they're gay. We were companions, friends. We became soul mates, if you will. It was something neither of us had ever had before in our lives. A good friend.

"I went to the police," the physics professor went on. "And they didn't understand either. But I told them, too. Your father would not have been with a call girl."

"And what did they say?"

"The usual cop stuff. 'Open-and-shut case,' they said. Your father had the same gun in his hand that killed the prostitute. He had gunshot residue on his hands and a bullet wound from that same gun in his chest."

"It sounds open and shut."

"He would not have been with a call girl."

"I have no reason to doubt the police."

"I'm sorry," Petersdorf continued. "This is a terrible time, I know. But do you really believe your father was some lonely, dirty old man? For godssake, he was a genius. He liked to talk science and politics. He liked fine wines. He loved my apple tarts." The professor's voice was firm now, rising, as if moving from a whisper to loud would convince her that his words were true. "Your father was very funny, too. He liked to sing and dance."

Now, Maggie was beginning to doubt his story. Her father was not funny.

"He liked to do Gene Kelly in 'Singing in the Rain,'" the professor went on. And he began imitating her father, dancing and singing around the pillars in the Stanford Quadrangle. "I'm singing in the rain. Just singing in the rain. What a glorious feelin', I'm happy again. I'm laughing at clouds, so dark up above. The sun's in my heart and I'm ready for love."

As a little girl, that was the one silly thing her father did with her, bouncing her about the house with her standing on his shoes while he danced and sang like Gene Kelly in that old Hollywood musical. But still, Maggie fought off this new absurdity. The circumstances of her father's death were already painful enough. She didn't need to hear more of the ridiculous. Murdered?

"Did he ever mention that anything was wrong?" Maggie asked.

"Nothing seemed wrong. And nothing was wrong—between us—except he was traveling a lot. But in the last few weeks, he was all of a sudden very . . . very obtuse."

"What do you mean?"

"He talked about things that were inconsequential, silly. You know, he was always a very witty man. We would speak about substantive issues. But recently he'd bring up silly things like the weather in India of all places, or how long some of his favorite foods could last frozen. And why, in the days before he ends up dead in bed with a call girl, would he remove all his computers and documents from his office? Why would that be?"

"You knew about that?"

"Sure."

"And the Lemuria Project?"

"The what?"

"The Lemuria Project. He didn't talk about that?"

"In the last few months, for some reason, he became very close-mouthed about his work. That was not like him, either."

Maggie closed her eyes for a moment. Her life was in a ruin, and this man was piling on debris.

"I have to go back to Boston and I really don't believe—"

"All right. All right. I know you want to put this behind you—but just meet somebody for me."

She was about to bury her father. All she wanted now was to heal. But she agreed to listen. *Let them throw one more spear,* she thought. *How much more could it hurt?*

———

Maggie Wagner had her luggage in the trunk and the ticket for her flight back to Boston sitting in the glove compartment of her rental car. She agreed to meet Nathan Stumpf at a local restaurant near the airport.

"Have to run. Can't miss my flight"—she had the words rehearsed. She wanted to be able to make a quick getaway from this lunacy.

Nathan Stumpf was a San Francisco detective hired by Professor Petersdorf to look into Julius Wagner's death. He was a short, scrawny fellow in his midthirties, with early balding; white, scaly psoriatic elbows; crooked teeth; and a bit of a W.C. Fields vein-mapped bulbous nose, a skin disease called rosacea. He fancied that a tan would make him look healthy, and his face had come to look like café-au-lait-colored leather. The only virtue of appearance he brought to the table was his stylish dress—his wardrobe was rayon baggy pleated pants, rayon classic fifties-style embroidered bowling shirts, a Robert Mitchum jacket, and, since he thought shoes mattered, well-shined Bruno Maglis. He thought the shoes had a bizarre panache. They were just what O.J. Simpson wore when he killed Nicole Brown and Ron Goldman.

Nate Stumpf lived in a third-floor walk-up just off the Haight, an area in San Francisco that was still emulating the 1960s. Although the area was gaining popularity among yuppies, it was nevertheless well populated with panhandlers and stoners, and tourists shopping in one of the many vintage stores, trying to achieve the retro look that Stumpf had perfected so well.

"Look," Professor Petersdorf had explained to Maggie, "I made a lot of inquiries about private investigators and got a lot of recommendations. But they all wanted big retainers and had pricey hourly rates. Nothing I could afford on a college professor's salary. Mr. Stumpf, well yes, he's a bit sleazy and crude, but I think he's sincere and he's honest. I trust him, and he works cheap."

Stumpf waved at her when she entered the restaurant, a small diner frequented by Haight-Ashbury locals just around the corner from the classic Red Vic Movie House and Jerry Garcia's old digs. A sign in big bold red letters in the front window read GOOD FOOD. She already knew what she'd order. Nothing. No place that advertised "good food" ever served any. She wondered if Stumpf recognized her from clips of the funeral on television or because she was the only non-morbidly obese woman in the restaurant. He was sitting in a booth at the rear of the family-style, low-cost eatery and had already started lunch. With every step forward, she thought about turning back. But she was here already, so she sat down. The waitress placed a glass of ice water and a menu in front of her.

"Chicken potpie's good," Stumpf said, gravy dribbling from the corner of his mouth. "I'm Nate Stumpf," he added, and held out his hand.

"I have to catch a plane," she said, politely shaking his hand. She was already setting up her getaway.

"Open-and-shut case, they said." He got right to the subject. "Uh-uh."

Stumpf pushed a photo across to her. It was a photograph of her father in the torched hotel room. A woman was lying naked in bed. Her father, clothes charred, body blistered from the fire, had a gun in his hand and was lying with his head at the dead woman's feet, his legs hanging over the bed.

"How did you get this?" Maggie asked.

"That's my job."

"And why is it that you and Professor Petersdorf think my father was murdered?"

"Did you read these?" Stumpf asked, pushing two autopsy reports to her.

"Yes, I did. I know how they both died. And—I have to catch a plane."

"Listen, he was your father. If your father's boyfriend cares more about him than you do—well, I don't give a fuck."

"Professor Petersdorf was not my father's boyfriend. He was just a friend and I don't think—"

"I'm ready to talk," Stumpf interrupted with deliberate calm, "when you're ready to listen."

"Listen to what?"

Stumpf cleared his throat and took a drink of water. Then he got up and moved to her side of the booth, sitting next to her—close. She tried to edge herself farther away. *What is that awful odor?* she thought. It was a mix of a strong citrus cologne and sweat. Stumpf's fancy shirts required dry cleaning. Dry cleaning was expensive. Looking good was what mattered, and as long as he looked good, Stumpf rarely cleaned his clothes. He picked up the photograph and held it right under her nose, pointing out the highlights.

"The hooker. See. She's lying naked in bed. Your father's lying there fully dressed. Now he either fucked her and he's getting ready to leave, or he couldn't fuck her and was getting ready to leave."

This is my father, Maggie thought. *For godsake, I don't need to hear this about my father.* She wanted to get up to leave, but he was blocking the way. Stumpf took a noisy slurp from his Coke and got to the meat of his case.

"I read the medical report. I read the crime scene report. They do an autopsy, and the hooker has no come in her vagina and they find no condoms anywhere in the place. So maybe you're thinking, he can't get it up. I know hookers. They're professionals. They'll try to help a guy who can't get it up. But your dad had no saliva on his dick. They check for that, too, you know. Doesn't fit."

Stumpf, who fancied himself a ladies' man, put on his most charming smile. He popped a Mentos and seemed about to say "Ta da!" to celebrate his ingeniousness.

"So, that's why you think somebody murdered my father. Because he couldn't consummate an affair with a hooker and didn't get a blow job?"

Stumpf shrugged. "That's one thing. And another thing." Stumpf tapped on a highlighted portion of the autopsy report. "Read that."

Maggie read the report out loud. "Five-centimeter gaping occipital scalp laceration with underlying hematoma."

"Picture this," Nate went on. "Your dad is sitting in bed, puts a gun to his chest, and shoots himself. He falls back onto a mattress and cuts the back of his head. Come on, 'open and shut' my ass."

"So what do you think happened?"

"I think somebody shot the hooker, coldcocked your dad, shot him, made it look like he did it himself, and then set the room on fire."

Maggie looked at her watch. She would have to leave now if she was going to make her flight. *What was it?* she thought. *Her father frequented prostitutes? Her father was gay? Her father killed a prostitute? Her father committed suicide? Her father was murdered? What should I wish for?* she thought, with burning bile welling up in her belly.

"How do you find out the truth?" she asked.

"I ask a lot of questions. And sometimes I get rough. I charge $300 per hour."

"Mr. Stumpf, I can't afford that."

Nate Stumpf leaned to the side a bit and stared at the young blonde. His eyes followed her curves from the arch of her neck to her knees. He took her hand and gently caressed her fingertips with his.

"I would accept other types of compensation," he said with a wicked smile. His upper lip was sweating.

Maggie pulled her hand away, and shoved him off the seat, so she could get out. She stood and strode toward the door.

Nate yelled after her. "I meant credit. Credit or barter. What did ya think I meant?!"

Maggie was out the door, but before she got to her car, she thought again. What if he was right? There was no way she would or could pay three hundred dollars an hour, but he said credit or barter, didn't he? She walked back into the diner. Stumpf was at the cashier's counter paying the bill.

"Mr. Stumpf—"

The detective turned around. He smiled broadly, exhibiting his yellow, crooked teeth, and looked like he was salivating.

"I didn't mean for you to get the wrong impression," he said with all the charm he could muster. "I'm really quite a nice guy, once you get to know me."

"Mr. Stumpf, my father bought a five-hundred-thousand-dollar life-insurance policy one year ago. It's uncollectible on a suicide. If you prove my father was murdered, I'll give it to you."

"Half a mil?"

"That's right."

Nate Stumpf thought a moment about how he'd pay his bills on potential earnings, but at this moment he had no other potential.

"Well then," he said, still leering at her, "you've hired yourself a private dick. I guess you won't have that plane to catch. Let's sit down again. I have questions to ask."

"All right."

"Can I change your mind about the potpie? They serve good food here."

Maggie had no appetite. She was still second-guessing her decision.

> *Science is always wrong. It never solves a*
> *problem without creating ten more.*
> —George Bernard Shaw

CHAPTER FOURTEEN

B esides the task of training his troops and refining their missions, Colonel McGraw was also directed to listen to a bunch of non-military folk who had very unique ideas on how to best utilize their special talents. While General Shell and his scientists chose what ideas would be presented, McGraw was generally given the leeway to choose if he wanted to buy into it and implement it.

While they waited for their lecturer to set up his presentation, Shell laid out McGraw's new mission.

"Link, your troops have done a superb job in annihilating small hamlets that we've targeted as terrorist camps. But we've started them off easy. Your missions have been in relatively open areas, easy to re-connoiter, well suited for quick attack and retreat. But we both know that most of our enemies are not hiding in little villages. They're hiding under rocks. And that's where the battle has to go."

Shell described McGraw's next target, a vast Al-Queda military base called Zwahar Kezar Al-Badr, or the "Worm Hole," an area of deep lattice caves inside the walls of a steep gorge in the Sodyaki Ghar Mountains, part of the Hindu Kush mountain chain that stretched from Eastern Afghanistan to the border of Pakistan.

"Intelligence from captured Al-Queda indicates that some of these caves are as deep as a hundred meters. Of course we've tried to bomb them. But not even bunker-busting smart bombs can fly down a narrow gorge and turn ninety degrees into the mouth of a cave. All we've managed to do is temporarily block the openings to a few caves. We've sent teams in to probe these hideouts, but it's virtually impossible for heavily armed troops to sneak up on a mountain site without the enemy knowing well in advance they're coming. And when they get there, all they find are booby traps. The enemy has plenty of time to run and plenty of other places to hide. I'm hoping you and your team can do better."

"I'm familiar with the terrain," Link told his general. "I've been there before."

"During the Tora Bora campaign?" Shell asked.

"No, sir. Two thousand years ago."

Shell smiled. "You want to give me a history lesson here?"

"I was there, sir."

"All right. All right." Shell waved him on, moving past being bemused. "What about the terrain?"

"Well, sir, Afghanistan has an arid climate. Its rivers are often dry for months. But during the rainy season, the caves in their mountains become natural cisterns. So, farmers dug down to the water table in the caves and built tunnels called *karez* to move the water from the mountains to their farms to irrigate their crops. Over centuries, the mountain caves became interconnected with thousands of these man-made tunnels. That cave and tunnel system was already in place in 328 BC. The natives fought from those caves then, too."

"They did?"

"Yes, sir. And when we marched into Afghanistan in 328 BC— it was part of the Persian Empire then—the natives fought us from those caves. But the history is written, sir. Alexander and I prevailed then. And I will this time, too."

Mack Shell was pleased to have a determined and optimistic commander, no matter where he found his conviction. His job was to give him the tools to succeed.

The current presentation was by a researcher from the University of California at Davis School of Engineering and Applied Science. He was a young man in his early thirties with a doctorate in micro-electronic engineering. He had a full beard, wore sandals, and had a T-shirt with the Rolling Stones big lips logo. He looked more ready to toss a Frisbee than present a proposal to a colonel, a general, and an assortment of PhD's. But he had an infectious exuberance for a project he had spent a decade researching.

"Magnometers," the engineer began simply, "detect the presence of metal. Metal distorts the earth's magnetic field and magnometers detect those changes. We all know that military equipment—guns, and tanks, and missiles—are all made of metal. Now, I know a soldier doesn't need a magnometer to tell him if somebody standing right in front of him in broad daylight is pointing a gun at him, but what if that gun is under a caftan? And what about whether there's a guy with a gun hiding in a concrete bunker or—"

"Or," McGraw piped in, "a hundred meters underground in some tiny tunnel?"

"Exactly. Or a hundred meters underground in a tiny tunnel."

Tired of being lectured like some simpleton, Link pressed the young man. "You can get to the point!"

"Yes, sir. Well, we've been able to detect metals deep underground for a while now—but the magnometers you need are big. They need a lot of power. And they're not practical for a soldier to lug around on a battlefield."

The engineer pulled a small, thin round disc from his pocket—thinner and smaller than a dime with several tiny wires protruding from it.

"This is a micro-magnometer. It can focus and detect the presence of metal—think military equipment like a tank, truck, or even a soldier holding a rifle—from a hundred feet away. And it is not meant to be powered by any outside source. It's designed to be powered by the normal acid-base chemical interactions in the brain. I've implanted it in pigs and monkeys. If you put it in the temporal regions, the animal gets auditory stimuli when any metal is detected. If you implant it the olfactory area, there's a taste or smell reaction."

"And how do you shut it off?" McGraw asked.

"A magnet. You wave a magnet over it and it shuts off. Another magnet, back on."

"Any problems?" General Shell asked.

"Seizures. Some of the animals have had seizures. There has, of course, been no human testing. But if the military has volunteers . . ."

McGraw stayed after the main lecture was over to watch the movies. The professor had filmed the procedure required to implant the magnometers. The animals underwent craniotomies—surgical drills cut through skulls to remove a flap of bone to access the brain. It wasn't a pretty picture.

The advantage of working on the Lemuria Project, however, was whatever questions one had, there were always experts to answer them and they were never far off. Minutes after the presentation, McGraw simply walked from the conference room to the third-floor offices of Marty White. Dr. White, formerly chairman of the Department of Neurosurgery at USC Medical Center, was now Lemuria's chief of neurosurgery. Just two years before, the forty-five-year-old handsome, athletic, egotistical surgeon had been at the top of his field, with a Ferrari F-430 Spider in his garage and starlets in his bed. And then, in just a few months, his career was over. He developed Parkinson's disease and a fine tremor. Although medications suppressed most of his symptoms, the results were not sufficient to allow him to perform the most delicate surgeries. Then he underwent his own brain surgery. Marty had a DBS, a deep brain stimulator, implanted in his brain. The device emitted high-frequency electrical impulses to block the signals that caused his tremors. It was like a "pacemaker for the brain" and completely relieved his symptoms. Unfortunately, patients were still hesitant to allow a surgeon with a history of Parkinsonian tremors and electrodes in his brain to operate on theirs.

"Marty, are you gonna waste away in this office reading journals?" Julius Wagner had personally confronted the surgeon. And then he teased his ego. "Or, will you let me put your golden hands to work on a project that will change history?"

Dr. White had indeed been kept busy by Lemuria. Mack Shell and Julius Wagner had put him into their business of genetic engineering. But most of what he did was postmortem work, measuring brain weight, examining pathology specimens, and accessing anomalies and cancers. When McGraw showed up with questions about micro-magnometers, Marty White listened enthusiastically.

"I like the idea, Marty," Link admitted, "but I don't like the idea of cracking the skulls on my soldiers or having them flopping around with seizures in the field."

"No problem," Marty replied. "I'll go through the nose."

The advantage of a military research project with almost unlimited funds and the security of a Manhattan Project was that ideas could reach fruition quickly. The next morning, Marty White had performed the first successful transphenoidal implantation of a micro-magnometer. His transphenoidal approach allowed him to reach the brain through the patient's nose rather than by cracking open a skull. And a week after the Davis engineer had first presented his idea, he was back at his UC campus actually tossing Frisbees. Within that same week, McGraw's troops had attacked two terrorist strongholds in the caves of the Hindu Kush Mountains of Northern Pakistan. There were several survivors—women, children, and a few old men—but no one carrying a weapon. And fortunately, Link thought, none of his troops had a seizure.

> *I had six honest serving men.*
> *They taught me all I knew: Their names were Where*
> *and What and When—and Why and How and Who.*
> —Rudyard Kipling

CHAPTER FIFTEEN

Nate Stumpf lived in pretty nice digs considering that most years his salary fell below the poverty line. But that was his declared salary. He made most of his money off the books. His was a cash business. He didn't take checks. And that's what made his living arrangement sweet. Some people were bicoastal. Stumpf was intrastate-al. He spent half his time in Northern California, and the rest in Southern California, splitting his business between spying on the peccadilloes of the nouveau riche in Silicon Valley and the Hollywood elite in LA. He had his place in the Haight and, in the summer, he lived in a rent-controlled apartment in Santa Monica, right on the beach. Summers at the seashore was a prize he was given by an old television producer he'd done some shady favors for in the past, shady meaning illegal, like wiretapping. His neighbors at the beach made millions, and yet he had the same view as they—the Pacific, a broad white sandy beach, and lots of buxom bikini-clad babes on roller skates.

Most of his jobs involved the sorry chore of tailing and photographing some harlot of a wife or playboy husband. He'd sit in his car and stare at a house for hours waiting for someone to come in or go out. Then, if they left, he'd sit some more, following behind in his car. Sometimes his libido would get stirred by one of his "vics" dry humping behind some restaurant or getting a blow job. But most of the time his gigs were simply ass callusing. Now, he thought, he finally had a job worthy of his talents. If he could catch the murderer of a Nobel Prize winner, he would not only have lots of bucks but the fame he deserved as well. He fantasized how he might get the girl, too.

He had to narrow down the suspects first. What was the big deal about what Professor Wagner did that earned him a Nobel Prize? And what was it about that research that would make anyone go through the machinations of faking a bizarre murder-suicide? Julius Wagner had worked in a field that could boost products worth billions for high-tech pharmaceutical companies. Stumpf suspected the obvious—money. It was the most common of motives in his experience. Stumpf first had to convince his client, the victim's daughter, about his theory, and she didn't look like anybody's fool. He wouldn't get paid unless he was right and proved himself right. Stumpf knew he would have to work for any reward, and so he read. He went to the UCLA libraries to bone up on Dr. Julius Wagner and his life's work. It was a tedious process for a fellow who was twelve units short of his AA degree but, after two days, he fancied himself an expert on genetics.

Dr. Wagner, he learned, chose his academic major, genetics, in 1955, the same year that another geneticist working in a lab in Bar Harbor, Maine, discovered that one of his experimental mice was limping in its cage. Examining it, he discovered a Ping-Pong ball–sized tumor in its scrotum. It was a testicular tumor, a cancer, a teratoma to be exact, and in it were an assortment of mouse parts, muscle, bone, teeth, and skin. He then transplanted pieces of the tumor into other mice. In some of the mice, the tumor tissue grew bone, in others muscle, or skin, or other specialized cells. These were embryonic or stem cells, the same kind of cells that were part of a primitive embryo and that eventually turned into the specialized cells of the body. The Bar Harbor geneticist had merely encountered them at the most propitious moment when some unknown stimulus was ready to turn them into a particular cell. Other scientists then worked for decades to learn what variety of stimuli would turn these primordial or stem cells into different functioning cells, such as nerve cells, which transmitted chemical and electrical stimuli, or heart cells, which beat. At first, the cells they used were from cancerous tissue. But the cancers, with abnormal chromosomes, could be expected to react abnormally. To grow normal tissue, they needed normal embryos. For another decade, stem cell research involved normal mouse embryos. But research on mice couldn't be transposed to human research. Existing human stem cell lines were aging. Using the leftover embryos from fertility clinics or therapeutic abortions posed ethical quandaries. Even when human embryonic research was not constrained by politics and moral debates, applying that research to human disease and using human volunteers continued to be a thorny issue. Dr. Wagner had taken a different approach. As had other researchers, he worked with primates. But while most had chosen the smaller rhesus monkeys, Wagner elected to work with chimpanzees, a larger animal but more genetically similar to humans. He had not only helped map the genetic code, or genome sequence, for chimpanzees, he'd developed methods to grow chimp stem cells, and had discovered several essential triggers that caused them to develop into particular tissue types.

Stumpf was convinced that Dr. Wagner's murder had something to do with big business. Maybe Professor Wagner had discovered a cure for something, maybe AIDS, maybe cancer. There was big money to be made in providing new treatments, and big money to be lost if old treatments went by the wayside. Pharmaceutical companies stood to make or lose billions and—well, people were killed for a lot less.

Nate Stumpf's second meeting with Maggie was at Denny's on Wilshire Boulevard. He thought about taking her someplace nicer, but he wasn't on any expense account and Denny's had a twofer. He was meeting to lay out his plan of attack and impress her with his research on her father and his scientific smarts. It wasn't long after he opened his mouth that he knew he had stepped in it—deep shit. He had made one grave mistake. He had failed to learn anything about his client.

"You see, Maggie," Stumpf began, "your father was this world-famous geneticist who worked with chimp genes. You know, chimps are a lot like humans, and he could manipulate chimp genes. I think he probably knew how to do the same with human genes. And with pharmaceutical companies in the game to make billions on human genetic research, well . . ."

"You don't think I know what my father did?"

"Well," Stumpf replied, trying hard to maintain his credibility, "he worked in a very esoteric field and I thought you might like some background—"

"Mr. Stumpf," she interrupted, and rapidly began to peel away his ego. "We are all members of the animal kingdom. We are of the metazoan subkingdom, chordata phylum, vertebrata subphylum, class mammalian, subclass theria, infraclass eutheria, primate order, suborder anthropoidea, superfamily hominoidea. This group includes modern and extinct humans and arthropod apes. Arthropod apes are tailless and include the gibbon, the chimpanzee, the gorilla, and the orangutan. And as humans, we share up to 98.6 percent of our genetic makeup with our closest relatives, and certainly yours, the chimpanzee. Don't tell me about my father's work, Mr. Stumpf. I know what he did. I have a bachelor's degree in biochemistry from Stanford, a master's in genetics from Cal Tech, and I'm working on my PhD at Princeton. Just tell me why he was killed."

Stumpf dropped his head, crossed his arms, and looked like he was trying to curl in a fetal position. "I don't know yet," he said, embarrassed. "Maybe it had something to do with his work."

"Of course it had something to do with his work!" she slammed him again.

The waitress returned to refill their coffee. He needed more of a stimulant than that to get his juices flowing. Maggie watched her sleuth pull a small silver flask from his jacket pocket to spike his brew.

"It's nine o'clock in the morning."

"I'm working on your case. Sometimes I need a little boost." And Stumpf quickly downed the Irish coffee. "Know what I think? It's right-wing nuts. You know those same people who think they've got God on their side, who bomb abortion clinics, who don't approve of manipulating genes and bettering humanity with genetic engineering. We need to look into whether he ever got death threats from those kinds of people."

"Think again. Those kinds of people liked my father. He worked with chimps. Not humans."

God, Nate Stumpf thought, *getting this fame and fortune ain't gonna be easy.*

"My father emptied out his office just days before he died. And in the weeks and months before, he was busy interviewing people for something called the Lemuria Project. But no one in his department at Stanford knows anything about it. Why is it that many of the best researchers in his field, people that he interviewed recently, are no longer at their old jobs and their universities and have no forwarding address? There's only one guy, tops in his field, who's still around, and I can't get him to take my calls. So, I don't know, but maybe my father's death has something to do with that."

"What was the name of this project he was working on again?"

"The Lemuria Project?"

Maggie watched as Stumpf straightened up like an inflatable toy. Either his morning cocktail was kicking in, she thought, or blood was finally getting to his brain.

"Do you know what Lemuria is?" he asked her. This time he wasn't going to step in it.

"I have no idea." Maggie shrugged. The more she talked to this man, the more pleased she was that she hadn't agreed to pay him by the hour.

With the waitress pouring another refill, Stumpf drank his coffee—straight this time. He smiled broadly. He wanted to be clearheaded when he impressed her. There were some things he did know. He knew he could hold his liquor. He knew he was great in bed. He knew he had a knack for this investigation business. And he knew mythology.

"I know *Lemuria*," he said emphatically.

Maggie flinched as if she had been slapped in the face. Maybe the little man would surprise her after all.

"You do?"

"Yes. *Lemuria* is from mythology. And I know all about myths. I know Greek mythology, Indian mythology, Celtic and Chinese mythology, and, of course, I know about the more modern mythologies like Tolkein's *Lord of the Rings* and C.S. Lewis's *Narnia*." Stumpf paused. He didn't want to her to think he was some crazy cultist. "And," he said, plying his finger in the air to make the point, "I knew all about them before the movies came out. I'm not one of these fad mythologists. I know about Oceanic and Pacific Island mythology. That's how I know about *Lemuria*.

"Lemuria"—Stumpf went on to explain while preening himself a bit—"was an ancient civilization that existed ten thousand years ago, some say fifty thousand years ago, long before the Egyptian pharaohs and their pyramids. It was a continent somewhere in the South Pacific Ocean, between North America and Asia and Australia. It was supposedly a very advanced and spiritual civilization until it disappeared at the same time as Atlantis, when the Great Flood came."

"Lemuria is like Atlantis?" she asked.

"Yeah, like Atlantis."

"The Great Flood? The one in the Bible?"

"Yeah, that one. Do you think maybe your father discovered Lemuria?"

This man's an idiot, Maggie thought.

How can I fuck her? Stumpf contemplated, quite impressed with himself.

> *Whatever it is that lives, a man, a tree, or a*
> *bird, should be touched gently, because the time is short.*
> *Civilization is another word for respect for life.*
> —Elizabeth Goudge

CHAPTER
SIXTEEN

Nate Stumpf wasn't the only expert on mythology. General Mack Shell surpassed him in every way. He was not only familiar with ancient myths but with ancient civilizations and ancient warfare, as well. As the military director of the Lemuria Project, he had named it. He had also adopted Alexander's battle scythe, albeit upon Colonel McGraw's recommendation. Apparently, the weapon, as McGraw would have him believe, was favored by Ptolemy, Alexander's general, who also studied under Aristotle. In recent months, Shell had also gained a fairly expansive knowledge of genetic engineering. He liked to think of himself as a Renaissance man and he likely was.

In the course of recruiting specialists for Lemuria, many people whose talents and expertise couldn't simply be bought by money were given great insight into the nature of the top-secret project to entice their participation. Most accepted the extraordinary opportunity to become a part of history. A few—very few—did not. Although they had agreed to keep secrets, General Shell felt that they needed an extra incentive to remain silent. He had flown back to the States from his Pacific headquarters to inspect and approve of two young men, FBI agents in Los Angeles, who had been assigned the mission to provide that "incentive" and protect the secret of Lemuria. He wasn't interested in personally meeting them. He'd know when he saw them if they were right for the job.

He had another reason for returning. The job of bringing Lemuria to fruition was a stressful one. He wanted to refill his spiritual tank. That's why, after his visit to LA, he planned to head to Sedona, Arizona—to relax, meditate, and reflect on his mission. Sedona, which of late had become a tourist mecca, had always been a spiritual place. Shell had been there many times before.

From Los Angeles, he flew into Luke Air Force Base, where a car and driver waited. He was driven two hours to Sedona—to a modern but rustic house set into red rock cliffs overlooking Boynton Canyon. The house was owned by the Pentagon, who offered it to its generals as a retreat.

Standing on a redwood deck overlooking the canyon below, he watched small groups of tourists hiking into the hills with local guides. He couldn't hear what they were saying, but he knew they would be speaking about the spirits and legends in this holy place. Shell learned the stories many years before from his own personal guide, Quilty.

Boynton Canyon was a sacred place for the local Yavapai-Apache Indians. The Apache legends paralleled biblical stories. Indian prophets foretold of a great flood and of a wise father who set his daughter adrift in a hollowed log boat. She was the only one of her tribe to survive when the boat came to rest on the sacred grounds of Boynton Canyon. The tribe was renewed when this last woman immaculately conceived with the help of the sun god. Although the U.S. Army had exiled the Apaches from their homes here in 1875, their descendants still returned each year to perform ceremonies to honor their First Mother and their creation. This place was their Garden of Eden.

The mountain air was cool and fresh. His only company was silence. Shell stood on the wood deck and raised his palms to the sky. "I am open," he whispered to no one. With the coming of dusk, he gazed up at the mist-shrouded red rock cliffs. It was easy to anthropomorphize the mountain, to imagine faces in the rocks—a screaming face, a pensive face, an Egyptian sphinx, reptiles, dogs, monkeys, lovers, whole families. Walt Disney had lived in Sedona from 1958 to 1969 and brought his artists there for inspiration. It was in Sedona where they created *Fantasia*. It was for that same inspiration that the general came time and again. And then Shell felt him. He didn't hear the door open, nor anyone call a greeting, not a footstep, nor a disturbing breeze. But Quilty had come.

Mack Shell had met Robert Quilty nearly two decades earlier on a tour of the U.S. Army Hospital in Landstuhl, Germany, where the most serious battle injuries were air-evac'd. Quilty was a patient. He was a lowly private, perhaps ten years Shell's junior, who had forsaken his job as a high-school English teacher to enlist. The young man with red hair and a ruddy, freckled complexion had been wounded in a friendly fire accident during the first Persian Gulf War. His company had moved more rapidly to a forward position than anyone had anticipated, and an F-14 mistakenly dropped its bomb load on them. He had sustained severe burns and had lost his left arm, but he would survive. With half his body still wrapped in burn dressings, Quilty meandered about the ward visiting other patients. He had a wonderful smile, an infectious laugh, and though it seemed absurd, Shell believed his touch could heal.

When Shell finally caught sight of Quilty approaching him from across the room, he smiled in pleased anticipation. His skin became warm and his body seemed to tingle as if being touched by a gentle hand.

Shell recalled their first meeting. He had sat next to the young man on a park bench at the hospital, and the conversation turned to how Quilty came to have such apparent inner strength and compassion. Shell listened as Quilty explained the legend of Lemuria.

"There was once a beautiful tropical paradise, a Garden of Eden if you will," he began. "This paradise was called Lemuria. Millions of people lived there tens of thousands of years ago, before any of the written history with which we are now familiar. Their civilization lived in peace, and harmony, and prosperity. There were no nations then, no borders, no language barriers, no religions."

Mack Shell listened politely at first but indifferently. Quilty, recognizing Shell's apathy, became quiet. He gently took Shell's hand and turned it palm up. He ran his fingers above Shell's hand. Startled, Shell pulled his hand away. He had felt Quilty's touchless touch and seemed to hear his unspoken words. *I know you will find it hard to believe, but do you want to believe?*

Shell heard himself answer aloud, "Yes." He was now prepared to listen.

"The Lemurians," Quilty continued his tale, "had no disease and lived to be hundreds of years old. They believed in the oneness of man and nature, and after centuries of evolution, they developed the ability to commune with each other and with nature by telepathy. They also had the ability of astral travel, that is, they could move beyond their bodies. They had no need for vehicles.

"The Lemurians sensed that a great cataclysm was coming—a great flood. While they hoped that some of them would survive to preserve their culture, they took precautions to preserve their knowledge and talents by burying sacred crystals throughout the world that could emanate the power of their knowledge to those prepared to receive it. Believers, like myself, describe these places as having a unique energy, a power from Mother Earth that enhances one's inner spirit. The Lemurians placed this extraordinary energy in special places—Stonehenge in England, Ayers Rock in Australia, Nazca in Peru, the Great Pyramid at Giza, and among these sacred red rocks in Sedona.

"We are all descendants of Lemuria," Quilty taught him. "Their powers remain within our very cells, in our genes—powers we call ESP, telepathy, teleportation, telekinesis. During the Lemurian civilization, these were all human attributes. They now remain dormant in our subconscious, but, with the right stimulus, they can be reawakened."

General Shell had renewed his spirituality alongside Quilty many times over the years. Each time, they would meet in Sedona overlooking the Apache holy places in Boynton Canyon.

"Boynton Canyon in Sedona," Quilty explained, "is one of the unique power spots on the planet, a giant conductor of psychic energy. Such energy is neither good nor bad. It just amplifies the space you're in. If you come here feeling anger, then you'll become angrier. If it's a creative seed you carry, it will sprout. If you feel love, it will make you feel more deeply in love.

"Today when people seek to find God or something loftier within themselves, they enter cathedrals, or temples, or mosques. The ancients built pyramids and stone temples to try to reach a higher plane. Some, like Native American Indians, sought out grand settings like this to commune with their creator, regal places that have unusual energy to bring them closer to God."

"Do you feel the energy?" Quilty would ask.

And each time he met him, Shell felt it even stronger.

To Mack Shell, Sedona became a spiritual mecca, a place for inspiration, soul searching, and soul nourishing, a place where there was harmony between man and nature. For a man who made war his life's work, this was his place of peace.

While Quilty described many places in the world where one could find remnants of Lemuria's spiritual energy, they were all trampled by tourists and real or fraudulent soul searchers. There was but one spiritual place that remained virtually untouched. It was the original land of Lemuria. It was Quilty who encouraged General Shell to choose Diego Garcia as the site for his greatest achievement, because millennia ago the island had been the tip of Lemuria's highest peak. Diego Garcia, Quilty taught, was the last vestige of the lost continent.

Mack Shell never articulated his beliefs in great detail to his friends or peers. Most would frown at his tales and describe his faith as sin. Christianity held such power in America, and particularly in the armed forces, that any belief that did not include redemption through Christ would make him out as some bizarre cultist. But nevertheless, he felt he could be a vehicle that would help reveal or release this ancient knowledge and perhaps return a harmony to earth—an earth scarred with wars, ripe with the seven deadly sins, with nature itself in disarray. The ancients had an innate wisdom and spirituality, a love and respect for each other and for Mother Earth. Perhaps, with a few billion dollars, and the talents of a bunch of scientists busy manipulating the secrets in men's genes, Lemuria, and everything it stood for, would rise again. Of course, in the meantime, a few people would have to die first. After all, Mack Shell was also a pragmatist.

> *He that can have patience, can have what he will.*
> —Benjamin Franklin

CHAPTER SEVENTEEN

Ding dong.

Dr. Kyle Evans held a prestigious chair in genetics at UCLA. The professor was a tall, lanky man in his early fifties. He lived alone in a posh Westwood neighborhood bordering the gates of Bel Air. He had never married, and other than his work, exercise was his life. He was most often seen in his neighborhood and about campus jogging or biking wearing Spandex shorts. Maggie Wagner knew him well. He had visited with her father several times at Stanford during collegial conferences. He was one of those health nuts who popped a dozen herbal supplements daily, drank only specialty vitamin-enriched water, and maintained one of those diet regimens suitable for rabbits and gurus on Indian mountaintops. Because he was such an exercise freak, she expected him to confound everyone by dropping dead unexpectedly—and ironically—one day, like Jim Fixx, the famously fit runner who wrote *The Complete Book of Running*. Maggie had found Professor Evans's name in her father's day calendar. Apparently, he had met with her father in the weeks before his death.

Maggie phoned the professor and then e-mailed him to inquire about that meeting and, perhaps, learn more about her father's Lemuria Project and any suspicions he might have. At first Dr. Evans didn't answer or return her calls. One day he inadvertently picked up his phone and curtly brushed her off by saying he had an appointment and would call back. He never did.

Ding dong. Nate Stumpf rang the doorbell again. Maggie stood by his side.

"Maybe he's not home," she suggested.

"His car's in the driveway. He's home."

Stumpf rang the doorbell again—and again, and again, and again.

Peeking through a side window, the professor could see a shady-looking, short, balding man ringing his doorbell with Maggie Wagner by his side. He didn't intend to answer and rubbed the back of his neck with apprehension.

Maggie watched as Stumpf rang the bell every five seconds. How long would he do this? Then he abruptly stopped ringing and walked to his car. He opened the trunk and retrieved a folding chair, a bottle of water, and an iPod and headset, and returned to sit down comfortably in front of Dr. Evans's front door.

"You can wait in the car if you want," he told Maggie. "If there's one virtue I have, it's patience."

He began to ring again. An hour passed, and then another, and every five seconds, twelve times a minute, 720 times an hour, he rang the bell. Stumpf sat on his chair with iPod earphones on and listened to a book on tape–motivational lectures on how to influence people and the power of positive thinking. He alternated ringing the bell using one arm, and then, when it tired, the other. In the course of this "investigative" endeavor, Stumpf began to ring Dr. Evans on his phone, as well.

The doorbell rang. The phone rang. The ringing was driving Evans mad. He thought of calling the cops, but then he'd have to answer the door and—well, what would this madman do? Two weeks earlier, he had thought of calling the police but didn't call then either.

It had been in broad daylight on a Sunday morning. He stepped out of his house to pick up his newspaper when two black men wearing nice slacks with shirts and ties walked up to him. The only black men he ever saw walking in his neighborhood were those who said they were selling magazines for college or were evangelicals proselytizing their religion. The only other blacks he ever saw in his neighborhood didn't walk. They were the ultrarich folks—mostly sports stars or entertainers—driving by in luxury cars. His only thought as the two men approached him on this beautiful Sunday morning was, *I'm not buying magazines and I have enough religion.*

General Mack Shell had eyeballed these same two young men a few days earlier from the confines of a sedan with dark-tinted windows. He was parked across from a liquor store on gang turf in South Central Los Angeles. He sat next to an FBI agent, Harley Fealkoff. Harley looked ten years younger than his fifty years, with a bushy mustache and well-coiffed hair. He was the photogenic guy the Bureau put out for the television crews when statements had to be made about touchy issues like manhunts for serial killers or sieges against villages of armed cultists. Fealkoff was also in charge of "street teams" for the Bureau. While Shell listened to the agent, he felt comfortable that he was with the kind of guy who was prepared for contingencies. Fealkoff had a .357 Magnum sitting at the ready on the center console of his car.

"I don't want to have to reach far," he said, "if the scenery turns nasty."

They were parked just down the street from the intersection of Florence and Normandie Avenues, the spot where in April 1992 the Los Angeles riots erupted and where a white truck driver, Reginald Denny, was dragged from his vehicle while parked at a stoplight and nearly beaten to death by a black mob.

"I knew Rodney King," Harley told him. "He was the ultimate asshole. You know his big quote 'Can't we all get along?' Well, with assholes you sometimes just can't."

"You see the one on the left?" Fealkoff nodded toward the taller black gangster with pectoral muscles that looked like armor plate. "He just got his law degree."

"Really?" Shell said with sincere surprise. The guy reminded him of a young, mean-looking heavyweight champ named Mike Tyson. Someone who would just as soon bite your ear off.

"In the sixties," Harley explained to his VIP passenger, "the Bureau infiltrated the Mafia and Costa Nostra with 'made men' they'd compromised. In the nineties, we started doing the same thing with black and Hispanic gangs that were edging into organized crime. We don't just pay off snitches. Just like we recruit the best and brightest out of law schools for the Bureau, we recruit the best and brightest youngsters in these communities, too. We train them and pay them to infiltrate the largest gangs in America's inner cities. Sometimes we've had to hire a few that have gone off the beaten track once or twice in their lives. We make some compromises. They make compromises. And we get the job done."

"You have FBI agents selling dope on the streets," Shell commented with some dismay.

"They're authorized to commit petty crimes. They have to fit in. Look, off the record, we don't even care if they kill rival gang members if what they're putting a stop to is really dirty. But anything big—major narcotics smuggling or bank jobs—they'd let the Bureau know about."

The men Shell saw looked like typical gangbangers. They wore low-slung jeans, with tight T-shirts outlining their rippled muscles, and were heavily tattooed. Like several others on the street, they were in the business of making side-window drug deals with cars that frequently drove up. But the FBI sedan parked across the street clearly looked like an undercover cop car. So, when cars did drive up, the "boys" just waved them on. They glowered a few minutes at the black sedan and then swaggered off down the street with a cohort of "homeboys" trailing behind.

"These men," Shell asked, "you think they're up to the job?"

"Absolutely," Fealkoff answered without hesitation. "I've trusted them with more. A law degree from a gangbanger growing up in the inner city, I think that's got to be a more noble and difficult task than my son or yours graduating from Harvard."

Shell nodded.

"You want to talk to them?" Harley asked.

"No. I'm good," Shell said. "Let's go." He was confident these two agents would serve his purposes well.

As Fealkoff drove off, he set his big gun safely under the seat again. Shell meanwhile was looking forward to Sedona.

———————

When the black men walked up to him, Professor Evans was prepared to politely listen to the first words of their "pitch" before telling them he wasn't interested. But their first words caught him off guard.

"Get on the ground, motherfucker!" One of the men pointed a shiny chrome revolver an inch from Evans's nose. He could see the bullets in the chamber. Then they shoved him facedown on the lawn.

My God, Evans thought, this is crazy. *It's broad daylight in Westwood. Don't they think someone will see? Someone will notice. Someone will help.*

"I don't have my wallet," Evans said, his voice cracking fearfully. "My wallet's in the house."

"Shut up," the second man said.

The first one pressed his mouth to Evans's ear. He could feel the moisture on his lips and the hot breath. "You've been warned," he said. "If you mention Lemuria, if you even whisper the word, we'll fuckin' kill you. And we'll mess up anybody you know or care about. You got it, motherfucker?"

The muzzle of a gun was pressed into his neck, his face pushed farther into the dirt, and then he heard a loud pop and a painful punch to the back of his neck. Was he shot?

The voice spoke into his ear again. "We've put a microchip into your neck. We'll know everything you say, everywhere you go." Then he was slapped hard on the back of the head. He felt dazed, maybe he'd pass out, but the pain passed, and when he looked up, he saw a car driving off, disappearing around the corner.

The FBI gangbangers smiled. Their marks believed they'd implanted some microchip into their necks. But it was just an air gun without pellets. Push hard enough and it hurt, bruised a bit. But there was no microchip. It was a trick that did the job. It shut people up.

Evans got up slowly and looked up and down his block. Someone was working on their garden at one end of the street. He could see a group of bike riders zipping past at the other corner. But the street was quiet. No one had noticed his assault. That's what made Shell's team seem even more fearsome. They were so brash, unafraid. Evans rubbed the back of his neck and slowly walked inside his house. He thought about calling the police. But he didn't. They'd be listening. Two days later, Julius Wagner was dead and Kyle Evans was glad he didn't call.

And now—now, some lunatic was ringing his doorbell—over and over, hour after hour. It was driving him mad. Okay, he thought, he'd open the door, tell the guy to go away, and slam the door again. Maybe—

When Evans opened the door, Stumpf shoved him inside and kept shoving until the professor found himself slumped on his couch. Stumpf was a foot shorter and forty pounds lighter then the professor. He was often puny compared to his adversaries, and he knew that to get the upper hand, he had to be decisive. *Throw the first punch* was always his first plan. Think next.

"What do you want?" the professor asked desperately. But he was subdued. He wasn't moving from the couch.

Nate Stumpf pulled out his cell phone and pushed *send*.

Maggie had been napping in the car across the street for two hours when her cell phone rang.

"I'm in. He's here," Stumpf said.

She jumped out of the car and ran inside.

Maggie got right to the point. "Dr. Evans, you knew my father. You were friends and colleagues. I know he met with you and talked about something called the Lemuria Project."

That word, Evans thought, sweat beading on his brow, *that word is going to get me killed.*

"My father didn't commit suicide. He was murdered."

She waited for his response. Evans knew it was true. But he wasn't going to say anything. His neck was still sore from that implanted microchip. He'd been well warned.

"I think it had something to do with a research project he was working on—the Lemuria Project. I want to know what it was."

Evans sat up on the couch and looked away. Stumpf thought about punching him in the face, just once. Sometimes that worked.

"Please," Maggie pleaded. "My father was murdered. His name has been ruined. I have to know. Does it have anything to do with one of the big pharm companies?"

No answer. But Stumpf was used to reading people. The professor averted his eyes, looking down and away. He knew something.

Stumpf wished he could just pull out a gun and shove it into the guy's face. A gun would work. But he didn't have a gun because he didn't have a permit to carry one. It was virtually impossible to get a permit to carry a concealed weapon in Los Angeles. You either had to have some political clout with a local sheriff or a lot of money. Stumpf had neither. Now, if he lived in Arizona, well, there he'd be packing on both hips. He'd been ringing a doorbell for hours. He was hungry, tired, and he was getting paid by results, not by the hour. Time for answers. He punched the guy in the face.

"What the hell are you doing?" Maggie yelled at him and ran to the refrigerator.

Nate looked the professor straight in the eye and held up his fist. "I want to know about Lemuria."

"I'm sorry," Maggie said, coming back with some ice in a glass and putting it to the professor's swollen cheek. "That won't happen again," she said, glaring at Stumpf.

Evans took the cold glass in hand and held it to his cheek himself. They all sat there quiet for several minutes. Evans was too afraid to speak aloud. Stumpf had effectively been told to shut up, and Maggie, now she was the impatient one. Then Evans set the glass down and, holding up both hands in a gesture urging calm, stood up and walked to a desk. Stumpf trailed him like a shadow. The professor picked up a piece of paper, wrote something on it, and handed it to Stumpf. In just the moment that Stumpf glanced at what he'd written, the professor bolted for the door. Stumpf rushed to give chase, but the professor was racing down the street with long limbs and a big stride. Stumpf knew he would never catch him, and anyway he was too tired. He looked at the paper the professor had scribbled on and handed it to Maggie. It had four letters written on it: *B I O T.*

"He wanted to tell us something, but for some reason, he couldn't," she lamented.

"*BIOT*," Stumpf muttered. "What's that? Short for bio or biotech something?"

"I don't know," Maggie said. "But you will find out, won't you?" Stumpf nodded. "I'll do my best."

"I'm depending on you," she said and proffered the first friendly smile she had ever given him.

I should've finished college, Stumpf thought to himself. He desperately wanted to please her, and not just for the payday.

> *And I heard the voice of a man between the banks of Ulai, who called, and said: "Gabriel, make this man to understand the vision." So he came near where I stood; and when he came, I was terrified, and fell upon my face; but he said to me: "Understand, son of man; for the vision belongs to the time of the end. . . ."*
> —Daniel 8:15–17

CHAPTER EIGHTEEN

They reclined back in their seats, napping side by side, her hand resting atop his.

Fala opened her eyes as a rumble disturbed the quiet din of engine noise and clinking glasses. She looked over at Krantz as his stomach growled loudly again.

"Sorry," he apologized, glancing over at the rest of the passengers in first class who were sipping on California cabernet and carving through Kobe beef filet mignons. An aroma of gustatory delights permeated the air and teased him.

Fala smiled and kissed him gently on the cheek. The colonel was hungry. It was late afternoon, and their flight from Paris was about to land in Teheran. They had not eaten since five a.m. It was Ramadan, and Fala was fasting. Muslims practiced sawm, or fasting, for the entire month of Ramadan. They ate and drank nothing, not even water, during daylight hours. Fala got up early for suhoor, the meal eaten before dawn. She broke her fast again at sunset with a meal known as iftar. The rest of the day, according to her faith, she fasted.

Although Krantz was Jewish, he didn't feel right eating in front of her, tempting her. Go ahead and growl, he spoke to his innards. We're a couple, and if a billion Muslims can fast for a month, so can one Jew. While Krantz was a secular Jew, he admired the Islamic devotion to Ramadan. The upcoming Christian Christmas and Jewish Hanukkah holidays were religious events that had become excuses for consumerism. Ramadan, on the other hand, remained focused on its theme of self-sacrifice and devotion to Allah. He respected that.

Joshua Krantz had come to know many Muslims while growing up. He went to school with some, did business with others, but none had ever been his friend. So, he never really learned much about their faith and never cared. He had been stuffed too full of the religious fables of Judaism during his youth to be interested in hearing about the tales and allegories of Islam—until he met Fala. He was receptive to listening to a lot of things while cuddled next to her warm body.

"Around 610 AD, a caravan trader named Mohammad was heading to Mecca thinking about God," she explained during one of their pillow talks.

"There's not much else to do when you're wandering in the middle of a desert on a camel," Krantz had responded.

She ignored his snide response. "One night a voice called to him. It was the angel Gabriel."

"Is this the same Gabriel that appears in the book of Daniel? The one Christians believe foretold the birth of Jesus?"

"Same one."

"He got around," Krantz joked. He'd always preferred to joke about religion rather than ever talk about it seriously. It was like a third rail. Step on it wrong and it would kill you, or a relationship.

"Gabriel told Mohammad that he'd been chosen to receive the word of Allah. It was during this month, the month of Ramadan, that Allah revealed those words to Mohammad, which would later be transcribed as the Qur'an."

Krantz was thinking about his lessons on Islam as their plane descended into Teheran's Mehrabad Airport. He remembered other lessons he had learned in school as a child, the story of Daniel in the lions' den. There the Bible referred to the messenger Gabriel as the "Left Hand of God." And here he was about to enter a lions' den to look for the "Right Hand of God." Is this my reward for loving history, he thought, to risk being eaten alive?

They both wore traditional Egyptian dress, the gown-like galabiya. His was simple gray; hers, black with some embroidery about the neck. Disembarking, Fala adjusted her head scarf, or hijab. This time they both held Egyptian passports. Krantz's was an exquisite forgery. A taxi drove them from the airport and through the capital's mishmash of skyscrapers and mosques. A religious parade snarled traffic in midtown before they broke through to the desert highway on the way to Qom, 130 kilometers to the south.

Although Fala knew little about modern Iran, she knew Islamic history.

"Qom is one of many Shiite desert shrine cities that stretch from Najaf in Iraq to Mashhad in eastern Iran," she explained. "Each is a crumbling old city with narrow alleyways surrounding a holy site. Qom's sacred site is a ninth-century golden-domed mosque built as the tomb of Fatima, the sister of the Eighth Imam."

"And that's important?"

"If you're a Shiite, it is," Fala went on. "Sunnis have tradition-ally followed a more secular view of leadership, a caliph-ruled one. Shias, on the other hand, believe that the Prophet designated Ali to be his successor, to be the imam or spiritual and secular leader of all of Islam, and that imams should rule. Ali was the first of twelve imams. Because the caliphs knew they were a threat to their power, they kept them secluded in Medina, a long way from their capitals. But in the eighth century, a Sunni caliph decided to put an end to the conflict between the two sects and asked the Eighth Imam to become his successor."

"So then why are the Shias and Sunnis still at odds?" Krantz asked.

"Somebody poisoned the Eighth Imam."

"Islam—I think it would make for a great soap opera," Krantz re-marked, shaking his head. He should have known better.

"And Judaism wouldn't?" Fala countered. "What with King David killing off his mistress Bathsheba's husband; one son raping a sister; another, Absalom, killed trying to usurp his father's throne."

Krantz kept quiet and turned to simply watch the passing scen-ery, the silver mirror-like reflection of one of the many salt lakes between the Teheran and Qom. Never parry swords over religion, he reminded himself. It would always be a losing battle.

Qom's golden dome of Fatima wasn't the most dramatic land-mark that caught the eye of Joshua and Fala as they drove into town. Two grand amusement parks were built on each side of the holy site, and it was surrounded by dozens of tacky neon-lit shops selling Qom's specialty, *sohan*—a saffron-flavored candy embedded with pistachio nuts, similar to peanut brittle.

While Teheran was the capital and home of government bureau-crats, the real power was held in Qom by the Grand Ayatollah. Qom was also the country's most prominent educational center for Shiite Islam. It had the largest *madrasa*, or religious university, Howzeh-ye Elmieh. The founder of the Iranian theocracy, Ayatollah Khomeini, had studied there. And so, it attracted Shiites from around the world who wanted to become mullahs, Islamic religious teachers. It would be a mullah who could tell Krantz if this new and ancient weapon, Alexander's battle scythe, was one of their creations and if the *Maimun*, the Right Hand of God, was also their doing.

They checked into a small hotel near the Fatima shrine. The streets were crowded with people shopping for *iftar*, their break-the-fast celebration. Turbaned clerics meandered among young men in American-style blue jeans, bearded and grimy Afghan migrant laborers, and women in modest but elegant long, embroidered jackets and designer head scarves. Qom, population one million, was a religious but eclectic city.

Among her peers in the world of Egyptian archaeology, some were religious. Fala had used one of those connections for an introduction to a prominent mullah in Qom. Krantz was confident of the outcome. The mullah would either provide them insight or shout to the crowd "Kill the Jew!" No matter, he was too hungry to worry. The sun was setting and the streets were emptying as people rushed home to be with their families when he and Fala sat down at an outdoor café for their *iftar*.

What he wanted was a beer or glass of wine. But he knew that not only were alcoholic beverages not served in restaurants, they were strictly forbidden in the entire country. He could order a nonalcoholic beer or a soft drink, but decided to stick with the national beverage and ordered *ckai*, a sweet tea sipped through a sugar cube. The menu had the classic Middle East staples—assortments of lamb, eggplant, yogurt, and wheat bread.

A young cleric, who could barely have been twenty, entered and sat across from them. He was turbaned but so young that his beard was only an irregular curly stubble. He sipped his tea quietly and said nothing as they devoured their meal. Only when they had finished did he speak.

"You are the friend of Mustafa Khalil?" he asked Fala.

"Why, yes," she answered, surprised. They had supposed that their contact would meet them later at their hotel.

"I am Danush," he introduced himself in Arabic. "You are Fala al-Shohada?"

"Yes."

"Where are you from?" the young cleric asked, turning to Krantz.

Krantz spoke a bit of Arabic, poorly. He intended to let Fala talk, and if spoken to, provide single word responses.

"*Al Kahira*," Cairo, he answered in Arabic.

The cleric simple shook his head no.

"He's British," Fala cut in. "We work together in Cairo."

The cleric smiled and again shook his head. He handed each of them his card. He was the Grand Ayatollah's secretary.

"You are very young to have such an important job," Fala commented. "You must be very smart."

The young man smiled. "There is perhaps a little nepotism. I am his son-in-law."

This young man must, indeed, be very smart, Krantz thought. The Grand Ayatollah would not allow his daughter to marry for love or marry just anyone. This mullah had to have wisdom and potential to perhaps someday become an Ayatollah himself. Krantz realized how exceptionally bright this kid was with his next sentence.

"M'davar Ivrit?" he asked. "Do you want me to speak in Hebrew?"

Krantz jumped up from his chair. They knew who he was. He was an Israeli in Iran, and he didn't plan on be shackled and tortured. While the Israeli government had often bartered for the return of their prisoners, he detested that policy. He didn't intend on being traded for some bomber who had killed dozens of innocents. He looked frantically about for the best direction to flee.

"Calm. Calm," Danush, the young mullah, said in English. "Please sit. I can guarantee you are safe here. Although you have been less then honest with me, I assure you I am being truthful."

Krantz sat again, slowly. The mullah poured him another cup of ckai.

"You will come to no harm—not in this holy city or in my country. The Ayatollah promises it is so."

The tension he had felt since arriving in this country passed like a great relaxing sigh. He had no reason to doubt this cleric's sincerity. He went from one moment feeling like a spy sitting on needles to a tourist pleasantly dining at an outdoor café enjoying the charms of an ancient city.

The cleric retrieved a small box from a leather satchel by his foot. He set it on the table and opened it. Inside was Alexander's battle scythe. This one, however, was clearly very old.

"Where did you get this?" Fala asked.

"May I?" Krantz asked, reaching toward the weapon.

The mullah nodded his consent.

"It is part of our collection of antiquities in the National Museum, from an excavation near Tabriz."

Krantz delicately examined the 2,300-year-old artifact. Only fine threads of its original leather remained, and the bladed fingers were broken or pitted with centuries of rust. But clearly the modern weapon and the old were of the same design.

"I have read your books, Dr. Krantz," the mullah smiled. "I found them very interesting."

They even know my name, Krantz thought. *Good intelligence.*

"I know very much about my country from the time of the Hijra—Mohammad's journey from Mecca to Medina. But I do not know very much about Al-Iskandar."

"Then you should ask Miss al-Shohada," Krantz replied.

The imam politely nodded to Fala.

"Alexander the Great conquered Persia in the fourth century BC," Fala began. "Qom was supposedly a great city even then, the center of the Zoroastrian religion. On his march to India, Alexander destroyed the city, and Qom wasn't fully restored to its former prominence until the seventh century, when it became a religious center for Shi'ism."

"The Ayatollah says that Al-Iskandar is called Dhu'l-Karnayn in the Qur'an," Danush interjected. "The two-horned one. He was Muslim, you know. He destroyed the city to cleanse it and prepare it for its holy purposes."

Krantz smiled. Islam was fond of usurping anyone of historical significance into their history. Moses was Muslim. Jesus was Muslim. Why not Alexander the Great? He would allow them to adopt anyone they wanted to be a Muslim. He would assent to them calling Ben-Gurion, Golda Meir, and Ariel Sharon Muslims if he learned what he wanted to know.

"We found a lot of dead people killed by a modern version of this ancient weapon." Krantz finally got to the point. "The only survivor said just one word to identify his assailants."

"And what is this word that brings you here?"

"*Maimun,*" Fala spoke up.

The young cleric was thoughtful for a moment.

"Only this word?"

"Yes," Krantz confirmed. "Do you know what it means?"

"The word literally means 'fortunate one,'" the young mullah began. "It came to mean 'right hand,' because the right hand symbolizes strength and all that is good and fortunate. It was also used in ancient times as a derogatory description. If you called someone a 'maimun,' you called them a monkey. A euphemism, since early Islam considered monkeys to be evil because many nonbelievers, the Hindus for instance, worshiped monkeys."

"We think it means the Right Hand of God," Fala interrupted.

"Do you know the Right Hand of God?" Krantz pressed. "Is it a Shia guerrilla group?"

"You Jews and the Americans, you just do not understand," the cleric answered, somewhat perturbed. "Islamic Iran is for peace and stability everywhere. We do not engage in hostile action against any country, any people. Look at our history. Iran has never attacked Israel. Iran has never attacked the United States. We defended ourselves against Iraq. We are maligned, but we are innocent. But if somebody attacks us, we will respond."

Krantz had no intention of jumping into a political debate—not here anyway. Iran may have never attacked Israel, but they financed most of Israel's enemies and their rhetoric continued to fuel the hatred.

"So who is responsible for making this weapon of Al-Iskandar?" Fala asked.

"Who? The people who have been killed, they are Shias. Why would we kill our own brethren?"

"A Sunni terror group, then?" Krantz followed up.

Like all clergymen, the Iranian mullah had to give his answer abstractly.

"We all come from different families. We are born and cared for, and few of us want to question what our parents and grandparents have taught us. The Hindus put ash on their foreheads and pray to an elephant-headed stone god. They do this because their parents taught them this. The Christians pray to a cross or an image of Jesus or Mary. You Jews don't pray to statues, but you rock back and forth in prayer toward an old wall in Jerusalem. And we Muslims, we pray toward a stone building, the Ka'aba in Mecca. What makes us believe? We all believe because we were born and our parents believed. So, if you are looking for the truth, question what your parents have told you. They know."

"You're saying Israel already knows?" Krantz asked, bewildered.

"Your parents know," the young cleric clarified. "Your parents, the Americans."

> *There is no gambling like politics.*
> —Disraeli

CHAPTER
NINETEEN

Even with the first-class accommodations aboard a VIP Air Force C-17, it was an arduous flight from Washington to Diego Garcia—or DC to DG, as Mack Shell described the trip. The general's job was not only to guide the success of Lemuria but keep those few government officials who were privy to the project, and who held its purse strings, informed. Today, he had two senior senators from the Intelligence Committee along to see the work in progress. He hated this part of his job. He didn't trust politicians, and he didn't like being a tour guide.

"Who in the world was Diego Garcia?" one senator asked.

It was the first question everyone seemed to ask, and Mack Shell had his answers down to rote.

"The island," he explained, "was discovered by Portuguese explorers in the early 1500s. There were two explorers on two separate voyages. One captain was named Diego, the other Garcia. They came upon it at different times, but both arrived back in Lisbon at the same time and both claimed to have discovered it. So, the king named it after both of them."

After seventeen hours of not much but clouds and blue ocean, they began their descent. Diego Garcia was a tiny island in the middle of the Indian Ocean. Its stamp from the air didn't seem much bigger than nearby supertankers. The tropical island was crescent shaped, a lush green narrow reef with forty miles of shoreline that wrapped about a turquoise blue lagoon. It had once been the home of natives called Ilois, but the British had moved them all off the island in the late 1960s, when they turned it into a military base.

"Diego Garcia is British Indian Ocean Territory," the general went on, "part of an archipelago called the Chagos Islands, also called the Oil Islands. There's no petroleum here. They're called the Oil Islands because harvesting coconut oil was their main industry for centuries. The few peaks, like Diego Garcia, that poke above the ocean are part of an undersea mountain chain known as Lemuria. Some say Lemuria was once part of a lost civilization like Atlantis with a culture far more advanced then ours today."

When Shell spoke of Lemuria, he spoke of it with reverence. He looked for a glimmer of insight or curiosity, but his guests today were interested only in the practical accomplishments of the work on the island, not in any history of lost civilizations. They knew that General Shell's job was to create a new genetically designed American soldier. They had no inkling of his grander dreams, to begin a revolution in human evolution.

"The Oil Islands," Shell continued to educate his guests, "were French colonies until they became British with Napoleon's defeat in 1814. When the British started giving up their colonies and gave

Mauritania its independence in 1964, we helped them negotiate a deal. For three million pounds and our agreement to give them a favorable exchange on sugar imports, the Oil Islands were excluded from the deal for independence. They continue under British control with us as their major silent partner. Today, DG is the most secure military base in the world. It's a thousand miles from anywhere else—India's north of us, Madagascar west, Indonesia east, and Antarctica south. The only way in or out is by military air or a navy ship. The island is now home to three thousand military personnel and, with work on Lemuria, twice that many civilians. Only fifty of that number are British. Mostly they handle the customs rituals at the airport. So, while Diego Garcia is a British colony, it's now clearly colonized by Americans."

His guests peered at the island below, growing ever larger in their windows. It looked a lot like a child's foot—a small heel to the south with the arch being the lagoon entrance winding into the web space of the big and second toes. There were two heavy-bomber-capable runways, each two and a half miles long, and an assortment of jetties and piers. A dozen navy ships anchored in the harbor. There was a clump of multistory modern buildings in the middle of the island, and on the rest were scattered bungalows, towers, space-tracking domes, fuel dumps, and training areas. As they approached for landing, they could read the writing on one large water tower. It read, "DIEGO GARCIA, The Footprint of Freedom."

It only took a thirty-minute drive to tour the entire island. Mack made it seem like a resort destination.

"The folks here like to windsurf off the southern shore, and I've heard they fish for two-hundred-pound marlin just east of the lagoon. If you snorkel or dive, you can see thousands of amazing tropical fish in shallow waters off the reef. And we've got a nine-hole, par-five golf course with ocean views on either side."

He wanted to encourage the senators to lull about on the beach or ride jet skis rather than bother with investigating his work. But they were not diverted. They wanted to know about the billion-dollar research being conducted in the high-tech military hospital in the center of the island.

Theodore Berger, the senator from Rhode Island, was also a physician. That was another reason his colleagues had chosen him to make the investigative trip to DG. They expected him to have the scientific know-how to ask the right questions. Senator Berger had a puffy face, the moonfaced look common among those on chronic steroid therapy. He was battling lupus. He looked jolly, but he took his senatorial duties seriously. As they walked toward the entrance to the hospital and research facility, he caught sight of half a dozen young male patients sitting on a veranda overlooking the ocean. He turned his gaze to Shell, and the unspoken question hung between them.

"As I told you, Senator, we're not experimenting on humans. Animal research is what we're about. Maybe months or years from now, when we know more, there'll be debate and—"

The senator nodded toward the young patients. "What's the matter with those men?"

"There are thousands of people on this island. Some of them get sick."

He didn't know if that answer satisfied the senator, but it would have to do. What would put the visitors at ease, however, was "show and tell." Mack found there was one reward for having to be away from DG periodically. Each time he returned, he was elated to discover the great progress being made on the Lemuria Project in these "show and tell" sessions. Researchers, who'd been hobbled for years with meager budgets and had spent more of their energies applying for grants than actually performing research, were incubating ideas faster than anyone could have ever expected.

In a darkened room he listened along with the senators to a computer PowerPoint presentation.

"We're working on synesthesia here," Xiang Sun, a researcher from Yale, began. She was a petite Chinese woman with a perfectly smooth complexion and an ageless quality. She looked fifteen, yet she was nearly fifty.

Senator Berger knew when to keep quiet. Sometimes the most intelligent thing to do was to shut up. But what the hell was synesthesia? And why was it costing the U.S. taxpayers twelve billion dollars?

"When young mammals are born, their senses are primitive, unrefined, and undifferentiated. It takes several weeks of development before the brain separates sight, smell, taste, hearing, and touch into distinct senses. These senses that are merged at birth can, even after separating, be merged again afterward. That merging of senses is called synesthesia."

A slide showed a graphic representation of the concept. "A sound can be seen. A touch can be a taste. A sight can be heard," explained Sun, who saw only bewilderment in her audience members' eyes.

The lights came up, and two assistants entered the room with two chimpanzees. One chimp wore a red collar, the other blue.

"We have been focusing on the most common forms of synesthesia and have had good success with color hearing and blind sight. It will be easier to understand when you see it," Xiang Sun went on.

While the general and the senators awaited the demonstration, two quasi-human faces stared back at them, with just as much curiosity. The general couldn't help but smile. Fish, the chimp with the red collar, grinned back. They called him Fish, Dr. Sun later explained, because he was fond of sardines. His handlers often accommodated his taste, and in return he suffered them with the most foul of breath. They had named the blue-collared chimp Talk, obviously because he talked so much or at least tried to mimic human speech. These two were of the latest generation of genetically engineered chimps to have reached maturity.

The attendants gave some softly worded command, and both chimps pirouetted quickly to face their handlers. Then they started to play catch. Fish and Talk were very adept at catching and tossing back a ball. Then the attendants abruptly stopped and blindfolded both chimps.

"Red has had the gene that separates the sense of hearing and sight blocked. He has blind-sight synesthesia," Sun explained. "Blue is a normal chimp with normal senses. Both have been trained to play catch, but that is all."

The attendants then tossed a ball at Talk, the blue-collared chimp.

"The normal one," Xiang Sun reiterated—although in the world of Pan troglodytes, neither chimpanzee was quite normal.

Blindfolded, Talk couldn't see it. The ball just hit his torso and fell to the floor. His handler tossed several more balls to him. The result was the same. None were caught by the blindfolded animal. Then they tossed a ball at Fish, the red-collared "genetically altered" chimp and just as he had played before being blindfolded, he caught the ball and tossed it back, each and every time.

"That, gentlemen, is not a trick," the Chinese-American Yale researcher said proudly. "That is blind-sight synesthesia."

Later, Shell and the senators walked through an indoor-outdoor jungle arboretum. Living there uncaged was a menagerie of chim-panzees. Most of the animals seemed busy with their own tasks—the usual feeding, play, and mutual preening activities that had always been the entertainment draws for humans gawking at monkey houses in zoos around the world. Others were more social and actually walked alongside their visitors, even reaching out to hold hands, as they walked the meandering path through their home. Suddenly, Senator Berger began laughing.

"What?" Shell asked.

"What did they name this one?" the senator asked grinning and screwing up his nose. The chimp walking alongside him and holding his hand was farting, loudly and frequently.

Dr. Sun, who also accompanied the VIPs, kept her silence. The gas-passing chimp was not called Fart, as the senator probably im-aged. He had been affectionately named Senator.

Senator Berger was actually an advocate of Lemuria, but he had a duty, too, to ask questions. He'd seen many a good idea become half-baked into a bad one once seasoned with enough federal dollars.

"And why," he asked, "have we chosen to use chimpanzees? Why not the bigger, stronger apes, like gorillas?"

"Well, there are several reasons, Senator," Shell began. "Chimps are man's closest living relatives. We had a common ancestor only about six million years ago. Scientists have sequenced the genetic code of several species—humans, as well as fruit flies, mice, and chimps. The genetic code of chimps is more than ninety-eight per-cent the same as ours. Between us, out of three billion DNA base pairs, there are only forty million sequences that are different. A little more than one percent."

"But one of our guys, Eichler, a geneticist from Brown in your state," Dr. Sun added, "has determined that we're even more alike. You see, a lot of those forty million different sequences don't matter. They're duplicates or silent. So we're actually 98.8 percent identical. And this is what's fascinating: in Eichler's research with our young chimps, he's noted that their genetic mutation rate, how fast they're evolving, is higher than ours. Now you hear the word *mutation*, you think cancer. But don't think cancer. They're not getting cancer. The genes that are mutating are evolving. The genes are those involved with transmission of nerve signals, the perception of sound, visual interpretation. Eichler thinks our chimps are getting smarter. And we're helping them along."

The senators were then brought into a room with a dozen chimps sitting in front of computers.

"Show them Einstein," Dr. Sun ordered.

A trainer ushered the senators around one chimp intently staring at his computer screen. The trainer hit a key, and on screen a series of numbers from one to nine popped up, scattered randomly on the screen. They appeared for only a split second. Then, the numbers in those same locations were replaced by a blank square. Einstein, named for obvious reasons, then quickly touched the squares on the computer screen in the exact sequence that the numbers had appeared.

"I've played this game dozens of times," Dr. Sun said. "Everyone has. And nobody can match the chimp's ability to remember those sequences. The numbers appear for just a half a second. I've managed to do the test with four of five numbers. Nobody can do ten. Our Einstein here has managed to do as many as fifteen. Most of the chimps can do eight or nine without any trouble."

"How'd you teach them to do that?" Senator Berger asked.

"It's an innate ability chimps have that we don't," Shell answered.

"A talent they've evolved. In the wild, they would've needed to quickly recognize the locations of multiple predators to survive."

"That's true," Dr. Sun smiled. "But we've helped. We've developed both chemical and electrical models to enhance LTP."

"LTP?" Even Shell was sometimes caught off guard by the rapid advances of his teams.

"LTP means long-term potentiation," she explained. "The strengthening of cell connections in the hippocampus, the area of the brain involved in memory, learning, tracking, and spacial awareness. I think our new drug works pretty well. Half our staff volunteered to take it. Everybody wants to compete with Einstein. Our simian friend here, I mean."

There were many other advances in chimp development that General Shell had passed over and some clearly of which he was unaware. They were becoming smarter, with each succeeding generation having measurably larger brain size. Lemuria's scientists had also manipulated stem cells to turn fat cells into muscle. While pound for pound chimps were stronger than humans, Shell's chimps were stronger still. His researchers had also genetically altered their hemoglobin, the molecule in red blood cells that carries oxygen throughout the body. This new hemoglobin had far greater oxygen-carrying capacity, giving the chimpanzees greater endurance. They could also perform better at higher altitudes and, as tests showed, remain conscious while holding their breath underwater beyond any human record.

"Are there any problems with these animals?" the other senator asked.

Shell paused. He wanted to be honest but at the same time not put off his benefactors. "They're smart and they train well." He would leave it at that.

"But no problems?" Senator Berger pressed.

"They do have one terrible attribute," Shell conceded.

"And what's that?"

"They kill their own kind," the general answered.

"That's not a small problem," Berger grumbled.

"No," the general agreed.

"Are you working on the problem?"

"We're working on it. I doubt we'll come up with a solution."

"Why not?" the other senator asked.

"Well," Shell went on, "there is only one other mammal that kills their own. And that's us—human beings. And we haven't been able to solve that problem in thousands of years."

On his flight home, Senator Berger wondered if this "monkey business" was worth billions of dollars. He had some ethical questions, as well. For now, however, he'd keep them to himself. No use providing fodder for those few U.S. senators who were borderline "creationists" and leaned toward a wacky dismissal of Darwin's theory of evolution. He smiled to himself imagining relaying the stories of the research he had seen with chimps named Fish, Talk, Fart, and Einstein.

"We're a few million years apart on the evolutionary tree," Shell had mentioned.

Many of Berger's peers in Congress would be quite displeased to learn that monkeys were climbing up fast.

CHAPTER TWENTY

Colonel McGraw had new orders: OD 9.12 0400. RP DG. FARP Davao. AOB Jolo. AFO auth. HUMINT. Translation:

> OD—Operational Detachment of his team would be at 4 a.m. on December 9.
> RP—Release Point Diego Garcia.
> FARP—Forward Arming and Refueling Point: Davao, Philippines.
> AOB—Advanced Operating Base at Jolo.
> AFO—Advance Force Operations or "black special ops in enemy territory" authorized.
> HUMINT—Human Intelligence, meaning the information was good, based on old-fashioned, man-on-the-ground spying.

This operation would take place on an island in the south of the

Philippines. Apparently stateside brass wanted to see if his crew could function in a different type of terrain, climate, culture, and battlefield.

He felt he was ready. More importantly, he knew his team was ready.

The Abu Sayyaf were Muslim separatists who had been a nemesis for the Philippine government for decades. They were few, but they were vicious, frequently beheading the soldiers they captured and holding hostages for ransom. And they were well armed. Most recently they had killed an American missionary and a dozen other hostages when an assault by the Philippine army failed. It was an American defeat as well, since the Americans had trained the Philippine special ops forces.

McGraw came to finish the task with just a single platoon, actually fewer troops than he'd used before. He was smart enough not to bring along the baggage of past successes. Fighting new wars with old strategies had always been the bane of military men. He had practiced a deployment of his troops in the same kind of terrain he would need to attack. As soon as his troops advanced on the training objective, the jungle came alive with screeching and screaming animals. The jungle would require different tactics. There would be no stealth here. But all of Colonel McGraw's troops now had a new weapon in their arsenal, a weapon Alexander the Great could not have imagined.

A Lemuria researcher at DG had developed a brain prosthesis—an artificial hippocampus. It was a microchip inserted into the brain that functioned as an accessory hippocampus, that part of the brain inside the temporal lobes that activated memory and spatial navigation. The name came from a Greek word—*hippokampos*—meaning "sea horse," because that's what that part of the brain resembled, and that's exactly what McGraw called his show: Operation Sea Horse.

Operation Sea Horse would take patience. It wouldn't be timed by the minute, but by the day.

When his troops entered enemy territory, the jungle came alive as expected. The screeching of wild animals was like an early warning system for the Abu Sayyaf. The rebels readied for an attack. None came. Every night the jungle would scream. The terrorists would move from one locale to another. Scouts were sent to look for the enemy. None ever returned. No grand attack ever came.

For ten nights, McGraw's troops hid and maneuvered in the trees of a Philippine jungle. With an "artificial hippocampus," they had a built-in GPS and an implanted memory of the rules and options for this engagement. While they waited for their go-ahead to attack, they ate leaves, seeds, tree bark, and flowers. They ate termites and ants. They ate young monkeys. And they ate even more. Then one night a signal came, a sound that no one else but they could "see," and they attacked the Abu Sayyaf.

Several days later the Philippine army came upon the blood-stained battlefield. As in the attack on the Pakistani Taliban, the enemy had been horrifically butchered, sliced apart with the blades of Alexander. There was one other interesting note in the report of the scene that McGraw read days later. The victims were found with limbs and other body parts partially chewed off, eaten. McGraw tried to shrug it off. His soldiers had gone into battle with no food, no water, only determination. They were taught to survive and win any way they could. War was kill or be killed. Why should this added bit of wartime horror make him squeamish? But it did.

> *Victory belongs to the most persevering.*
> —Napoleon Bonaparte

CHAPTER TWENTY-ONE

Several days after the Abu Sayyaf massacre, General Shell received a call from the vice chief-of-staff at the Pentagon, who imagined himself to be Shell's "handler." Shell viewed him as simply a nemesis bureaucrat. He was someone who had succeeded in rising through the ranks by simply saying "no" to everything, lauding his own judgment when things went wrong and, when they went right, somehow making others believe he'd actively supported the mission from the sidelines. Like many men he had run into in his years in the military, he substituted bravado for brains.

The VCS ranted. He used phrases like "indiscriminate killing" and "a total breakdown in morality."

"When this gets out," the VCS said, "it'll be no different from the atrocities of war that have undermined our missions in the past, like Mai Lai and Abu Graiv. We can't condone or ignore cannibalism."

The VCS liked "yes men," so Shell answered "yes" to anything he had to say. When that call was finished, General Shell made his own call—to Colonel McGraw.

"You won't get one, Link, but you deserve a medal for this one." That's all he had to say. There was more work to do on Lemuria. The military would not toss out the use of their new troops because of one misstep. They would just train them better.

At 1600 Pennsylvania Avenue, someone else was dealing with the problem. The president was briefed on the Philippine Lemuria mission. By all accounts it was a success. No U.S. troops had been lost, and forty-one vicious terrorists were slain. There were women and children among them, but intelligence confirmed that they were carrying weapons as well. That was how terrorists fought. They had no hesitancy in hiding among civilians or using women and children as part of their arsenal. The United States and other nations had to fight with moral handcuffs. The president was actually pleased to have this new, albeit still imperfect, weapon in his war on terror.

There was another, perhaps bigger problem with which his staff would have to deal. The *New York Times* would headline the story of the Abu Sayyaf "massacre" the next day. There were three hits the administration would take.

The story would say Americans were involved. That came from a Philippine military source. The U.S. Army clearly had to remove any Filipino troops from the area before pursuing their agenda. They couldn't be trusted anyway. Many were either susceptible to bribes or sympathetic to the terrorists. It was expected that it might leak that U.S. troops undertook the mission. But it was a fight against terrorists, and taking any fight to the enemy anywhere was not going to pose a problem. So, it was decided. They would admit to involvement.

The story would go on to mention words like *atrocity*, *barbarism*, and *cannibalism*. The responses to that story, the president's national security advisor said, would require some fine-tuning, a euphemism for "denial."

And finally, the story would say that an American soldier had been taken prisoner and unless the U.S. government paid reparations to the Abu Sayyaf, the soldier would be tortured and sent back to America "piece by piece." That was a bit more troublesome. But after a quick and thorough investigation, the military returned with an answer. Bogus. No troops were taken in the attack. None wounded. None captured. And, after a lot of number counting, the generals concluded that unless one of the few dozen navy personnel on leave in Manila had been captured by hookers, there wasn't an American soldier or sailor missing in the Philippines. And with orders going out canceling any leave, they, too, would soon be accounted for.

A plan of action was agreed upon. Admit that Americans were involved and successful in a fight against terrorism. Deny any American soldier involved in the attack was captured. Reiterate that America did not negotiate with terrorists, succumb to their threats, or pay ransoms. And deny any atrocities.

"And," the president would jokingly say later at a press conference, "there are no cannibals among our soldiers." And that was the truth. Cannibalism was defined as eating your own kind. McGraw's chimps ate humans, not other chimps.

"I'll have the Office of Reconciliation handle this," his chief-of-staff declared. The president nodded his assent.

In the last several decades, the government had become adept at manipulating the press. They became magicians in controlling the dispersal of information and with it public opinion and interests. Truth no longer mattered. Reality could be altered, and history could be rewritten.

In the nineteenth century, it was actually the press that rewrote history and manipulated America into its wars. They demonized the American Indian and ignored an American genocide. At the end of the century, William Randolph Hearst's newspapers ignited the Spanish-American War by riling up public opinion against Spanish colonialism and creating a war theme—"Remember the Maine." It was the beginning of America's own colonialism. The press held hands with the government as it pursued its interests in World Wars I and II. It was only in the 1960s that an independent investigative American press actually began to hold the government to task for its actions and deceptions—Vietnam, Watergate, American-instigated insurgencies in Latin America. The end of the press' successful onslaught against government excesses came perhaps during Ronald Reagan's tenure. The "Great Communicator" was almost undone by Iran-Contra when the press tried to hold the government and the president to task for "trading arms for hostages." Like many government machinations, it was a shrewd plan that went awry. The United States sold arms to Iran for the release of Middle East hostages and funneled the money to unpopular right-wing Latin America governments to suppress native Communist insurgencies.

Unfortunately, the policy resulted in barbaric tortures and mass executions in Nicaragua, El Salvador, Guatemala, Honduras, and Argentina and propelled a radical Iranian theocracy into power. United States government policy was "the end justifies the means." The elite reasoned that in a world with limited resources and billions of undereducated, underfed, indigenous people, there was no instant solution to their suffering. American society could not survive by actually living up to humanistic slogans. Slogans were meant for politicians to pacify an electorate and for theologians, pundits, and editorial writers to provide "feel good" emotions to their listeners.

Reagan's great legacy following the debacle of Iran-Contra was not only ending the cold war and defeating Communism, it was the Office of Reconciliation. Hardly anyone had ever heard of it. It was buried in the Department of Commerce, one of many offices in the Federal Department of Consumer Information. While some of the staff of the Office of Reconciliation busied themselves with providing information to the public about mundane topics like the differences between natural or genetically modified corn, most were involved in the ever more important task of targeting the government's "message." The department had many directors over the years, but the folks working there jokingly referred to each new boss as Goebbels, as in "I've got to meet Goebbels to push my project." They named the director's office after Joseph Goebbels, Hitler's director of the Nazi Ministry of Propaganda. Since Reagan, the White House had used the Office of Reconciliation to turn the Washington and national press corps into tabloid media. They didn't manipulate information. Their job—and they did it exceedingly well—was to move the media and the public's attention to other interests. They tamed the national press by pushing them to pursue sexier subjects or scandals. Sometimes they failed. They couldn't help William Jefferson Clinton or divert the media from his sexual indiscretions with Monica Lewinsky. The story was just far too alluring. But most of the time their efforts were astonishingly successful. Just hours before the story of the Philippine massacre was published, Internet sites around the world began to receive reliable gossip about a Washington congressman involved in child pornography, a Russian oligarch given U.S. asylum after being indicted for manipulating

Russian oil prices that favored American corporations—and someone would discover Jimmy Hoffa's body. More titillating stories would go out and the Office of Reconciliation would allow the chips to fall where they may. Whatever story the American media chose to run with was fine—just as long as they were diverted from another, in this case one that involved the Lemuria Project.

There were some, however, who could not be diverted from interest in the stories of massacres in the Philippines—*Aman*, Israeli military intelligence. The details of the encounter in the southern Philippines were too similar to the slayings in the Hindu Kush Mountains of Pakistan. The brutally successful outcomes were also noteworthy. If this was the Americans and they had a new tactic and new weapons— even if they were two thousand years old—Israel wanted to know about them, and perhaps, if necessary, emulate them.

> *It is strange but true; for truth is always*
> *strange, stranger than fiction.*
> —Byron

CHAPTER
TWENTY-TWO

It was a Google day. Maggie Wagner and Nate Stumpf sat alongside each other in her father's home, munched on chips and sipped diet Coke, and said barely a word as they searched the Internet for anything meaningful connecting the words *LEMURIA* and *BIOT*. She was sure that *Biot* was also a valid clue in the search about the truth of her father's death. She had looked closer at the few documents he had left behind. And there was one mention of *Biot*. It was apparently somewhere he had been before and someplace he intended to go to again.

LEMURIA seemed a dead end. All that ever turned up were stories of a mythological "lost" civilization. And nothing connected the two words together.

BIOT, however, turned up some interesting possibilities.

"Was your father ever in France?" Stumpf queried. Biot was a medieval picturesque village in the French Riviera.

"No," Maggie was quick to respond. "He had no interest in medieval French villages. He went to Paris once on his way to Stockholm for his prize. But that's it."

"Jean-Baptiste Biot. He was a nineteenth-century French physicist." Stumpf was reading off the Web. Not a lead.

Biot was a Dutch pharmaceutical company. But they didn't do any high-tech research. They made generic drugs.

Biot was an acronym for British Indian Ocean Territories. They both searched the online world maps to find the place. "Why would my father fly ten thousand miles to a dot in the middle of the Indian Ocean? It'd take him a week to get there and back." That didn't seem a likely lead either.

But *BIOT* was also the name of a yearly symposium on biotech research that attracted researchers from around the world. Maggie had never attended, but several of her professors had been guest lecturers on genetics at BIOT conferences in years past. And her father had spoken there in 2005. The next BIOT was being held in three days in Oregon. She called the director of the conference. Had her father been scheduled to speak there? He had not. But he had been expected to attend.

Maggie turned to Stumpf and quickly hated herself for asking. "Do you ski?"

> *The mountains through which the rivers pass . . .*
> *to sepulcher rock are high, broken, rocky . . . covered with*
> *fir white cedar, and . . . exhibit very romantic scenes . . .*
> *cascades tumbling from stupendous rocks . . . into the river.*
> —Meriwether Lewis, April 14, 1806

CHAPTER
TWENTY-THREE

Nate Stumpf had never been to the Pacific Northwest. He traveled often between LA and San Francisco and occasionally to Las Vegas. But other than that, he hadn't been much of anywhere. He thought he might have visited Seattle once when he was a young child visiting a great-aunt. But he wasn't sure. His parents were long dead. Both had died in a car accident shortly after he finished high school. He was an only child, and there was no extended family with whom to reminisce. So, he came into the habit of making up childhood memories, unsure if he was pulling them from repressed memory or imagination. He didn't know, they might be valid—or not. As years went by, the habit continued and his life's story became an amalgam of reality and fiction. After a while, not even he could tell them apart. It would be easy to label Nate Stumpf as just a pretentious asshole, but he was more complex than that. Sure, he would regale folks with stories of all the women he fucked and big shots he had "taken down," with most of those stories having been well-cooked in a brain often stewed in tequila, but he did work in the seamy side of Hollywood and Frisco and, even for a fellow who was missing good looks and charm, there were plenty of opportunities for there to be an inkling of truth to his tales. Even if his life was mostly a lie, being with Nate Stumpf was an experience. He looked at once insane and wise, sad and joyful. He was a fellow whom you could hardly stop looking at and desperately wanted to avoid looking at. And Maggie Wagner had him as her partner.

Portland, Oregon, was a short two-hour flight from Los Angeles. Nate and Maggie rented a car at an agency conveniently located just across the street from the terminal. They drove along Route 26, southeast from Portland through evergreen forests and pastoral villages with peculiar names like Zigzag and Rhododendron. The BIOT conference was being held at Timberline Lodge, a ski chalet hotel at the base of Oregon's highest peak, Mount Hood. The stone and timber hotel was built by Franklin Roosevelt's Works Projects Administration, the WPA, during the Depression. It was intended to be a grand ski lodge then and was still. Although it was already late September, snow was still on the slopes.

They drove up a tortuous mountain road to their destination, and as soon as the hotel came into view mid-mountain, Nate remembered the place.

"I've been here before," he said. "They've got night skiing, but the place can get really spooky at night."

He had melded his recollection of the Timberline resort brochures he had read with subconscious images of blood seeping from its walls and Jack Nicholson's maniacal and fearsome smile. The memory flashed through him because Timberline Lodge was the exterior setting for Stanley Kubrick's classic horror film *The Shining*. Stumpf had never been to Timberline before, but now it was his new reality.

The conference was scheduled to begin in the evening over wine and cheese in the hotel's main lobby. After check-in, Maggie and Stumpf settled into adjacent rooms and then met for lunch. The plan they hatched was simple. They would confront guests at the conference—particularly those who had known Julius Wagner—with questions about Lemuria and see whose interest sparked. In the meantime, just to be polite, Maggie asked Nate if he wanted to ski together.

"Nah, I sprained my ankle a couple of weeks ago jumping over a hedge on an investigation. It's been actin' up. I'm gonna take a rain check though. Hey, snow check, I mean."

Stumpf stumbled over his words, trying to be charming and witty and succeeding at neither. In fact, he didn't ski at all. He didn't know why he made up that story, but now that he had, he would have to feign a limp for a day to make himself appear honest. He limped alongside her as she rented skis. She wore one of those Gore-Tex stretchy outfits that accentuated her beautiful round derriere. Nate Stumpf was an "ass man."

When they met later that evening, her face was ruddy from a day on the slopes and the sun had brought out some childhood freckles. Nate couldn't help but notice that she was even more attractive without makeup. He had put a stone in his shoe to give his limp a little more authenticity. The conference was being held in the resort's great room—a hexagonal area that surrounded a grand ninety-eight-foot-tall chimney with six individually blazing fireplaces.

"We'll circle in opposite directions," he instructed her.

Their plan was to interrogate guests about Lemuria. If anyone seemed interested at all, they would compare notes when they met after completing the circle and then consider pursuing the "marks" together.

"We'll get to the bottom of this Lemuria business soon enough," he smiled reassuringly. "I'm an expert at rattling cages."

Stumpf had a few drinks and nibbled on hors d'oeuvres as he circled. He'd insinuate himself in the midst of a group and listen intently for a minute before making his inquiry. He understood very little of the conversations between these scientific types and hoped they wouldn't suspect him of only having a junior college education.

"Anybody here working on the Lemuria Project?" he would ask offhandedly. "I hear they're running with a lot of interesting stuff. We should talk."

No one showed a glimmer of enlightenment. He knew they were talking about him as he moved on from one group to another. *Buncha nerds*, he thought. He shoved his hands in his pockets and, curling his fingers into fists, thought how in "less civilized" society he would get his point across.

When he finally met up with Maggie again, he found her with an entirely different demeanor. She beamed at him with more teeth than he had ever seen in his life. She took hold of his hand and sat him down next to her on a two-seat couch in front of a roaring fireplace.

"I got nothing. But more are registering tomorrow. I thought tonight we'd just take a break," she said, taking his arm and squeezing. She stared into the flickering orange, red, and blue of the great fireplace for a quiet moment and then turned to look Stumpf deep in the eyes. Her mouth seemed to be edging closer to his.

Stumpf knew what he thought was happening wasn't happening. It wasn't true. He was just imagining her newfound interest in him. He knew he'd get bitch slapped if he leaned in closer. But he did, and he kissed her. And rather than a sudden sting on his face, he felt her tongue explore his.

It's the fuckin' mountain air, he thought. *Why didn't I ever learn to ski?*

Stumpf put one hand under her sweater, pulling her closer to him, feeling the warm skin of her flanks. With his other hand, he took the rock out of his shoe.

They held hands as they walked back to her room. Stumpf held his sweater over his arm. He wanted to hide the erection he had on display. She said little until they entered her hotel room.

"Nate Stumpf," she said, holding his face gently in her hands, "you are an incredibly fascinating man." And she kissed him hard again, aggressively pinning him against a wall.

"You're pretty interesting yourself."

She undid his shirt and began touching, then kissing his nipples.

Holy Fatal Attraction, Stumpf thought. He didn't have a mound in his pants anymore. He had a mountain. And then the part of his brain that he wished he could suppress kicked in.

"Give me a minute, babe." He set her down on the bed and went into the bathroom. This wasn't real. This was out of character for her. As much as Stumpf liked to act out the fantasy of himself as some lothario, he knew deep down that he wasn't. She wasn't seeing him. She was seeing something else. Maggie Wagner was on something—acid or ecstasy, something.

Stumpf splashed some cold water on his face. He peeked out the bathroom door. She was lying on the bed. She had taken off her blouse and bra, and her firm, large breasts were just lying there beckoning to him. *Get in there and suck her tits,* a horny voice on one side of his head yelled. The other was calling him an asshole. He started hammering at his groin to put out the green light on his manhood. Then, with his libido somewhat suppressed, he suddenly knew exactly what was going on and what he had to do. This was a dirty trick that he himself would have done, and he knew just where to look. Storming back into the bedroom, Stumpf avoided looking at the enticements that awaited him in bed. *For godssake*, he was telling himself, *you're here for a bigger payday than that.* He went from mirror, to lamp, to—the sconce on the wall. And there it was—a wireless micro-camera. He yanked it out. Were there others? Was his room bugged, too? He looked over to Maggie in bed. She wanted him and titillated him by playing with her breasts.

"Be right back, babe," he said.

Stumpf ran down to the lobby and slapped Maggie's room key onto the check-in countertop.

"I need another room," he announced breathlessly to the receptionist, a young man wearing the hotel's requisite blue tie and ivory blazer.

"I'm sorry, sir. All of our rooms are booked."

"You've got rooms that are booked for tomorrow. I just need a different one tonight. Tomorrow morning, I'll be back in mine."

"I'm sorry, sir. Our policy—"

Stumpf got into his pissed-off mode, the kind where his whole face turned beet red, and his voice cracked deeply, like someone possessed in *The Exorcist.*

"Listen to me. I'm gonna tell you once and only once. You've got a room. I know you've got a room. You're gonna gimme the key now. I'm gonna pay you for the room. And we're all gonna be happy." He paused a moment to let logic sink in. Then he let the devil out. "You don't, I'm gonna punch you in the face, piss in your lobby, and shit in your kitchen. You're gonna call the cops. We'll both be wastin' our time in court and, in the end, you'll be black and blue, and your hotel will have a shit-and-piss reputation for years. All for a fuckin' room. So what do you want to do?"

The desk clerk's jaw dropped. He seemed speechless. Stumpf had little patience. "Don't call my bluff," he said, and he undid his fly. A second later, the desk clerk handed him another room key.

———

Stumpf opened a Mac laptop in his "new" room and angled it to face the bed. He set the Apple's built-in camera to *record* mode. Then he went to bring Maggie back to his new "bug-proof" room.

———

At dawn, with sunlight shimmering off the snow-covered ski runs just outside her window, Maggie Wagner slowly awoke. A haze seemed to cover her eyes and her mind. And then it began to lift. She remembered little of the night before. When she rolled over in bed, she found herself facing Nate Stumpf's hairy back.

He awoke a moment later with her standing over him wrapped in a sheet and screaming.

"You bastard. You drugged me."

"No, no."

"You raped me."

"No. No. I didn't."

Dashing about the room, she flailed about looking for her clothes, and once retrieving them, went into the bathroom to change. And shortly, she came out dressed.

"Someone drugged you," Stumpf tried to explain, pulling on his pants. "But it wasn't me."

"And how did I end up in this room, naked in your bed?"

"We had to sleep somewhere. They bugged our rooms."

"You're fired. Just—just get out of my life."

"Nothin' happened, babe. Really."

"I'm not your babe."

She hurried out of the room, and Stumpf rushed out after her. He held out her laptop computer.

"Take your computer. It's yours. Look at it. You'll see. Just look at it."

She grabbed the laptop and ran off down the hall to her room. Maggie had looked at him in disgust, like a roach too disgusting to stomp on, something you just wanted to get away from quickly. Stumpf had thought that maybe, just maybe, it wasn't drugs and she would awake in the morning to cuddle close to him and smile that toothy smile. But she ran off without even a "thanks" or a "good-bye." And he had done nothing. *The little princess*, Stumpf thought. *I should have fucked her.*

When Maggie got to her room, she hurried into the shower. Her hands were trembling, her heart pounding. She wanted to wash away that weasel's stench. By the time she finished, she had calmed. Her breathing slowed. And when she walked back into the bedroom, she saw it—a tiny camera with a lens as big as a dime sitting on the bureau below a wall sconce. The lens was cracked, as if somebody had smashed it. She opened her laptop. An image of her in bed lying alongside Stumpf was frozen on the screen. The pervert had recorded them using her computer's built-in camera. And then she played back the night. But it was she who was the seductress—disrobing, dancing naked, and lasciviously trying to entice him into bed.

Who was this woman? It wasn't her. She had been drugged. But, except for an occasional kiss and a caress, Stumpf did not respond to her invitation. He never responded to her advances. He was clearly doing his best to restrain himself. And it didn't look easy. The video showed her finally tiring of trying to seduce him. She got into bed and slept. It was only after she had fallen asleep that he had gotten into bed next to her. Nate Stumpf, it seemed, was telling the truth. *Gentlemen*, Maggie thought, *come in strange packages.*

Maggie knocked on Nate Stumpf's door. She had brought along breakfast. Some cinnamon rolls and coffee. There was no answer. In the lobby, the morning session of the BIOT conference was beginning. Perhaps he was pursuing leads. But he was nowhere to be found. She asked the desk clerk if he had checked out. Apparently not. She spent the next hour sitting by the picture windows overlooking the slopes of Mount Hood. She wondered if she would ever discover the truth of her father's murder. Having been drugged, it was clear there were people who didn't want that truth to be known. And now, she had tossed away the one person she discovered she could trust.

And then she saw him. Nate Stumpf, wearing a baggy orange ski bib, was taking ski lessons—falling alongside five-year-olds on the bunny slopes. But he got up and kept trying. She watched as he finally succeeded in completing the short run without falling, raising his arms and his poles in ecstatic triumph. In years to come, Nate Stumpf's selective and imaginative memory would change that bunny slope achievement into a great slalom victory—and Maggie Wagner would not dispute it.

> *If I have ever made any valuable discoveries, it has been owing more to patient attention, than to any other talent.*
> —Sir Isaac Newton

CHAPTER
TWENTY-FOUR

Colonel Krantz and Fala reported their conversation with the Iranian mullah in detail to *Aman*. They spoke individually, first with a captain, then a major, and then with a civilian, a psychologist they presumed. The idea was not only to flesh out every detail of what they had seen and been told, but to mine for any discrepancies, lies that is. And then, finally, they met with General Echod again.

"I hate to agree with an Ayatollah," the general said, biting his lower lip, "but I think he's right. The Americans are behind this business."

He handed Krantz some documents detailing the massacre of Islamic rebels on a southern Philippine island.

"The descriptions of the carnage at the battle scene match those from the Hindu Kush. The Americans, they're not denying their participation," the general went on, "but they're busy trying to bury the story and minimize their responsibility."

"With all their technology," Krantz asked, "why would the

Americans arm their special ops teams with primitive weapons like the Alexander battle scythe? And, considering the size of the weapon, are the soldiers they're deploying children?"

"I don't know, Colonel." Danny Echod shrugged. "But I need to know."

"General," Fala said, staring him straight in the eye, probing for a direct answer, "the Americans are your allies. I can't believe you haven't simply asked them. I know you have lots of friends in the Pentagon and the American administration."

"Of course we have asked. But we got nothing. They say we are simply wrong in our assumptions."

"Do you believe them?"

"We need the Americans," Echod answered. "But we don't rely on them for our survival. I believe, more likely, the Americans know. But the information is being closely guarded."

"But why?" Krantz asked.

"But why?" The general smiled, just a little wickedly. "That is why I have hired you and your lovely lady."

Although Krantz was feeling a bit jet-lagged, he was a lot more relaxed traveling to the Philippines than to Iran and Pakistan. Israel had had good relations with the Philippines since its founding. In fact, the Philippines was the only Asian nation to support the creation of the Jewish state at the United Nations when the partition resolution was brought to a vote on November 29, 1947. The two countries had had full diplomatic relations since 1957. And, next to the United States, Israel supplied more weaponry to the Filipino army than any other country. There were also more than sixty thousasnd Filipinos working in Israel. With their coming and going over the decades, that meant for a lot of friends.

Krantz found first-class sleeping berths on the Lufthansa flight quite to his liking—and, after a few bourbons and water, he slept well. But Fala was uncomfortable and had abdominal cramps during most of the twenty-two-hour flight from Tel Aviv to Manila. Joshua suggested it was just the long flight. Fala knew the difference. She had had these discomforts before. It was *mittleshmerz*, a nice German medical term for mid-cycle ovulatory pain. The timing meant she was fertile, but it was pain nevertheless. When they arrived at Aquino International Airport in Manila on the morning of the next day, Krantz and Fala were ushered through customs like VIPs and into a waiting limousine. *What a difference a continent makes*, Krantz thought.

The hotel manager himself ushered his special guests to their luxury suite in the Peninsula Hotel. Fala was clearly exhausted.

"Stay here and rest," Joshua insisted.

"I can take a couple of Advil," she said. "I'm fine."

"Sweetheart, as much as I enjoy your company, your Muslim roots and Arabic fluency are not important here. We'll discuss anything I find when I get back." He kissed her gently on the forehead and closed the drapes, darkening the room. "You just need a dozen hours of sleep. I'll have the hotel doctor come up and give you something. Don't worry. I'll be back in a few hours."

He was right, and she didn't argue. She closed her eyes and was asleep moments after he departed.

———————

Aman had arranged for the Filipino army to answer any questions Joshua Krantz would pose. A Filipino major was assigned to be his host and guide. Krantz had the timetable fixed in his head. An army helicopter would take little more than an hour to travel the three hundred kilometers to the "scene of the crime" on Jolo Island, south of Mindinao. He would inspect the site for a few minutes, discover the same slaughter he had seen before, and fly right back. He could accomplish his mission and return before Fala awoke.

The site indeed looked like a terrorist camp in the middle of a jungle—a scattering of thatched-roof huts, tunnels, and lookout towers in trees. The bodies were gone, but the dark red stains of a bloody carnage were everywhere—in the huts, on the ground, splattered on the surrounding vegetation.

"Did you find any unusual weapons?" Krantz asked.

"Nothing but the usual—Kalashnikovs."

There were no witnesses to speak to. No survivors. No need to stay any longer. But Krantz knew his job was incomplete.

"I have to see the bodies."

"We have plenty of photos."

"No, I have to see them."

"There were many," the Filipino major responded. "They've been buried."

"All of them?"

"In the heat they rot. It's a terrible odor. And there are vultures here and bugs as big as birds."

Krantz shrugged. "How hard would it be to unbury them?"

"Are you a *bissil meshuga*?" a bit crazy? the major responded with the little Yiddish he learned from his time training in Israel.

"Yeah, a lot of people I know would say that. But I can't go home and say I saw a bunch of pictures. You've got to know that."

"*Meshugana*," the major grumbled again. But he made no more arguments and began making some calls.

Krantz imagined that this disinterment was going to involve some expensive quid pro quo. In fact, it did later involve some expensive bargaining. To encourage Israel's silence regarding what Krantz would subsequently find there on Jolo, the United States subsidized the Philippines in their purchase of Israeli armaments. As opposed to Krantz's expectation that his request would "cost" Israel, the Jewish state actually made a hefty profit on the deal.

The same bulldozers that had dug the trench and buried dozens of rebel bodies two days earlier now dug up the same site. Krantz jumped into the trench when the bodies appeared. The face mask he wore did little to blunt the stench of death, that malicious and sulfurous odor of rotting flesh and feces. There was also the noxious smell of lye that had been tossed over the corpses. The Filipino major stood far back and even his eyes watered. One after the other, Krantz looked over the bodies. They all appeared horribly shredded by a weapon consistent with the Alexander scythe. What was even more interesting was that some had their limbs literally torn from their bodies. What kind of strength did these American soldiers have? About to move on, he noticed one body whose face and lips had been torn away. But there was something held between the corpse's clenched teeth. It looked like a piece of tissue. Krantz pried the mouth open and found what looked like a piece of an ear. It was thick, black, and coarse, perhaps from exposure to weather or lye—but no other tissue on any of the victims' bodies seemed to have discolored the same. It was in the victim's mouth. Maybe that's what saliva did to tissue? He would have to find out. Joshua put the fragment into a small plastic envelope and tucked it into his shirt pocket. He spent a few minutes more turning over bodies and finally decided he had enough and perhaps had found what he needed.

"Anything?" the major asked.

Krantz shook his head no.

The bulldozers were covering over the burial site again when their helicopter lifted off. It was an even quicker return to Manila. He had been gone less than six hours and expected Fala to be still sleeping.

Krantz asked to be dropped off first at the Peninsula. He wanted to see how Fala was feeling. But his major got a cell phone call en route and drove him instead where he was ordered—to the Israeli embassy.

Krantz was cordially ushered into the ambassador's office. Like all Israeli missions abroad, it was an inner sanctum, a windowless office—secure from being targeted from outside snipers and well insulated from any electronic eavesdropping. After some polite introductions, Krantz quickly presented the evidence he had found at the Jola island site and asked that it be sent to *Aman* for identification and possible DNA analysis.

"Could you get me a driver back to the hotel?" he asked. "I think my business with *Aman* is done. They no longer have any need for an archaeologist."

"Colonel," the ambassador began, trying to calmly explain an unpleasant and perplexing problem, "Miss al-Shohada is not at your hotel."

"Is she ill? Did they take her to a hospital?"

"No. No. The hospital doctor went to the room as you arranged. But he found the room in disarray, and Miss al-Shohada was not there. He called the police, and our people have been involved, too.

But she is nowhere to be found."

"And you're sure she just didn't go out for a cup of tea?"

"The room was torn apart. She clearly struggled. We are sure she was taken. We suspect she has been kidnapped, but there has been no ransom demand, no messages, no threats. In these cases I can't say for sure, but we don't know if she's still alive."

Krantz felt like a fish caught on a hook. He ached. It was a terrible painless pain. He was being pulled to where he didn't want to go, but he knew he had no choice.

No, I am not an archaeologist, Krantz thought to himself. *I am a fucking spy. And this business working for* Aman *is not yet over.*

> *There is no rule more invariable than that we are paid*
> *for our suspicions by finding what we suspect.*
> —Thoreau

CHAPTER
TWENTY-FIVE

Krantz spent three days in Manila with the Filipino police and military looking for Fala. They were thorough and not insensitive to his concerns. He was an honored guest in their country, and understandably they felt responsible. But Fala was nowhere to be found. There were video monitors at the hotel entrance. She certainly did not leave through the main entrance. How was it possible that a tall, beautiful Egyptian woman could disappear so completely? But no one had seen her. No struggles had been reported. No large packages carried out. There was no forced entry into the room. Desperate, Colonel Krantz even made inquiries at the Egyptian and American embassies. They were sympathetic but just as unhelpful.

On his final day, Krantz decided to review the tapes of everyone who had checked into the Peninsula from the time of his arrival and two days prior. An archaeologist's talent was being meticulous in sifting through material, looking for clues to the past, tossing aside the detritus to find the bones of history and the truth. He finally discovered one person of interest. A businessman, an American, had checked into the hotel the day before their arrival. He had two oversized pieces of luggage with him, and two porters had struggled to load them onto a cargo rack. Although the American checked out the next afternoon, he left without luggage. Where had it gone? And why leave without it? Could he have managed to stuff Fala into a suitcase? It wasn't possible. Krantz provided the American's name, photo, and passport information to the Americans and of course, to the Israelis. No one had a record of the man. His identity was a forgery. So Krantz had a suspect but still plenty of questions and no answers.

If she had been taken, it had to be because of this spy business. And he was responsible for getting her involved in that. It had something to do with Alexander's battle scythe, Maimun, the Right Hand of God, terrorists, the Americans, or—well, he didn't know. But Krantz had spent years searching for obscure clues about ancient civilizations, for knowledge that lay hidden for hundreds or thousands of years; he would make no less an effort to find the woman he loved.

On his flight back to Tel Aviv, he read through several newspapers. He was thorough in reviewing the standard world bad news—typhoons, terrorism, political corruption, global wars, economic downturns. He even glanced through the fluff about celebrities and bizarre events. Nothing was enlightening. There was a clue in a small column in the back pages of the *Manila Times*—unfortunately, Krantz didn't recognize it.

The *Manila Times* reported: "The United States embassy today issued a warning to Americans traveling in the Philippines to avoid the Asecuro Chimpanzee Sanctuary. Several chimps escaped from the fenced shelter on Sunday. Two fled through the park and still elude capture. Several others attacked tourists in a taxicab, causing the passengers minor injuries. Those animals were shot by local police. 'We don't know how the chimps were able to escape and why they became violent,' said animal keeper, Marco Gutierrez. 'Chimpanzee attacks are rare but not unheard of,' he explained."

At about the same time Krantz's flight for Israel left Manila, Fala was awakening four thousand miles away. She knew she had been kidnapped and probably drugged, but she had no idea of how, or why, or where she now was. The room her captors had placed her in looked like a modest hotel room, nothing luxurious like her lodgings at the Peninsula, no flat-screen television, five-hundred-thread-count *frette* linens, marble floors, or lavish furnishings. She had a queen-sized bed with clean linens, a coffeepot on an old scratched bureau, a television with a remote, and a minibar—comfortable but not lavish accommodations. But she wasn't restrained. She splashed cold water on her face to shock herself into a little more astuteness and then she tried the door. Unexpectedly, it was unlocked. She was not a prisoner. Looking out, she viewed a sterile hallway with a lot of other serially numbered hotel room doors. There was an ice machine in the middle of the corridor and an elevator at the end. She thought she might run. Perhaps her captors had forgotten to lock her room and would be coming back. But where was she and to where would she run? She parted the curtains in her room to reveal a glass door that led out to a balcony. When she opened it, a rush of dry, incredibly hot air almost smothered her. She was on the third floor of a building that overlooked a broad white sand beach and an oasis of palm trees surrounding a pool populated by sunbathers. And there was a distinct odor of something cooking below, something familiar but unfamiliar. She was at some resort, she thought. But was this some beach in the Caribbean or the Pacific? Was she in the Middle East or Africa? She thought about yelling for help, but the door was unlocked. She could walk out and simply ask for help. She was about to do just that when her phone rang.

"*Ahlan*," she said "hello" in Arabic.

"*Ahlan bik*," came the polite Arabic response; "and hello. I hope you're feeling better."

"I would feel better if I knew where I am and why I'm here."

"All in good time, Miss al-Shohada. Why don't you take your time, get dressed, and I'll meet you in the lobby. There's a buffet breakfast right outside."

"Who are you?" Fala asked.

"Oh, I'm sorry. My name is Dr. Joshua Jaymes and I've been assigned to show you around. I'll be waiting for you in the lobby. Take your time. Good-bye."

The accent was American and that odor of something cooking below—she recognized it now. It was bacon and eggs. The mullah was right, Fala thought.

> *Grant I may never prove so foolish*
> *To trust a man on his oath or bond,*
> *Or a harlot for her weeping,*
> *Or a dog that seems a-sleeping,*
> *Or a keeper with my freedom,*
> *Or my friends if I should need 'em.*
> —Shakespeare: Timon of Athens I.ii

CHAPTER
TWENTY-SIX

Colonel Krantz was hoping that Israeli intelligence would un-cover a DNA match to the tissue he had found at the Jolo island massacre site. He hoped, but knew it was unlikely. Although they had DNA profiles on tens of thousands of individuals, this was a world of billons of possibilities. He really didn't expect a particular person to be identified, but he expected their forensics experts could certainly narrow the field. He would at least learn gender, ethnicity, and perhaps some family connections. As he drove from Ben Gurion Airport to *Aman*'s headquarters, all he could think about was Fala—and with an aching knot in the middle of his chest, he wondered if she was still alive. Where would *Aman* send him next? And would it lead him to her?

Krantz did not receive the polite welcome-home he expected when he arrived at the offices of Israeli military intelligence. Instead of handshakes or commiserations, he was curtly escorted by several armed soldiers to a small, stark windowless room. There were several chairs and a solitary desk in the middle of the room. Two men awaited him. One was a technician in civilian clothes, a thin, bespectacled fellow who busied himself with setting up an assortment of electronic gadgetry and a laptap computer on the desk. The other was a uniformed major, a handsome young man with piercing blue eyes and wire-rimmed eyeglasses that gave him an intelligent, professorial look. Initially, the major said little and simply pointed for Krantz to take a seat. Joshua Krantz was familiar with the setting. He himself had brought "enemies of the state" to rooms like this. He was to be interrogated.

"This is just routine, Colonel," the major began. "I know it's insulting and an inconvenience but after any incident, it is required."

Krantz made no objection. The polygraph that he was attached to was not the simple lie detector system seen on the average television cop whodunit. Lie detection, particularly for Israeli intelligence, had become a far more sophisticated science. After all, *Aman* dealt with spies, and spies were probably the world's best liars. They had to be to stay alive. The old polygraphs attached the subject to medical instruments that monitored changes in the body—measuring heart rate, blood pressure, and electrodermal activity, or sweatiness. All this information would play out as squiggly lines on rolling graph paper. What it meant was left to the sometimes arbitrary interpretation of a polygraph examiner. It was a very primitive and often arbitrary and unreliable method of deducing the truth. That's why courts were loath to accept lie detector evidence.

Aman's system used digital equipment with the old-fashioned paper scroll human interpretation replaced by a sophisticated computer algorithm. Krantz was connected up, as with the old system, to blood pressure monitors, electrodes to measure heart rate, and electrodermal connectors to measure skin resistance and sweating. The system, however, went far beyond that. Sensors were also attached to his face and scalp that measured brain signals called "event-related potentials," or ERPs, and were tracked by an electroencephalograph, or EEG machine; and his eyes were pried open and anesthetized so that his pupillary reaction could be assessed. Although the science of polygraphy had plenty of skeptics, the scientists with the Israeli Department of Defense Polygraph Institute claimed a lie-detection accuracy of 97 percent. If the 3 percent error meant a few innocent people would die, well, that was the price of preserving a country surrounded by enemies sworn to destroy it hand-in-hand with their God.

Krantz didn't resent the test or its implications. He just resented having his fate determined by a bunch of chips and wires in a box. After the major asked some routine identification questions, the rest of the queries came at him fast. A quick yes or no response was required.

"Did you see a replica of an ancient weapon in Pakistan?"

"Yes."

"Do you know who is responsible for the weapon?"

"No."

"Did you speak with an Iranian mullah about this weapon?"

"Yes."

"Are you cooperating with the Iranian government?"

"No.

"Have you been paid for any services by an Arab or Islamic government?"

"No."

Krantz expected all these questions. He would have asked them, as well. After all, he was an Israeli who had traveled to Iran, spoke with the Ayatollah's secretary, and returned home without a scratch. That alone would make Israeli military intelligence suspicious, even if they had encouraged the venture. The Iranians had an excellent intelligence service. Their Ministry of Intelligence and Security (MOIS) was the Islamic Republic's successor to the Shah's vaunted and dreaded secret police, SAVAK—and they were just as capable. Aman suspected that MOIS had moles within Israeli intelligence. It would be far easier for MOIS to allow Israel to pry a secret from their allies, the Americans—and then learn it from Israel—rather than attempting the more difficult task of trying to discover for themselves what the Pentagon was up to.

"Did you kill your wife?"

Krantz hesitated.

"Answer the question."

"I don't have a wife."

"Fala al-Shohada."

"She is not my wife. Maybe someday—but she's . . ."

"Did you have something to do with her disappearance?"

"No."

"Are you involved with any other women?"

Krantz popped the lid separators from his eyes and yanked off the cables attaching him to the polygraph. Some questions he would not tolerate. Accusing him of infidelity was one of them.

"We're not finished, Colonel."

"Then I suggest you shoot me, Major. Or let me speak with the director."

The young major quickly departed, and soon two other soldiers appeared to escort Krantz to another room, this one a bit more comfortable with a plush leather couch, beverages and snacks set out on a table, and plenty of magazines to peruse. He had his cell phone in his pocket and thought about calling Cairo and talking to Fala's parents. He was sure the Egyptian embassy in Manila had made the contact, but still he ought to tell them something. He started dialing his cell phone and then hung up. Sometimes even a wise man does foolish things. Would a call even go through to Cairo from *Aman* headquarters, and if it did, how would it look?

He was not to see the director. The major returned and informed him the general was unavailable.

"Anything you can tell me about the tissue sample I found?"

"It was nothing useful," the major replied. "If we discover more, we'll be in touch with you."

And with that, he was dismissed—as ignominiously escorted out of *Aman's* headquarters as he had been into it. And he knew what the suspicious minds in Israeli intelligence must be thinking. Perhaps Krantz's lover had not suffered any foul play; perhaps her disappearance was planned—with or without his involvement. If Krantz was not a double agent, perhaps he was a simple dupe. Fala could be in Cairo now giving information to her Egyptian handlers. What better place to spy upon Israel than alongside a famous Israeli war hero?

Krantz thought that while Israeli intelligence may not have found anything useful in the tissue sample he found, since they suspected his trustworthiness, even if they had, he would not be privy to the information. But he had other resources.

Dr. Krantz drove to work the next morning, to Bar-Ilan University in Ramat Gan, Israel's fourth largest city, adjoining Tel Aviv. As a professor of archaeology, it was where he was entitled to be, although lately nobody ever expected him. He received lots of cold looks from associates, mostly resentful of the privilege he had managed to obtain. He had an office and a title on the door: *Julius Krantz, Professor of Military Archaeology*. Quite inflated, most felt, for someone who didn't teach, rarely published, and was hardly ever present on campus. Krantz didn't disappoint them. He was in his office only a few minutes, just long enough to make an extension call to a friend and associate in the Life Sciences Department, Professor Malko Waldenkoff. Krantz had helped the Ukrainian immigrant biochemist and geneticist obtain his position at Bar-Ilan. He was not a man who would refuse anything Krantz asked.

Waldenkoff watched with curiosity as Krantz unscrewed his Timex dive watch. Krantz had worn the cheap but reliable watch for half a dozen years. It had served him well, with features like a depth gauge, barometric pressure indicator, water temperature gauge, and dive memory. It was waterproof to a hundred meters, although the deepest that Krantz had ever dove was seventy meters, to Greek ruins off the coast of Turkey, near ancient Ephesus. He would have to get a new watch now. It was no longer waterproof since he had unscrewed and pried off the back of it to hide away a postage stamp cellophane envelope containing a small piece of the tissue he had found on Jolo island. If *Aman* would not help him identify the people who were slaughtering terrorists with the Alexander battle scythe, perhaps Professor Waldenkoff could. He might not discover name, rank, and serial number, but knowing race, sex, ethnicity, and other hereditary quirks might help. And anyway he had no better idea on how to find Fala except to keep sifting through clues.

It was late afternoon when Waldenkoff called him back. Krantz suggested they meet at the campus outdoor cafeteria to talk. With the chatter of students and the blast of rock 'n' roll from nearby speakers, their conversation could be public but yet very private.

"What can you tell me?" Krantz got right to the point. "Can you narrow it down to somebody black, white, Middle Eastern, Asian, European, or some mixed American?"

"It's not human tissue," the professor began.

"What is it? A piece of meat?"

"I don't think so. This tissue you gave me has forty-eight chromosomes. Human beings have forty-six. The DNA belongs to a chimpanzee."

"Do Filipinos eat monkeys?"

"Maybe, but I don't think this was a meal."

"Why not?"

"This chimpanzee DNA is very unique and identifiable."

"What?" Krantz asked, clearly bewildered. "A famous chimp? Like Cheetah from Tarzan or the one on the *Beverly Hillbillies*?"

"No, no, Joshua," the genetics professor explained. "It is not from some famous ape."

"What then?"

"The DNA matches a chimpanzee stem cell line developed in the 1990s by Dr. Julius Wagner, an American scientist. He won a Nobel Prize for his research on mammalian genetics."

"Maimun," Krantz mumbled.

"What's that?" Waldenkoff asked.

"Maimun," Krantz explained, recalling the Iranian cleric's explanation, "is an Arabic word that means 'fortunate.' It was also used in ancient times to mean a monkey."

"Oh? I'm not sure what you mean."

But a fog had lifted. Joshua Krantz at last had a clue, one that might lead him to Fala.

"Where can I find this American doctor?" Krantz asked his associate.

"Unfortunately, I read he died in a murder-suicide earlier this year."
How coincidental was that? Krantz thought.

———————

He spent the next several days in the Hebrew University medical
school library reading about Julius Wagner and his research. When
he thought he had learned everything he could about the man and
his work, he knew that he needed to go to California to learn more—
from Wagner's colleagues, and perhaps from his daughter, who was
also a geneticist. But would the Israeli government allow him to
leave? Why should they? If he was in their shoes, he wouldn't.
There was just no percentage in taking the risk. But Krantz needed
to get to America to find out exactly what this monkey business was
all about. More importantly, he hoped the information would lead
him to Fala.

He couldn't simply fly out of the country, and he couldn't just
walk out. Israel, despite suicide bombers and cross-border shelling,
still, of all nations in the world, had the most secure borders. But
Krantz had a boat and a well-forged Egyptian passport. What he
needed most now was a new dive watch.

His boat was moored in the harbor at Netanya, a quaint beach
resort, which was also well known, like a lot of other Israeli towns,
as the site of a particular suicide bombing. Netanya's was the Pass-
over Massacre. That's why forgiveness was so elusive on both sides.
Towns were not just thought of as seaside resorts, agricultural communities, or industrial centers; they were also memorials.

Krantz slowly motored his cabin cruiser out of the harbor. Just
a quarter mile offshore, he turned north. He was running slow, no

more than ten knots. The coast of Lebanon was about eighty kilometers away. He had been cruising just thirty minutes when he saw the Israeli gunboat taking a position a half mile astern. If it wanted, it could overtake him in a couple of minutes, and shoot him out of the water sooner than that. It kept its distance until he cruised past the Israeli coastal town of Nahariya. He was now less than thirty kilometers from the Lebanese border. Krantz gunned his engine. His twin inboard Chrysler engines could do twenty-five knots. The Israeli gunboat could make forty. When he sped up, the gunboat closed its distance. When they were a hundred yards away, their loudspeakers demanded he stop. When he didn't, fifty-caliber machine guns sprayed the water on either side of his boat. It was then that Krantz's boat turned around and with just as much speed, headed south again. The captain of the gunboat could make out someone at the helm.

Krantz's boat ran out of fuel two hours later. It had been on autopilot. The boarding party from the gunboat found a store mannequin at its controls. Krantz had slid overboard from the stern when his boat had turned around and was as close to the Lebanese border as the Israeli navy would allow. He had on scuba gear and had dry clothes and his papers in a waterproof bag clipped to his belt. He stayed underwater until the gunboat was out of sight, and then began the longest swim of his life. He had calculated the offshore winds and tides. They blew in from the southwest and would carry him north. He would catch sight of a Lebanese beach in a few hours. There were sharks that made a home in these waters. But he wasn't worried about sharks at sea. He was worried about the sharks of Hezbollah on land.

Krantz came ashore at An Naquarah. He had been in the small

fishing village years before during the Israeli occupation of Southern Lebanon. That had been a frustrating time. The Israeli army was sent there to put a stop to Hezbollah's shelling of Israeli cities and incursions by suicide bombers. But Hezbollah melted in with innocent Lebanese civilians, who often had to be displaced or suffered in the line of fire. The incursion raised the ire of the international community and was unpopular with many Israelis as well. That was one of the reasons that Krantz had moved on to another career. He was actually fed up with democracy. My God, they were at war with madmen and you couldn't fight madmen with words. The fact was, bullets killed. While they were aimed at the enemy, they unfortunately often killed the innocent. He resented that the world wanted apologies from Israel all the time simply because Israel was trying to defend itself. He had thought 9/11 would awaken Americans and Europeans to the realization that victory in a war against Islamic terrorism did not come wrapped up in morality. How could there be morality in war, particularly against an enemy who fought, as all armies did, with God on their side, but with the added conviction that death and martyrdom were to be sought after, and prized? Death was their goal, not life. America was now mired in the same ethical quagmire Israel had dealt with for generations. They agonized over the loss of innocent lives, flagellated themselves over small moral lapses in their armies, all the while fighting an enemy that gloated over innocent death and sought their own. How could they win that battle?

Krantz sat quietly sipping coffee at a busy café in Tyre. He knew that the best way to remain inconspicuous was not to hide but to become part of the crowd. He eyed his new watch every now and then and, at the last minute, hurried to catch the bus to Beirut. From

Beirut he flew to Qatar, then to London, finally arriving in the U.S. in New York. From there he would head to Los Angeles.

"Are you here on business or pleasure?" the customs officer in New York asked, looking over an exquisitely forged Egyptian passport.

"I am here to learn," Krantz replied. Among the many lies he was prepared to tell, that was the only truth.

> *Man, however well behaved, at best is but a monkey shaved.*
> —Gilbert and Sullivan

CHAPTER
TWENTY-SEVEN

D r. Jaymes had been a very amiable host. He had given Fala a thorough tour of the research facilities and, even without an escort; she was allowed free rein of the island of Diego Garcia. There were no electric fences, no walls, no moats, no guard dogs, no armed security keeping tabs over her. She was free—but she was not. She was on an island surrounded in every direction by hundreds of miles of water. No cruise ships or recreational boats stopped there. No commercial flights flew in or out. Passage to and from the island was only by consent of its military overlords. It was still, in effect, her prison.

"This is paradise," Dr. Jaymes said after they first met, trying to make her feel comfortable. How could anyone be disenchanted with paradise?

While he was forthright in answering her questions about their work on the island, every other question she asked was the same.

"When will I be able to leave?"

By the end of their first day together, Jaymes had become more curt. "For the time being," he responded to her persistent inquiry, "you will be our guest."

He provided her with a cell phone.

"Call me if you need anything or if you have any more questions." He added one caveat in an effort to put an end to her annoying quest for freedom. "Unfortunately, I won't have all the answers."

Phone communication on the island was available. But phone and Internet access that allowed communication off the island was well secured.

They were desperately trying to be gracious hosts, Fala thought. There was the initial faux pas of offering her pig meat, or sausages, for breakfast, but clearly they were making every effort to treat her if she were a VIP at some luxury resort rather than a captive, which in reality she was. They provided for her every need. Her closet was stocked with every garment she could want—from bathing suits to shorts to modest Arab *chadors*.

In the shade of a beachfront cabana, Dr. Jaymes had candidly explained the Lemuria Project. Although the Americans had thought she and Colonel Krantz were close to knowing the truth, Fala now knew they were so very far off. She smiled to herself, somewhat bemused and saddened. Joshua was probably desperately searching for her and perhaps still searching for the Right Hand of God. If, instead of rushing off on his mission, he had only stayed in their hotel room to recover from the jet lag of a long flight as she had, he, too, would probably have been kidnapped and would be sitting alongside her now—sipping margaritas and fine-tuning his tan. And, of course, resenting his imprisonment.

After their morning chat on the beach, Dr. Jaymes had walked Fala through the modern research facility in the middle of the island. Every building looked new—all stainless steel, concrete, marble, and glass. And army engineers were busy building more. White-jacketed doctors and technicians in surgical scrubs were busily meandering through the halls. When they arrived at Dr. Jaymes's office, she noticed the nameplate on his door: *Major Joshua Jaymes*.

"You're a major in the U.S. Army?" Fala asked. "I thought you were a doctor."

"I am a doctor. I have a PhD in embryology and biogenetics and was chair of my department at MIT. But everybody here is in the army. It was part of the deal. As soon as I signed on, they made me an officer. No basic training. No marksmanship tests. I just had to raise my right hand and 'solemnly swear.' They just want us under their chain of command, to understand that while we're free to do our work, we're still subject to taking orders."

"And I suppose, if you don't," Fala added, "they can shoot you."

Jaymes just smiled. "No one's been shot yet." Clearly he didn't take his military role seriously.

"No regrets then?" Fala asked.

"Just sometimes I think," Jaymes joked, "I should have held out for being a colonel."

On the way to his lab, they passed several huge, windowed rooms. Inside were dozens of caged chimpanzees that appeared to be in various stages of pregnancy. In another room, she saw caregivers playing with chimps like children in a nursery school. When they arrived at Dr. Jaymes's lab, his staff was ready for him. He was about to demonstrate his personal expertise.

Staff brought in a female chimp that had already been sedated.

They set the animal on an examining table and then, in the ignominious way that woman are always examined "down there," they spread the animal's legs over the stirrups of the gynecological table. Jaymes turned on an ultrasound machine and manipulated an instrument into the animal's vagina.

"We're doing a transvaginal oocyte retrieval. I'm using this sonographically guided needle to maneuver through the vaginal wall to the ovaries, and there, you see, we recover her eggs. We prep the animal a few weeks before by giving fertility drugs, and then do blood tests and ultrasounds so that we know the optimal time to retrieve the eggs from the ovaries—just before ovulation when the oocytes are primed for fertilization.

"We use chimpanzees because they're so similar to us physiologically. The statistic they like to throw around is that we have ninety-eight percent of the same DNA. And even though our two species branched off the evolutionary tree six million years ago, they're like us in many ways psychologically, as well. They're intelligent, and they cooperate for mutual benefit. They're very smart. They pass on knowledge—like herbal self-medication and how to use tools to find food. They have families. They adopt orphans. And they mourn their dead."

Later, under a dual high-power microscope, Fala watched him inject those same chimp eggs with what he called "designer DNA." With a micro-needle in one hand and a glass pipette in the other, Jaymes pressed the tip of the pipette against the egg and with a subtle poke of the needle, pierced the membrane of the chimp's egg. Then, pushing farther with the pipette, he prodded the cell until the nucleus oozed out like jelly from a doughnut. The nucleus from a specially prepared stem cell line was then removed from its membrane and slipped through the tiny tear in the emptied egg cell. Out with the bad, in with the good. A small electrical charge was enough to patch the hole and fuse the new nucleus and engineered DNA into the egg. The fertilized eggs were then placed in petri dishes with special nutrients designed to duplicate the nurturing environment of fallopian tubes. These were placed in large incubators, perfectly set to the body temperature of a chimpanzee.

"In a few hours," Jaymes explained, "the cell will divide, and later divide again, and again. In about four or five days, it will enter its blastocyst stage with enough cells so that we can pick out which embryos are most likely to thrive. That's when we implant them in our fertile female chimps."

"And, *inshallah*, you end up with healthy baby chimps that you can use for spare parts," Fala said cynically.

"We don't do that," Jaymes rebutted. "We're not part of that scientific community that butchers animals. Look, we treat these animals as if they were people."

"You treat them like people, but eventually you do kill them. Or torture them."

"We don't."

"Dr. Jaymes, I have a PhD in archaeology. Part of my study was learning about animal anatomy, especially mammalian anatomy. I have to be able to identify a monkey's bones from a man's. And I know what the biomedical community does. I know that chimps are physiologically similar to humans and that the experimental findings on them are likely to apply to us, as well. That's why for years they have used these animals. They give them AIDS. They transplant their organs. They give them spinal cord or brain injuries. They give them cancer and try new chemotherapy or radiation treatments.

And now, you're doing gene therapy—the latest paradigm of modern medicine. How is that any different?"

"We are not harming these animals. We are creating a better species."

"You said that these animals are ninety-eight percent like us."

"That's right."

"I suppose you're working on making that closer to ninety-nine percent."

Dr. Jaymes smiled wickedly. "I firmly believe that someday one of our chimps might engage you personally in answering that question."

He was being facetious again, Fala thought. She had more to say and more questions to ask. Where were these soldiers who were being trained to use the battle scythe of Alexander? Were they chimpanzees, too? Chimps different from those baby chimps or their mothers that she had seen? She had come very close to alienating her host and decided to hold her tongue. She would now play the demure Arab maiden and bide her time. After all, this was her first day as a prisoner in "paradise."

CHAPTER
TWENTY-EIGHT

On the other side of the island that General Mack Shell called Lemuria but the world knew as Diego Garcia, there was another research center called ATAA—the Advanced Training, Acculturation, and Analysis Center. This was a training ground for the mature animals. There were no high-tech multistory research centers there. The place looked more like a World War II bivouac area with a multitude of pup tents and a few larger tents for officers. There were specialized canteen vehicles that provided meals to troops on the move. And there were cages, of course. They were McGraw's version of a brig. Having spent some time himself in a cage, he was loath to use them, but there were occasional discipline problems. There had never been a human-chimpanzee conflict—only those of chimp versus chimp. And in an army, that could not be tolerated. Soldiers had to work together, or they would die together.

Chimpanzee newborns, like human babies, were helpless at

birth. But just a few days after birth, they could hold on tight to their mother's hair, and in a few months, they were riding jockey-style on her back. By two years they were walking. They reached puberty in about seven years. When the Lemuria-bred animals reached that milestone, they were brought to ATAA.

General Shell's nascent genetic research on Diego Garcia had been making progress for almost a decade, since its inception shortly after 9/11. Unhampered by the usual government or academic oversights, or financial constraints, the research involving the manipulation of the chromosomes of man's closest relative, the chimpanzee, had advanced rapidly. But it was only in the last year that their "research product" had matured. Each new birth had been a refinement of the past. The animals were maturing sooner. They were progressively bred physically larger and, with each new genetic modification, they were subtly more complex creatures.

"The chimpanzee is a naturally aggressive mammal," McGraw would often explain to scientists new to the project or military or political brass who had a need to know. "In fact, in their natural habitat, they can and do kill other animals. They also often kill their rivals, sometimes even their own children. Here in ATAA, we don't aim to remove that aggressive bent. We just want to control it by creating a human-dominated leadership. Our goal is that they kill our enemies, not theirs."

———

Colonel Link McGraw was just stepping into his trousers when he heard a knock on his door. He looked at his watch. It was six a.m. and his adjutant was right on time. The young captain had been handpicked by General Shell for the job. He had combat experience and had once been a veterinarian. He did a good job, but McGraw had no illusions. He knew his adjutant reported directly back to the general. That never struck him as a problem. After all, they both had loyalty to the same man.

Another day of training was about to begin. It was a short walk from McGraw's modern, modular beachfront cabana to the bivouac area where several dozen orderly tents housed his troops. It was dawn. A morning mist hung over the ground. He could hear the surf pulsating nearby, but the shore was hidden by incoming fog. He wore well-pressed combat fatigues; his boots had a spit-and-polish shine. His shirt was adjusted to a tight tuck, and the silver eagle of his rank glistened on his garrison cap. In a few months, his command had grown from a few platoons to a company. More than a hundred troops were under his authority now. McGraw also knew how breeding was progressing on the other side of the island. In another few months, he would be commanding a thousand—a regiment-sized force. And soon, an army.

As he walked past each tent, with his adjutant trailing obediently behind, he could hear the murmurs of his troops. They were rising and knew their commander was passing, by the sound of his step and by his smell. Link had studied the ways of war and warriors during his academic years at the Citadel. He knew about the swagger of Patton, the calm demeanor of Eisenhower, and the camaraderie fostered by Napoleon. But of all the great military leaders he'd studied, it was Alexander the Great who most excited his passion.

"Another perfect day," his adjutant said, making small talk.

"Yes." McGraw nodded. "It's time."

The adjutant waved his hand and a bugler blew assembly, a sound familiar to every soldier, a tune perfectly fit for that lyric: "There's a soldier in the grass, with a bullet up his ass, take it out, take it out, like a good Boy Scout!"

In less than a minute, nearly two hundred chimpanzee soldiers were standing stolidly in front of their tents, and McGraw slowly began his review. He was surprised each time he saw these creatures, his troops. At first, he had difficulty telling them apart. They had all looked alike. But no longer; he now knew them all, by their character, as well as by their names. Many had already been given names by their earlier handlers. Some names, he found need to change. Their personalities called for it.

"Look thee out for a kingdom equal to and worthy of thyself," McGraw said aloud.

"What's that, sir?" his adjutant inquired.

"You know, Captain, I once rode alongside Alexander the Great."

"I've heard those stories, sir," his captain smiled.

"There are a lot of legends about Alexander," McGraw began, walking slowly before his troops. "Plutarch, the great Greek historian, created many of them. 'It was in 344 BC,' he wrote, 'when a ten-year-old Alexander watched the most skilled horsemen in his father's kingdom try and fail to ride a great steed named Bucephalus. The horse was untamable. Alexander begged his father for his chance. Reluctantly, King Phillip agreed. And, with a soothing voice, a kind touch, and some firm urging, Alexander succeeded in riding Bucephalus.'"

"King Phillip," McGraw went on, "is said to have told his son, 'Look thee out for a kingdom equal to and worthy of thyself for Macedonia is too little for thee.' And so, Alexander set out astride Bucephalus to conquer the known world."

"Do you think of this as your little kingdom, sir?" his adjutant asked, somewhat impolitic.

"Do you know the tale of the Gordian Knot?" McGraw said, ignoring any affront.

"Yes, sir," the captain replied quickly, from habit. Then he corrected himself. "Not really, sir."

"Another tale of Alexander was the legend of the Gordian Knot. According to that fable, the ancient land of Phrygia had lapsed into civil war. The elders of the land were unable to decide which faction should lead them until a great oracle came before them and predicted that the next man to enter the kingdom would be riding an oxcart. That man, he declared, would put an end to their bickering and become their king. While the Phrygian high council was discussing the oracle's prediction, Midas, a peasant farmer, rode into town on his father Gordias's oxcart. With the prediction having come true, Midas was anointed king. In gratitude, he dedicated Gordias's oxcart to Zeus, set it in the center of a temple, and tied it to a post with an intricate knot made of bark. The oracle then prophesied that whoever untied that knot would someday rule all of Asia. Years went by and the bark of the knot grew together. Though many tried, no one could untie it. And so, the legend of the Gordian Knot, the unsolvable puzzle, grew. In 333 BC, Alexander came to Phrygia and attempted to untie the knot himself. He could find no end to the knot, and it seemed that he would fail, too. Then, with a single stroke of his sword, Alexander sliced the knot in half, revealing its ends."

"Sounds like he cheated, sir."

"Well, maybe," McGraw conceded. "We could dispute the legend. But what is undisputed is that Alexander the Great did go on to conquer most of Asia. There's a lesson to be learned here, Captain."

"Sir?"

"Do whatever needs to be done to accomplish the mission."

With the events that had unfolded in the last several months, McGraw couldn't help seeing his own fate replayed in these Greek fables. Like Midas, for no rational reason he had been raised up from his lowly position as a prisoner to become a virtual king over his own army. Just as Alexander had tamed Bucephalus, he, too, was taming the untamable. And when his superiors remained bewildered how he would take his new army into battle, well, he untied the Gordian Knot. The generals were uncomfortable with arming chimpanzees with high-powered automatic weapons. Despite the animals' dexterity, they were not yet capable of the fine touch required to aim and fire a weapon that could potentially spray death out at six hundred rounds per minute. McGraw remembered the stories of the Alexander battle scythe. Perhaps it was a recollection from his former life. He told the idea to Mack Shell and had no problem giving the general credit for the idea.

In the fourth century BC, Alexander the Great molded a great army by creating a persona of invincibility. He made himself a legend, and then a god. McGraw knew that to command soldiers to fight and die, a leader, even a modern one, had to generate that same godlike aura—engendering awe, fear, and a prideful worship. As he trekked through the campgrounds and his troops stepped out, as Alexander did to Bucephalus, he gave one after another a gentle touch, but his voice was firm, decisive, and demanding of obedience.

In a former life, Link McGraw knew he had been Ptolemy—not Alexander. But Ptolemy, the childhood friend of Alexander the Great, went on to become his greatest general. And, with Alexander's death, Ptolemy himself became a king, the pharaoh of Egypt and the first of his own dynasty, which lasted three hundred years. McGraw, too, knew he had more noble things to accomplish in his life. But he would never speak of such imaginings. He was sure General Shell would laugh at his arrogance.

"You see," he would remind Link, "I told you no one imagines themselves reincarnated as a 'nobody.' And why imagine being a general, when you can be a king?"

> *Facts are ventriloquist's dummies. Sitting on a wise*
> *man's knee they may be made to utter words of wisdom;*
> *elsewhere they say nothing or talk nonsense.*
> —Aldous Huxley: Time Must Have a Stop

CHAPTER
TWENTY-NINE

The black 1995 Mercedes 600 SL coupe had seen better days. It had been bought new, but like its owner, was older, world worn, and in need of a lot of refurbishing. It was parked across from Dr. Julius Wagner's house on a cul-de-sac street in Palo Alto. For over a week it had been parked there every night and often during the day. Maggie Wagner knew it was there and ignored it. The neighbors were not so magnanimous. They had called the local police several times. After all, the stranger who sat all day and slept in the car night after night was suspicious and made them uncomfortable.

"What are you doing here, sir?" the police asked. Stumpf efficiently and coldly passed over his driver's license, his insurance certificate, and his photo ID as a licensed private detective.

"Working," he'd answer curtly.

And the police would depart after taking time to explain to anxious neighbors that the interloper was not a thief or a pedophile but a private detective. Learning that Stumpf was "on the job" actually made many of these upright citizens even more nervous as they contemplated which of their indiscretions was the subject of his attentions.

Maggie felt she had no more need of the man. Clearly she was meddling in a business where she could get hurt. She had been hurt. Someone had drugged her and clearly wanted to defame her. And while she believed Stumpf when he denied responsibility, she also believed he was incompetent and a little strange. While the video demonstrated that he hadn't raped her, he couldn't hide his lascivious glare and a subtle fondling as he put her to bed. So, she ignored his presence outside her front door. She would continue her pursuit of the truth about her father in a more mundane manner. She made telephone calls and sent lots of e-mails. None bore fruit.

Stumpf, on the other hand, believed he still had a job, or wanted to believe that. And anyway, for the time being he had no other gigs. Finding out what BIOT was, was the key to this case. As at other times in his career, he expected the heavens to part and good fortune to suddenly shine upon him. Like the time he found a ten-thousand-dollar Rolex sitting on the bedside table of a hotel room quickly vacated by the wife of a client who had hired him to catch her in flagrante delicto. While he had missed "catching" her with the philanderer, he was able to provide his client with a "name" by tracking the registration number of the watch. And he kept the watch. So, Stumpf, a bit of a manic-depressive with an optimistic bent, expected to become suddenly enlightened or have good fortune stumble upon him again. Either that, or Maggie Wagner would solve the clue of BIOT and he would latch onto her to follow it. He did have a contract after all, and if he had any part in proving that her father did not commit suicide, well, it would be a big payday.

Stumpf left his "stakeout" one evening, driving off for dinner to get his usual drive-thru burger and Coke. When he returned, he was a bit put off to find another car parked in his usual spot in front of the Wagner home. It was a car he had not seen before. After scarfing down his dinner, he decided to forgo his usual after-dinner smoke and take a closer look. The sedan, he quickly noted, was a rental. Was this a friend visiting? He didn't like snooping so close to homes in broad daylight, but he was working for half-a-mil. He went back to his own car to retrieve two tools of his trade. He decided to leave one, the camera, behind.

From a side window, he had a good view of the living room. No one was there. *Damn*, he thought, *I hope they're not upstairs in the bedroom doing tummy slaps.* He had climbed trees and patio trellises before to get a view of a second story, but he hadn't expected to do any second-story work on this job, and anyway he was wearing his good shoes, not sneakers. Nate Stumpf slipped through the side gate to see if he could spy anyone in the kitchen. And there they were. A swarthy-looking man with a military crew cut was standing over Maggie, who sat in a kitchen chair. He had his hand on her shoulder as if he were keeping her in place. Stumpf crunched down and crawled snake-like to put his ear to a small crack at the base of rear door. He could hear just snippets of conversation—the context was unclear, but one thing he knew for sure, this visitor had an accent and it sounded Middle Eastern. *Shit*, he thought, *are Arab terrorists involved in this?*

Stumpf knew that whatever edge he lacked in size, he could always make up for in decisiveness. At least that's the way he succeeded most of the time. Maggie bolted up from her chair when her kitchen door flew open as Stumpf kicked through it. He cracked the wood and tore the door off one of the hinges. It was a karate kick, he told himself. It had come in handy for him before—although he had never bothered to actually learn karate. He held a .38 Smith and Wesson revolver in hand and pointed it at Colonel Joshua Krantz.

"Back off, motherfucker!" Stumpf bellowed at him. "And put 'em up. Hands on your head. Come on! Hands on your head!"

Krantz complied.

"You all right, babe?" Stumpf said with a wink to Maggie.

"I thought you said you didn't have a gun?" Maggie replied, still startled.

"I never give away all my secrets."

"She was not in any danger from me," Krantz interrupted.

"Shut up."

"I'm okay," Maggie confirmed.

Krantz looked closer, eyeing Nate Stumpf up and down. And then he put his hands down.

"Put 'em up, asshole."

Krantz began walking toward him.

"*No comprende ingles?*" he said, mustering his meanest growl. "I'll fuckin' blow your head off."

But Krantz kept coming. He simply ignored the gun, picked the diminutive detective up by the collar of his shirt, and set him gently on the couch. Then he turned to Maggie.

"Please," he said, and pointed for her to sit on the couch next to Stumpf. She complied, and Krantz pulled up a chair and sat opposite them, knee to knee.

"Dr. Wagner," he went on, "you have nothing to fear from me. I believe we are on the same side. Searching for the same answers."

"You know," Stumpf said, still waving his gun, but now with far less bluster, "I could fuckin' blow you away."

Krantz hesitated a moment and then simply leaned over, slapped the gun aside with one hand, and yanked it from Stumpf's hand with his other. Krantz hefted the weapon for a moment and manipulated the trigger.

"This is a very good replica," he said. "You know, you could go to jail for having a toy gun like this. Your federal law requires that a yellow plug be visible on the barrel. You have taken it out."

Nate Stumpf smiled sheepishly. "I wasn't going to shoot you. I was just protecting my client."

"Perfectly understandable."

"How did you know the gun wasn't real? I got it from a friend who works props for the studios. The gun has gotta look real for close-ups. Nobody can tell the difference."

"The trigger action is different," Krantz replied and demonstrated.

"But how could you know that with me pointing it at you?"

Krantz just smiled. "I am an expert on weapons. But I am more of an expert when it comes to judging people. Please do not take offense, but you do not look like the kind of man who could 'blow my fuckin' head off.' Mister, mister?"

"Stumpf. Nate Stumpf," he replied, extending his hand to shake. "I'm a private detective. I work for Ms. Wagner."

"No, you don't," Maggie snapped back.

"We have a contract," Stumpf reminded.

Krantz ignored their tiff and introduced himself. "My name is Joshua Krantz."

"It's Colonel Krantz," Maggie clarified. "He's a spy. He works for Israeli intelligence."

"As I told you, I am not so much a spy. I am an archaeologist. And I am here because understanding why your father died will help me find my—my wife." Sometimes, he thought, it was simpler describing Fala as a wife than describing their complex relationship.

"Do you know why Professor Wagner was murdered?" Stumpf asked excitedly. He was counting his money already.

"I know nothing of that."

And poof, Stumpf was broke again. "Then why are you here?"

"The clues have led me here."

Krantz went on to explain the last month of his life, beginning with what seemed his long-ago former life—his suntanned tranquil explorations off the coast of Acre. Then he described the convoluted events that led him to Southern California—the discovery of the Alexander battle scythe, which led him to a survivor in the Hindu Kush who spoke of his attackers as Maimun; to his search in Iran for a nonexistent terror cell called the Right Hand of God; to a massacre in the Philippines and the disappearance of Fala there; and finally to his dismissal by *Aman*, his furtive flight from Israel, and new evidence that the soldiers who wielded the battle scythe were genetically similar to a chimpanzee stem cell line that a Nobel Laureate, Dr. Julius Wagner, had created.

"I am no longer working for *Aman*, or for Israel," Krantz stressed. "I am working now only to find a woman named Fala al-Shohada."

"My father was working on something called the Lemuria Project," Maggie told him. "Do you know anything about that?"

"No. What is this Lemuria Project?"

"That's what's so damn unusual. No one knows. Or no one is saying."

"We think it refers to an ancient civilization," Stumpf piped in. "Like Atlantis, Lemuria was a place that disappeared in a great flood thousands of years ago."

Stupid man, Krantz thought. "That is a myth. What else have you learned?"

Krantz clearly focused his attention on Maggie; after all, she was the daughter of the next link in his "dig" for the truth. Stumpf, however, resented being ignored.

"Do we really want to talk to this guy?" Stumpf interrupted. "We only know who he is from who he says he is."

Krantz leaned forward, putting his face inches from Stumpf and staring at him with a gaze that Stumpf understood quite clearly. It said, *don't fuck with me*. It was sufficiently sudden and threatening to silence Stumpf. And just as quickly, Krantz relaxed.

"Please, I am not here to hurt anyone. My wife, the woman I love, has disappeared, and the information I have has led me here. I would like to be a patient man, but I am impatient. You must understand."

"We talked to an associate of my father's who was clearly very scared to talk about Lemuria," Maggie went on. "So it must be important. He gave us one word and ran off, and I haven't been able to find him since."

"And what did he say?"

"He didn't say a thing," Stumpf said, again wanting to be a team player.

Krantz looked him over and decided to be more tolerant of the annoying detective.

"I slapped him about a bit, and this is all he gave us before running off," Stumpf said, trying to regain his gravitas. Then he pulled the scrap of paper from his pocket and handed it to the colonel.

"We thought *Biot* was this biomedical convention, so I took my client there to make inquiries, but some people plainly didn't want us looking into this and we got screwed there. They drugged us."

"I got drugged," Maggie corrected.

"That's right," Stumpf said, still apologetic. "She was drugged."

"B-I-O-T," Krantz read the letters aloud. They were all caps. Working in military intelligence, he had seen reports about BIOT before and they never referred to anything about biotechnology.

"Do you know what it means?" Maggie asked.

"BIOT. I think it's a place," Krantz said, and then added, somewhat surprised himself, "a place like Lemuria."

"Hey, buddy," Stumpf sneered, tired of being put down. "I know Lemuria is a myth, a legend, like Atlantis. I know it doesn't exist. I'm not stupid."

But Krantz, an archaeologist and historian, had his own wealth of knowledge about ancient legends and myths.

"Many people think it did exist," Krantz continued. "Plato's stories put Atlantis somewhere in the Aegean near Crete. Lemuria is supposed to have been in the Pacific, somewhere near Asia or Australia. And some believe it is in the Indian Ocean. Today, I am sure Lemuria is in the Indian Ocean."

"You're sure?" Now Maggie was surprised.

"The only BIOT I have ever heard of in all my years working with Israeli intelligence always referred to the American and British secret military base on Diego Garcia. It was called BIOT because it is a British Indian Ocean Territory. BIOT and Lemuria, I think they must refer to the same thing."

Ka-ching. Jackpot. Stumpf was counting his money again. Now this made sense.

"So," Stumpf verbalized his conclusion, "Dr. Wagner was murdered because he knew too much about some secret military project called Lemuria on a secret military base in the Indian Ocean?"

"Possibly," Krantz agreed.

"So how do we find out for sure?" Maggie asked.

There was a long lull—at first to allow them to emotionally absorb that the three of them were now collaborators, and a bit longer to conceive of how to proceed.

"We need to shake the tree." Krantz was first to respond. "We need to ask questions. By e-mail and on the blogs, we need to mention this information we know about Lemuria and BIOT and Dr. Wagner and his research. And then we must wait and see if important people become uncomfortable. And then we will know for sure. But if we do this, we should do it from a safe house."

"I have a safe house," Stumpf jumped in.

"You do?" Maggie asked, surprised.

"Where?" Krantz asked.

"Anywhere," Stumpf replied, feeling puffed with power again. "It's a twenty-four-foot Fleetwood Tioga and it sleeps six comfortably."

CHAPTER THIRTY

In 1999 a newly assigned Russian diplomat walked into the Harry S. Truman Building a few blocks from the White House in the Foggy Bottom neighborhood of Washington, DC. The Truman Building, which housed the offices of the Department of State, was built as one of Roosevelt's make work construction projects during the Depression. The old building was in a perpetual state of remodel. The diplomat was scheduled for a routine introduction with the secretary of state, a moment of polite face time. During a minute alone in the secretary's office, he simply pried back a piece of molding on the floor and planted a powerful listening device. No one took notice of the warped baseboard. Cracked molding, half-finished newly painted walls, and dangling wires were a consequence of work performed by the lowest bidder. It was only during more routine renovations six months later that the bug was found. Everyone in government agreed that security—in the White House, the executive

offices, the State Department, and especially in the Capitol building—places where both the public and foreign dignitaries frequently
tread, was leaky. If the president really had something to say that he
never wanted to hear played back, he said it on the south lawn with
the noise of Marine One's chopper blades in the background.

"I think we've got a problem," Senator Berger told the president
as he was preparing to board his helicopter. "The Israelis know about
Lemuria."

"They're allies," the president responded. "I think I can shush it
with the prime minister."

"And people are calling their congressmen about it. Congressmen who are not our friends."

"You are Congress. You need to meet and figure this out before the
press makes it a headline. And put General Shell on it. It's his baby."

The "people" calling their congressmen were easily identified.
They were Margaret Wagner and Nathaniel Stumpf. A dozen select FBI agents were tagged with a simple mission—gather them up.
They first knocked on their doors, and then, with no answer, they
broke them down. Lots of inquiries were made; phone records and
credit cards were checked. Surveillance monitors in the neighborhood
were reviewed. They were not to be found in the "usual places."

One of the benefits of being pretty near broke was that Stumpf
had never bothered to register his motor home when he took it over
several years before from a deadbeat client. So, of course, the feds
never thought to check out the beachfront motor home sites along
the California coast. Stumpf's rundown twenty-four-foot motor
home was one of several dozen parked at Carpinteria State Beach,
just twelve miles south of Santa Barbara on Highway 101. Krantz
felt right at home. It reminded him of the some of the beaches in

Israel. And the climate was very much like Israel's. Los Angeles and Tel Aviv shared the same latitude.

That same evening, two senators and four congressmen, the leadership from the Armed Services Committee, met in secret to discuss Lemuria. They met after hours at Ciao, an intimate Italian restaurant in Arlington owned by the senator from Rhode Island. Everyone agreed that what they said there would be more private than any speech could be in the Capitol Building, where past talk held in "secret sessions" had ended up as quotes in front-page head-lines. There were, nevertheless, no guarantees to secrecy anymore with an increasing array of sophisticated listening devices—that ranged from a tie clip to microwave antennae on satellites a thousand miles up. And while these men all felt they were "honorable," they were all worldly enough to know that too many elected officials had sworn to uphold the nation's secrets and later simply decided that they had a special privilege to ignore that oath. Secrets leaked and oaths were no longer sacred. They were confident, however, the words said here would be as secret as possible because to reveal them would be political suicide and these men were all professionals—professional politicians. Not one had spent less than two decades in one high political office or another. And they were disciplined profession-als—meaning they knew how to raise funds, were comfortable in the business of coddling special interests, and could adjust their positions to run with any political wind. It was not that they didn't have strong opinions; they did. But they were survivors. If the game of politics was like playing rock, paper, scissors, they would always win—be-cause they were water.

Most of the men in the room were septuagenarians. The youngest, Congressman Adler from California, was sixty. All were balding or gray haired. They sat around a long table in the empty restaurant and picked at several huge bowls of baked ziti set in the middle of the table. And there was plenty of wine. They looked more like Mafia bosses planning a hit than a congressional committee in secret session.

Theodore Berger, the senator from Rhode Island, the committee chair, and their host, began the discussion. Although he was a Republican, the conservatives in his party still thought of him as some East Coast liberal—and he probably was except for when it came to the armed forces. He gave the military anything they wanted. And General Shell and his fellows in the joint chiefs wanted Lemuria.

"People who shouldn't know, know," Berger began. "The Israelis know. And Dr. Wagner's daughter has probably figured it out."

"The Israelis are allies," Congressman Adler entered the fray. "And eventually we share information with our allies."

"And this Egyptian woman we're holding," the congressman from Wyoming asked, "does that mean the Egyptians know and by extension the rest of the Arab world? Maybe we should think about shutting this business down."

"I don't know," Berger responded solemnly.

"We ought to shut nothing down," Senator Leland Bruce spoke up. He was the senior senator there. Of all the congressmen sitting around the table, he was perhaps most intimate with the results of the Lemuria Project. He had arranged to receive firsthand reports on progress from the "formerly disgraced" Colonel McGraw, whom he admired very much. Senator Bruce considered McGraw a maligned hero who had risen, phoenix-like, to an even greater heroic status.

"Nobody likes to say it," he began, "but we've been involved in one war or another since the end of World War II. We've gone from the Nazis, to the Communists, to petty dictators, and now we've got the fanatic Islamo-fascists to deal with. Would any of you boys have shut down the Manhattan Project if the secret got leaked and a few pussies in the press made scare headlines about the dangers of radioactivity? Or if the environmentalists objected? Secrets don't stay secrets forever. What'll count in the end is results."

"I agree with Leland," another congressman entered the conversation. He used a common political ploy of announcing agreement and then disagreeing. "Any new weapon will have its detractors. And this one will, too. But an awful lot of people in both our parties are not going to like this. We should step back a bit and maybe introduce the idea more slowly, over a few years, to adjust the public. Maybe later—"

"Congressman," Leland responded. He only used first names when he liked people. "Horses have been battle scarred for centuries. We've given medals to dogs for heroism on the battlefield. Animals have always been used in war—horses, camels, elephants, dogs, cats, birds, and now chimps. We can't go backwards on this."

"I am not advocating going backwards. Just going forward more slowly."

The congressman from Wyoming, a real cowboy, with big pointy-toed fancy alligator boots and a thousand-acre ranch back home, finished off a tall glass of wine and decided to confront the old man.

"I don't disagree, Leland, that we've benefited from using animals in war, but what nobody has talked about here is that we've gotten ourselves onto that proverbial 'slippery slope.' The one the religious right has been so noisy about. Everybody is for using genetic research to cure disease but scared at the same time that we'd use it to engineer a new human being."

"We're not engineering a new human being," Leland corrected.

"Maybe what we're doing is worse," the Wyoming congressman continued. "We've created a chimera."

"A what?" Senator Berger asked.

"I'm not ignorant of all this scientific stuff. I've been reading the reports. They're doing research that people call transgenesis, the creation of a chimera. A chimera is a composite animal."

"Like a mule?" Senator Bruce cut him off. "Half horse, half donkey. What's the big deal? We bred mules for special jobs and nobody ever got in an uproar about that. There are hybrid cattle and sheep and, well, we're just breeding chimps to have special characteristics, to do a special job, as well."

"Leland," the cowboy said, softening his speech. "We all know we're not making another mule. Half horse, half donkey. We all know the half and half they're making on that island."

The conversation quieted. Everyone knew what the cowboy meant, but no one was ready to speak the words aloud: "half man, half chimp."

Halfway around the world, Colonel McGraw was having a similar conversation with a "guest" on his island.

Fala had spent the morning watching him train with his troops. Nearly two hundred chimpanzees ran along the beach with McGraw in the lead. She was familiar with monkeys in a zoo and monkeys in the wild. They scampered around in haphazard ways. They were either playful or sedentary. But McGraw's chimps were different. She had never seen animals like this exhibit such discipline. They were larger than chimpanzees she had seen in the past, at least five feet tall. They also exhibited more of a bipedal motion and stood more upright. And their right hands wore special gloves that never touched the ground. The Alexander battle scythe she had seen had been a right-handed weapon. But what was most curious was their chant. It was almost as if these animals could speak. As McGraw ran, he sang out army running cadences.

"One, two, three, four. If you don't sing, we're gonna run some more. One mile—won't get it," McGraw sang out.

"Oon mah," the chimps responded.

"Two miles—stickin' with it." Again McGraw.

"Too mah," the chimp company answered.

"Three miles—lookin' good," McGraw sang.

"Tree mah," they responded.

"Four miles—knew you could."

"Fo mah."

The company came to a halt on the beachfront where Fala sat on a knoll. McGraw's chest heaved from the exertion. His T-shirt was drenched in sweat. His chimps weren't winded at all, and in fact, they seemed eager for more. Colonel McGraw brought his troops to a disciplined attention and then dismissed them. They instantly appeared more like monkeys, scampering into the sea to play, back into the jungle to their tents, or into nearby trees. McGraw sauntered over to her. Curiosity piqued, Fala was the first to talk.

"They speak?" was her first question.

"They mimic speech, like parrots," Link answered.

"They stand more upright and they're larger than any chimpanzees I've ever seen."

McGraw smiled. "Good breeding." And he changed the subject. "Are you enjoying your stay on our island?"

"Do I have a choice?"

"Sure you have a choice."

"It's been interesting," Fala conceded, somberly.

McGraw sat next to her. "Well, we don't all get dealt the cards we want. You can choose to be happy with your lot in life right now or simply be miserable over things you can't change." He picked up a handful of sand and let it flow in a slow trickle out of his hand. When it emptied, he picked up another handful. "Unlike an hourglass where time seems so finite, it can seem endless here. You ought to try to enjoy it."

"Well then, I can't think of a more beautiful place to be a captive."

"I knew I'd find an optimist in there somewhere." Link smiled.

"So, you are using these animals to fight your wars," Fala got instantly to the heart of the matter.

"Why not?" McGraw quickly conceded. "Man has always used animals to fight. It may have even been your relatives who started it. The ancient Egyptians loosed leopards and hawks and snakes on their enemies."

"But you are creating a new kind of animal."

"We've made a hybrid."

"No. A mule is a hybrid, a cross between a horse and a donkey. You're creating a chimera."

"A chimera? That's just mythology. Man has always worked to breed better animals—faster horses, fatter cattle, hardier chickens. Chimeras are bizarro things, like animals with the body of a goat, the head of a lion, the tail of a serpent."

Fala added her wisdom. "The Greeks had centaurs—half man, half horse; and harpies, a falcon with the head of a lion; and the minotaur with the head of a bull on the body of a man."

"Exactly. My soldiers look just like chimpanzees to me. We don't have a chimera here."

"Just a smart chimp?"

"Exactly."

"But with the body of a chimpanzee and the genes of a man."

She was not so dumb, McGraw quickly realized. And she was beautiful.

"Swim?" he asked her, taking off his shirt. He was prepared to swim in the buff and hoped she'd do the same. He looked down on her. His eyes—and his six-pack lean, muscled abdomen—enticed her.

"I'll have to change." She smiled.

"You'd have to drive halfway across the island. You can swim in your underwear." And he was down to his.

This soldier made her uncomfortable. But he was beautiful, she thought.

"Don't worry," McGraw added. "There'll be no monkey business with me."

"No monkey business?"

"Absolutely not. This is a great place to swim." He had goggles and snorkels in his backpack. He handed her a pair. "We can snorkel off the reef. It's shallow and just about fifty meters offshore. There's a world of colorful fish down there. And who's gonna see? Just me and a bunch of chimpanzees. Come on."

He smiled one last time, then quickly took off his shorts and ran naked into the surf. She watched his torso and buttocks undulating, butterflying through the surf. She could not help but look. This man was testing and teasing her. She had never done anything like this before. She thought for a moment that she would strip down to panties and a bra and run after him into the sea. Or should she just become naked like him? Oh, what crazy thoughts this man had her thinking. She imagined what her uncles would think. They would stone her. *Allahumma-gh fir-lee*, she thought. God forgive me. She took her shoes off but left on all her clothes. She was a Muslim woman who could be respectable and enjoy life, too, and she ran into the surf after the handsome colonel.

They swam together for a while pointing out to each other the drama of the world below. Fala looked up when she heard the loud regular staccato yells of animals onshore: "Whoop, whoop, whoop, whoop." She saw several chimps in the trees holding some bright red object in their hands. She swam over to McGraw, who seemed oblivious to the racket, and tapped him on the shoulder.

"What are they doing?" she asked.

McGraw lifted off his goggles, wiped the saltwater from his eyes, and looked ashore. Then he looked closer at Fala. The water had pasted her blouse taut to her body. Her breasts were high and full, her nipples erotic beacons. From the trees onshore, his chimps were watching Fala and masturbating.

"They're just playing," he lied, and to divert her attention turned her seaward to urge her to watch a manta ray below.

Like Ptolemy and all great generals of history, McGraw knew leading troops involved both discipline and reward. When they performed well, he rewarded his soldiers with leisure time, better food, more comfortable shelter, and at times—the company of females. McGraw clearly had anticipated all the needs of his soldiers. Although the scientists of the Lemuria Project were somewhat chagrined over his request, they nevertheless provided him what he needed. The colonel had a bevy of infertile chimp prostitutes at his disposal. It was one duty that he didn't fancy—being the chief "chimp pimp."

And, as he watched his soldiers dealing with their needs, he realized he was feeling needs, as well.

————————

The congressmen were finishing their meeting at Ciao. The ziti and the wine were long gone, and Senator Berger summed up the consensus.

"Genetic research is not going to stop even if we close down Lemuria. I remember people playing with genetic manipulation as early as the sixties. Remember that guy who collected sperm from Nobel Prize winners to create super-intelligent kids? It ain't going to stop. We've just got to convince our colleagues that we've achieved the best balance possible between science and ethics. And I think we have.

"Gentlemen, the most abused animals in the world are young men. Why should there be any outrage if we manipulate an animal to fight our wars instead of manipulating our young men—and women? Is it better to brainwash kids to pursue our political and economic goals on the battlefield or genetically modify an animal to do it for us? To me, there's no question. I don't care if these chimps are chimeras or not. All I care about is whether or not they can save our children and preserve our nation."

And so, they all agreed. The Lemuria Project would continue, fully funded. They would give the scientists more time to create new soldiers and General Shell more time—to patch a leak. But Berger was a practical politician. After the meeting, both he and Senator Bruce spoke personally with General Shell. They were emphatic: "One more leak, Mack, might be the straw that breaks the monkey's back."

> *Things don't turn up in this world*
> *until somebody turns them up.*
> —Garfield

CHAPTER
THIRTY-ONE

While Stumpf kept "house" in their beachfront motor home, Maggie and Krantz spent several days moving from one local library or Internet café to another, in Carpenteria, Ventura, and Santa Barbara. They wrote e-mails to congressmen, sent text messages, started fires in some blogs, all in an effort to "rattle some cages" in Washington. By bringing what they knew out in the open—and possibly making those in the know furious or others simply curious— they hoped they would learn more about the Lemuria Project. When they did get a reply to their persistent inquiries, however, they were usually automated responses about some bill a congressman was sponsoring that had nothing whatsoever to do with their inquiry. They figured the government could monitor their computer use, even from a library, so they limited their time at each site. They kept an eye on the newspapers and listened to the news. But Lemuria did not appear to spike anyone's interest.

Their efforts seemed to have come to a dead end, and in the back of his mind, Krantz wondered if Fala was even still alive. But that doubt disappeared over morning coffee and a danish at an Internet café in Isla Vista, the seaside student residential community of the University of California, Santa Barbara. He logged on to his own Web site just to see if there was any activity there. If Fala was a captive, he didn't expect her to be able to communicate with him. But somebody might be trying to contact him. And somebody was. Rushing back to Stumpf's motor home on Carpenteria Beach, he felt as exhilarated as if he had dredged up some priceless relic of a long lost civilization. The past—and hopefully his future—had come alive.

"My Fala's a genius," he announced. "She has managed to tell me not only that she is still alive but where she is."

Krantz explained. His Web site included entries of all his research articles. There were dozens of pieces, most of interest only to a handful of archaeologists. But one esoteric article written over eight years ago had eighteen recent hits. Why? The article he recalled had been full of unsupported hypotheses and had less than an enthusiastic response from his peers. It mentioned his undersea findings on the Greek island of Milos. It was a low point in his career because it was critiqued negatively by the prestigious French research institute, the Centre National de la Recherche Scientifique. At first he was bewildered why anyone would show interest in his most discredited work and then, he remembered that critique. The French had called his efforts "an inane search into substantiated myths—like Atlantis or Lemuria." While Fala may not have been allowed access to communicate with anyone, her captors were allowing her to read and search the Internet. The meaning of those eighteen new "hits" on that particular article on his Web site was unmistakable. The number eighteen when written in Hebrew letters means "life." Fala was trying to tell him she was alive and being held in Lemuria, or more accurately in BIOT, on the island of Diego Garcia.

In Washington, meanwhile, the persistent probes by Joshua Krantz and Maggie Wagner had powerful people asking questions, and Senator Berger, Senator Bruce, and their cohorts on the Armed Services Committee were busy putting out a lot of little fires.

"Do Israelis eat barbecue?" Stumpf asked, poking at some glowing briquettes on an outdoor grill. There was a special aura to the beach at night—a mystic quiet painted with the perpetual whoosh of the surf and almost florescent foam lit by moonlight and a billion stars in a pitch-black sky.

"We invented barbecue." Krantz smiled. "How do you think we cooked manna from heaven while wandering in the desert for forty years?"

The colonel got up to lend a hand. "Here, let me help. We call Israeli barbecue *mangal*. It is very popular, especially on our Independence Day. But we do not just cook hot dogs and hamburgers. We like kebabs, or *shipudim*."

Krantz looked around, found some small twigs, and cutting up a bit of chicken, some hot dogs, onions, and peppers, he skewered them and tossed them on the grill.

"We refer to this as *al ha'esh*. Means 'on the fire.'"

"*Ah ha'esh*," Stumpf repeated, tossing a few burgers "on the fire."

Maggie was lying on a blanket staring up at the stars. Krantz sat next to her.

"A dying man talked about the soldiers who killed him and said one word, *Maimun*," Krantz began. "My Fala and I, we are archaeologists and of course we thought that it referred to the Maimun of the twelfth century, the fiercest warriors of Salah al-Din, called the Right Hand of God. But now we have learned that it is a little used Arab word that means 'monkey.' It did not make sense at the time. And then I found a piece of an ear, bitten off in battle, in the mouth of a dead man. And this ear has the DNA made by your father in his work with monkeys. Do you think your father has made monkey men?"

"No, of course not," Maggie answered, but then she qualified herself. "I don't think so. He wouldn't do that. He used chimpanzee DNA to avoid the ethical concerns that people have about manipulating human genes. Out of tens of thousands of genes in the human genome, there are perhaps just fifty that are responsible for the major differences between humans and chimpanzees. All DNA is written in a language with an alphabet of just four letters, four peptides that some refer to in shorthand as GATTACA. And long strings of DNA, which act as code for the attributes of all creatures, can be altered by simply moving around Gs and As, Ts or Cs. Moving just one letter can have a huge effect. So, since chimps are so similar to us, one way to determine how a human gene works is to put it in a chimpanzee and see what happens. My father's work determined which genes made the animals vulnerable to HIV and cancer, malaria and the flu; and what changes in those letters could make them less vulnerable."

"But could he make a monkey man?"

"What are you talking about? A man with the body of a monkey? No. He put human genes into monkeys for research. He didn't experiment with people. He wasn't Dr. Moreau creating monsters. He didn't put monkey genes into people. That kind of trans-species experimentation would be completely unethical."

"But he won the Nobel Prize. He *could* have made a monkey

man. And maybe that's why they killed him. Because he did or because he wouldn't."

Nate Stumpf brought over dinner—kebobs and burgers.

"Leave her alone, willya? She told you he wouldn't and that's it. The burgers are ours. You can eat the chicken and veggies on a stick."

"The soldiers that used those weapons you described—could they have been chimpanzees?" Maggie asked.

"They'd have to be pretty smart chimps. They attacked experienced, well-equipped, well-organized terrorist groups in their home bases. That requires troops that are disciplined and well trained, and, more important, able to communicate and adjust to changes in the field."

Maggie gazed at the stars a moment in quiet thought and then she thought out loud.

"My father wrote a controversial article in the journal *Science* in January 2005. He said that among the few genes that establish the key differences between humans and chimps, the ones that affected hearing were the most significant. How humans hear affected the evolution of speech, and with speech, the evolution of the higher centers in the brain. My father found three genes in the human genome that were not present in chimps and that he believed dealt with the development of human hearing. The most significant was one he called alpha-tectorin. Alpha-tectorin is critical for the development of the fine bones and membranes of the inner ear. Although he wasn't positive that that particular gene gave us the gift of speech, people with mutations of alpha-tectorin inherit deficits that make it difficult for them to speak and understand speech. My father hypothesized that if chimpanzees could adapt a gene to make alpha-tectorin, they would develop finer hearing mechanisms, and in time could evolve the ability to speak."

Maggie and Krantz stared at each other a long moment. They were both thinking the same thing. And so was Stumpf.

"What the hell are they doing on Diego Garcia?" the detective mumbled, his mouth full of burger. "Maybe they *are* making monkey men."

"I don't know," Maggie answered.

"And nobody wants us to know," Krantz said.

"Well then, there's only one way we're gonna know," Stumpf fired back. "We've gotta go see for ourselves. We can't live with sand fleas forever."

Joshua Krantz raked his fingers through his hair and clutched hard at the back of his head, as if trying to squeeze out the answer. "Diego Garcia is a secure military base in the middle of the Indian Ocean. It's ten thousand miles from here. There are no commercial flights there. How could we get there?"

"We could sail there," Stumpf suggested.

"They would see us coming from a hundred miles away. The island is like an aircraft carrier in the middle of the ocean. You don't just sail up to an aircraft carrier."

Krantz got up and walked to the water's edge.

"He's supposed to be a big-shot spy?" Stumpf remarked to Maggie. "My ass."

"He's an archaeologist," Maggie corrected.

"You know, he and I are a lot alike. We're both spies and archaeologists."

"How's that?"

"He searches through garbage that's thousands of years old. I search through modern garbage. We're both lookin' for the truth."

Maggie just shook her head. "His truth smells better."

There was still a distance between them, Stumpf thought. But he was patient and hopeful that she would someday see him in a better light. Someday Maggie Wagner would see him as he saw himself—charming, intelligent, and a great lover.

Krantz walked back with a bit more vigor in his stride.

"It's not moving," he said.

"What's not moving?" Maggie asked.

"Diego Garcia. It's not an aircraft carrier. It's an island. And it doesn't move."

"Man's a fuckin' genius," Stumpf smirked.

"I read a lot about rich people in Hollywood. Do you know some of these rich people?"

"I know a lot of people," Stumpf boasted. "Some of 'em are rich."

"Do you know one who owns a Gulfstream?" Krantz pressed.

Stumpf was quiet and toed the sand. He didn't like not knowing the answers. He particularly didn't like looking stupid. Why did this Israeli colonel want one of those toaster-shaped all-aluminum trailers?

"Well?"

"What kind of fucking Gulfstream?" Stumpf roared back. When in doubt come back with a "fuck" and another question.

"A Gulfstream IV or V. A big private jet."

Stumpf's free fall was over. He was back in his realm.

"All the big shots in Hollywood own jets. It's de rigueur. You've got to have a beach house in Malibu, a home screening room big as a movie theater, a trophy wife—and a big jet."

"So?" Krantz queried. "Is this something you can do? To get us to meet one of these people?"

"Maybe," Stumpf said with a distinct lack of confidence.

"Maybe yes? Or, maybe no?"

"Well," he answered, clearly his throat uneasily, "I'll have to use a little finesse."

"What does that mean?" Krantz asked.

"It means I may have to kiss some ass."

"Then kiss."

> *I am not covetous for gold; but if it be a sin to covet*
> *honor, I am the most offending soul alive.*
> —Shakespeare

CHAPTER
THIRTY-TWO

The gate guards at Malibu Colony would not let Stumpf's motor home pass.

"If you don't have an invitation, we can't let you in."

"Sir, just please give him a call," Stumpf insisted in his most saccharine manner. "He knows me. I'll talk to him. He'll let me in."

The guards were all too familiar with stargazers, stalkers, and freaks trying to get close to celebrities. They would try anything—even just to hear the voice of their favorite star on an intercom or phone.

"Give them twenty bucks or something," Maggie whispered.

Stumpf just shook his head. "This is Malibu Colony, not some fancy restaurant. Besides, a twenty won't even get you in the door at Patina. That's all right. I've got another idea."

With the annoying beep-beep of his motor home moving in reverse, Stumpf backed out from the entry gates at Malibu Colony and headed up the Pacific Coast Highway. While they couldn't get access to the gated community of Los Angeles' celebrity elite through the front door, the back door was entirely open. California law required that the public have access to the beach. Stumpf found a place to park on a shoulder alongside the Coast Highway about a mile up. Reaching Malibu Colony's beach would require a trek along meandering trails, down a steep cliff, along a narrow beach, and over some man-made obstacles—but it was access nevertheless.

When the trio arrived at the beachfront backyards of the homes of Hollywood's elite, they found a path through a side yard and made their way to the street front. The house Nate Stumpf sought was a fifteen-thousand-square-foot Cape Cod–style estate owned by Sullivan Key. Sulli Key, as his fans knew him, was part Thai, part Puerto Rican, part African American, with exotically handsome features that seemed to appeal to all three genders. He had sold millions of records to teenyboppers in the early nineties, had parlayed that fame into an Emmy-winning TV series, and now was a big box office movie star. He had a flare for romantic comedies and was a current Oscar favorite.

"Just having his name attached to a script, gives the picture a green light," Stumpf explained.

Krantz had seen the star once or twice on screens in Israel.

"He is not so funny dubbed in Hebrew," Krantz remarked.

"I can believe that," Stumpf, the movie critic, responded. "The comedy leap from English to a foreign language works better when there's more slapstick. If they fall down a lot or do a lot of silly double takes, people laugh. Sulli Key goes for charm and funny lines, and most of the time, just translating witty words isn't funny."

"How do you know Sulli Key?" Maggie asked.

"I spied on him once."

"You mean you worked for him?" Krantz asked.

"No. I spied on *him*. I worked for his wife's attorney, who was trying to get something on him to jack up the divorce settlement."

"Does he know that?"

"Sure. I took a lot of pictures. And sometimes I had to get in his face."

"And," Krantz said, somewhat dumbfounded, "that's why you think he's gonna let us into his house to talk with him."

"You asked if I knew anybody with a jet. He's got a jet. I'm gonna do the best I can."

They came to a large iron gate, dramatically embossed with undersea scenes—dolphins, whales, and fish. The gate cost more than most people's homes. With video surveillance cameras peering down on them, Stumpf rang the bell on the intercom. There was no answer. After annoyingly ringing for several more minutes, a tactic he was quite adept at, a voice finally came over the intercom.

"Who are you and what do you want?"

"We need to speak to Mr. Key."

"He's not home. Please leave before we call Security."

"He's home. I know he's there. Tell him it's Nate Stumpf. I used to work for Gennie, his ex-wife. His ex-wife, uh, a couple back."

After a few more minutes, the intercom came alive again.

"Mr. Key is not home at this time. We have called Colony Security. I suggest you leave immediately."

"Now what?" Maggie asked.

"Colonel, bend down. Let me climb up on your shoulders," Stumpf commanded.

"What?"

"Just do it. Bend down. Come on."

Krantz reluctantly crouched down, and Stumpf piggybacked on his shoulders.

"Get me over to the camera."

Krantz waddled over toward the surveillance camera. Stump pulled a photo from his pocket and held it up to the camera. A golf cart with Malibu Security was just turning the corner when the great electronic gates began to slowly part.

Two black women wearing colorful bare-midriff saris opened the front door. They were supermodel gorgeous—both over six feet, with exquisite figures, large breasts, wearing heavy makeup. They said nothing but invited them to sit in the cavernous living room with picture windows overlooking the beach.

"They're not women," Stumpf whispered conspiratorially to Krantz. "They're transvestites."

"How do you know?"

"I've lived in this town all my life. Telling the difference between pricks and pussies is second nature to me."

Krantz walked about the living room admiring the furnishings and artwork.

"It is like a museum in here," he remarked.

"This guy has so much fucking money, he doesn't know what to do with it," Stumpf said, shaking his head in chagrin. "Look at that scribble over there. A kindergartener could do better."

"That's a Picasso," Krantz said.

"What was the picture you held up?" Maggie asked.

"He is a homosexual," Krantz surmised. "You have compromising pictures of Sulli Key."

"Of course, I do. But nobody in Hollywood cares if he's a fudge packer. You've got to be a fag—or at least pretend to be a little gay—

to succeed in this town anyway."

"So, what enticed him to let us in?" Maggie asked.

Stumpf was hesitant to reply. He tried to avoid Krantz's gaze.

"Show me the picture," Krantz asked.

Stumpf stuffed the photo deep into his pocket and moved away from Krantz, to the other side of the vast living room.

"What's the big deal?" Maggie said. "Show him the picture."

Stumpf hesitated. Then, morphing into his most charming smile, he turned to Krantz.

"I showed him pictures of you."

"Me?"

"Yeah. I took naked pictures of you. In the shower, on the beach—I thought they might come in handy someday."

"What?" Krantz said, astonished, moving closer to the impudent detective. "You took naked photos of me?"

"It's no big deal. I take pictures. That's my job."

"You want me to be with a homosexual?"

"No. No. I just wanted to get us in to talk. And hey, what's the big deal if you have to flirt a little bit, if it gets you closer to the love of your life?"

Krantz came toe-to-toe with Stumpf.

"If he tries to kiss me, I am going to kill him. No, no, no. I am going to kill you."

"Hey, back off," Stumpf replied defensively, demonstrating with every ridiculous flailing imitation karate motion he could conjure. "I can defend myself."

Retired Israeli Colonel Joshua Krantz made a single fleeting movement with the side of his hand, *krav maga*, or "contact combat" it was called, and Nate Stumpf found himself sprawled on the floor panting.

"You didn't need to do that!" Maggie pounced back, kneeling down to help the detective.

"Hey, don't forget, don't forget," Stumpf said, looking up, still winded, "Mr. Big Shot Spy—"

"What?" Krantz said, fed up.

Nate Stumpf put an end to the conversation by bringing home the most important point. "Sulli Key," he said, "he's got one of them Gulf Creek jets."

> *Few love to hear the sins they love to act.*
> —Shakespeare

CHAPTER THIRTY-THREE

In the week that Fala had been on the island, Colonel McGraw had been a frequent companion. Except for the serenity of living on a beach, she found Diego Garcia a rather boring place. You could hike around the entire island in a single day. She found McGraw's company enjoyable—picnicking, swimming, and, of course, discussing politics, archaeology, and genetics. She was learning a lot about genetics. Dr. Jaymes had given her free rein of the research facilities, and she had a lot of questions.

Everyone on the island had a mission. McGraw's mission was to train his army of chimps. And the biotech workers on the island were ecstatic with their life. Their social agenda with their peers was full. And professionally, every day brought the gossip of a new breakthrough. They had given up an academic world of backbiting for limited research dollars in exchange for the incredible freedom of having whatever they needed to accomplish a task whenever they wanted it. The answer to their requests was never, "Why do you need that?" but "How soon do you need it?" Fala also had a mission. She was probing for a way to get off the island. Except for a few select military officers, everyone on the island had contracted to stay there for at least three years. Flights or sailings from the island were few and well secured. The research facility had a world-class library, which, of course, required access to information available on the Internet. She could search out any resource of interest. But the system blocked anyone from unauthorized communication. She did have one idea, though. She serially accessed Joshua Krantz's Web site. She didn't know if he would look at it and, even if he did, whether or not he would understand her message. It was unlikely.

After a week of amiable chats and picnics on the beach, McGraw invited her for dinner at his home. His was one of a complex of pre-fab bungalows set up for officers. The "neighborhood" fronted the beach. But this was a small island; almost every structure fronted a beach. McGraw had only one request.

"Please, do not wear perfume."

It was a strange request. They had supplied her with a wardrobe and plenty of cosmetics. She often wore perfume. She enjoyed the scents. But perhaps the colonel liked his women unadorned. She wore a simple white summer dress with spaghetti straps. She wore no makeup and no perfume.

McGraw gave his guest a polite kiss on the cheek when she arrived and invited her to sit at a table on a small enclosed patio. A center tapered candle was lit. There were two glasses, an open bottle of wine, and one of Perrier.

"This is an Australian Shiraz," he said. "It's very good. I didn't know if being Muslim, you would drink with me, so I have some water if you want."

"No, I love wine."

Link poured for each of them.

"I'm glad you're not religious. I didn't want it to be a problem."

"Oh, I believe I am religious."

"Really?"

"I believe Mohammad did and said many good things, just as did Jesus. But people who came after the Prophet sometimes made his words into something different. There were very few things that the Prophet called *haram*, that which is forbidden. Of course, swine meat is one of them—"

"We're having chicken," McGraw smiled.

"But I believe wine is wonderful."

McGraw raised his glass. "Then to your health—and happiness," he toasted.

"And to yours."

"I've seen them flog people in Pakistan for drinking wine," he said.

"I have seen that, too. But wine—and I have read the Koran, it does not forbid wine. 'Draw not near unto prayer when you are drunken,' it says. It doesn't forbid wine; it forbids intemperance. It is just that over the centuries the mullahs have made it a sin. Eighty lashes is the standard punishment for drinking a glass of wine. But nowhere in the Koran is such a punishment prescribed. They flog people for drinking alcohol, but in Pakistan alone there are two million drug addicts. You can't sell alcohol there, but you can buy hashish or heroin right on the streets. The stench of urine on the streets there is from addicts, not drunks."

"I know," McGraw began, "that you abhor what we're doing."

"And what is that?"

"Training animals to kill."

"I don't approve of training men to kill, either."

"You should know I have discovered other benefits to our research."

"And what is that?"

McGraw reached under his seat and retrieved a dinner bell. He rang it gently three times. A moment later two chimpanzees came out with dinner plates in their hands. As are all animals, McGraw's chimps were naturally naked, unclothed—except for white bow ties that McGraw had placed about their necks for a formal touch.

"You trained them to be waiters?"

"It wasn't very hard. They're very bright. They pick up tasks quite quickly."

The chimps carefully set dinner plates in front of their guests, and for just a brief moment Fala made eye contact with her waiter. The animal had the classic high-sloped forehead and great overriding arched brow with the close-set eyes of his species. But there was also an electricity in his gaze, Fala thought, almost as if there was—what was she thinking?—a soul behind those eyes. She flashed back at memories of her earliest studies as a young archaeologist.

The chimps stepped back, like diligent waiters, as their "guests" began to dine.

"What are you thinking?" McGraw asked.

"I was just remembering an internship I did with a French paleontologist during my early training in the nineties. We were at a dig in the Algarve, in the south of Portugal, where he thought he had found remains of Spanish sailors from the 1500s. The men had short, sturdy skeletons with small skulls, prominent arched brows, and coarse features. Not unlike your chimpanzees. But they weren't sixteenth-century sailors. It wasn't until we did carbon dating that we determined the skeletons were those of Neanderthals.

"Neanderthals are classified as a separate species. They disappeared about thirty-five thousand years ago. The first human fossil remains—the first homo sapiens—were found in Africa and date from about one hundred thousand years ago. So, the Neanderthals and modern humans lived together for thousands of years. The guy I worked with, and several other paleontologists, believe that Neanderthals—a not too distant relative of the chimpanzee—interbred with the earliest humans. And I think it's obvious that a lot of people today still have those same prominent features—sloping forehead; heavy brows; stocky, big-boned physiques."

"Yeah, I know a few modern-day Neanderthals," McGraw said cynically.

"I was just thinking how chimp faces look a lot like the Neanderthals."

Fala caught the glimpse of a smile from her "waiter" and reflexively she smiled back.

"For centuries," Fala mused, "the cliché admonishing bad human behavior has been 'don't act like an ape.' How ironic is it to see apes act like men . . . gentlemen."

Fala took a taste of her dinner. "This is very good."

"You're surprised?"

"Don't tell me they cook, as well?"

"My chimps? No. At least not yet. I cooked."

"Well, I figured you could open a can. But this is a surprise."

"I'm a soldier with a lot of talents—besides culinary."

"And what would those be?"

"We'll have to see where the night takes us. You look very beautiful, by the way."

"Oh, and now it starts. Flattery is one of your talents. And maybe seduction?"

"Is that *haram*?"

"I gather you prefer your women plain. No makeup, no perfume."

"Is that what you think?"

"'No perfume' was the only request you made of me for tonight."

"I love beautiful women—and makeup and perfume just enhances their beauty. Nothing wrong with that."

Without asking, one of the chimp waiters moved forward and filled each of their wineglasses again. Fala was surprised. Even McGraw seemed a little taken aback.

"The scientists here have been working a decade to enhance the genetic capabilities of these chimps," McGraw began explaining. "But it's been millions of years since chimps and humans parted on the evolutionary tree, and during that time they developed different survival mechanisms from us. We have no interest in removing those attributes. You see, while we don't rely on smell to survive, chimps do—in detecting enemies, seeking out food, choosing a mate. In a way, I think we've been robbed of a wonderful sense. I've been told my chimps have thirty percent more genes dedicated to the sense of smell than we have. So, it's not your perfume I didn't want. I just felt that this evening was not the time to provide them with extra olfactory stimulation. I think you've already seen how some visual stimulation can excite them."

Fala recalled their first day cavorting in the water and watching the chimps onshore playing with "red" objects. She blushed with that enlightenment.

The evening progressed with more wine, pleasant conversation, and finally something she knew was *haram*. The punishment for this, she thought, would be stoning.

> *War is cruelty. There's no use trying to reform*
> *it. The crueler it is the sooner it will be over.*
> —William Tecumseh Sherman

CHAPTER
THIRTY-FOUR

During the first weeks and months that McGraw had assumed his unusual command, General Shell had been a daily visitor to his encampment, surveying his successes, his failures, his skills. And when progressively more political duties took him away, McGraw still exchanged daily reports and received useful suggestions from his general, and his patron. And he remained quite aware that this was the one duty that kept him out of Leavenworth prison.

When he had only six chimps in his command, and the first had reached maturity after years of research, genetic manipulation, and breeding, he had four enlisted men assisting him as handlers. They provided for the chimpanzees' shelter and feeding, and they performed the unpleasant tasks of cleaning up their toilet. When his troops reached one hundred, he still had those same four enlisted men. He didn't need any more. And now, with a force of nearly two companies, his human crew had little work to do at all. His chimpanzees had their own chain of command. McGraw had given the brightest of them rank. And the chimps trained each other in the tasks he had taught them. There was one recent element in their training that McGraw had wanted to communicate with General Shell. The general, however, was just too preoccupied lately. He had pressing business in Washington. McGraw put his comments in a report and wondered if the general was even reading them anymore. He wrote:

"Training has progressed with my second company at a pace far faster than the time required by the first force. Their peers have been instrumental in teaching them the required behaviors and preferred techniques. Recently, however, several of the animals have made dramatic adaptations to their training that have clearly improved the team's performance. They are no longer copying behaviors; they are inventing new and better ones."

"What other animal can do that?" McGraw wanted to say in his report. But he didn't. He knew the obvious answer already—humans.

General Mack Shell had been ordered to appear at a secret session of a joint congressional oversight committee. He sat alone at a mahogany desk whose edges had been gouged by the fingernail scratches of the myriad of people who had nervously sat there before him to face scrutiny. Congressional oversight committees have existed since the Revolutionary War, ostensibly to weed out abuses in government. They were formed when the flames of scandal became public and disbanded when they smoldered away. But since 1976, in the wake of the Nixon Watergate abuses, congressional oversight committees had been made permanent as the Senate Select Committee on Intelligence (SSCI) and the House Permanent Select Committee on Intelligence (HPSCI). Their interests had stepped beyond just monitoring the intelligence community and began intruding on other committee jurisdictions, like budgets, military appropriations, and homeland security. Many of the folks in the intelligence community and most in the military felt that congressional oversight was counterproductive. Members of the oversight committees were elected officials who acted out of partisan political interests and were swayed by the winds of fickle public opinion. Serving the national interest most often seemed secondary to serving their own.

"Ladies and gentlemen," the committee chair began, "we are here to seek a vigorous review of military activities and expenditures that have not been privy to the vast majority of our colleagues or to the public."

Shell looked about the room. There were a dozen congressmen on the dais. He was the only witness. No one was in the gallery behind him except security guards at the door. This was a secret session of a congressional committee, and yet its chairman was speaking as if he was talking to the press. Shell locked his jaw and again reminded himself to hold his temper and give a reasoned explanation and review of his project. But he knew he sat before a bunch of shortsighted meddlers in a business they didn't understand. And he knew that what was said here—in secret session—would not be secret very long.

The questions were fired at him rapidly, and he was frequently interrupted. These men and women seemed more interested in making a point than in listening to his explanations.

"It has come to our attention," one began, "that you are not just doing genetic research, but rather creating chimeras—composite animals."

"Are you introducing animal genes into humans?"

"Are you crossing spiders with chimps so that they can weave webs?"

"By introducing human genes into animals, aren't you creating an entirely new being with a significant human component?"

"Why are we spending billions of dollars for the army to play God?"

General Shell had formulated his answer in a fashion he thought they would understand most—dollars and cents.

"I didn't make up these numbers, Mr. Chairman," the general began. "These are conservative figures from a Nobel Prize winning economist. In 2006 dollars, it cost $400,000 annually to put a soldier in the field. For every casualty sustained in combat, it costs $2,000,000 for care and rehabilitation. What is the cost to your communities when we call away your firemen, policemen, salesmen, and farmers? When a soldier is sent abroad to fight our battles, what does that cost in the damage done to marriages and families? The cost in lost productivity, lost life, and the renting of our social fabric? I would measure it in the trillions.

"Gentlemen, what is the essential quality of humanity? How do we differ from other animals? I'll tell you how. We have the ability to make rational decisions, to reason. We have the ability to use our brains and not just our brawn. Over the years, humans have all agreed that it is unreasonable for a man to do the work an animal can do, and so we had oxen pulling plows. As technology evolved, we made machines to do the work. But to fight our political and economic battles, we still use and bloody young men and women. What a waste. We made the ox pull our plows. Why not have a distant relative, the chimpanzee, fight our wars? Patton said it best: we go to war not to die for our country, but to make the other guy die for his. I'm in the business of winning wars, and the Lemuria Project is one way to win."

There were a lot of nods of assent about the room. But after listening quietly for most of the session, the senator from South Carolina, who had served longer than most of his colleagues had been alive, made his remarks, his accent exaggerated with buttery smooth long vowels, and agonizingly slow.

"General, I remember other generals who have come here. Long ago, they said the tank would win our wars, then the airplane, the aircraft carrier, then missiles. It was always a new technology. And now you have another new technology of sorts—the genetic manipulation of an animal to fight our battles. But you have talked about this 'new technology' using interesting words. Let me see, I have it here, you say these new soldiers are 'smart, adaptable, determined, decisive.' They have some innate intelligence. Maybe they don't have a system of ethics, or morals, religion, a written word, or a spoken language yet, but they think. Do they not?"

"Yes. But they're trained and bred to—"

The South Carolina senator interrupted. "This is the same debate we've had for years about what's more important, 'nature or nuture.' But I want to cut through the rhetoric here. I want us all to remember that regardless of this genetics business, or breeding, or training, what we as humans do in life is still determined by something else. And what we decide here is determined by that something else. And that's free will. I don't care if you've been born in a ghetto or born with a silver spoon in your mouth. Each of us has free will to decide what's right and wrong. And so I want to know, General, before we exercise our free will here, what happens if your chimps ever come to have free will? Who wins, if they ever think about fighting us?"

Shell was used to being decisive. After all, he was a general who made decisions that put men's lives at risk. When he spoke, his answers had to be unequivocal. Men don't fight well, and certainly don't fight to die, when their leaders express doubt.

"Who wins?" the senator asked again.

"We do," Shell finally answered, after some hesitation. "We win, sir."

But Shell could tell he had left doubts in the room, and some of them were his own.

> *Once we have a war there is only one thing to do.*
> *It must be won. For defeat brings worse things*
> *than any that can ever happen in war.*
> —Ernest Hemingway

CHAPTER
THIRTY-FIVE

The Gulfstream 350 filed a flight plan from Van Nuys Airport in Southern California to Pretoria, South Africa. The only passengers listed were Sulli Key, his pilot, his bodyguards—two lovely black transvestites—and Nate Stumpf. Although Sulli had a pilot's license and was instrument rated on his jets, he preferred to copilot the business jet so he could socialize with his guests whenever he wished. The private plane cruised at 45,000 feet, flew nearly Mach 1, had a range of 3,800 miles, and could accommodate a dozen passengers in decadent, beyond-first-class luxury. Sulli had his own aft stateroom with exercise bikes designed to handle two-G bank angles. The cabin was soundproof. You could speak in whispers. There were wide plush leather armchairs and couches that folded out into beds, multiple flat-panel video monitors and a surround-sound entertainment system, and a full bar and galley suitable for preparing gourmet meals. Not bad for a kid born in a small brick row house in northeast

Philadelphia. As a child, his mother removed him from the temptations of the streets by taking him on long, tedious bus and subway rides to a charity arts school downtown. There he learned to play piano and guitar, to sing and dance. He even took art and fencing lessons. The more talents he acquired, his mother admonished, the better his chances for success in life. He performed in cafés and bars, on street corners, anywhere people would watch and listen. And just as his mother had promised, fame and fortune arrived. He had been a "star" for more than thirty years, and still everything he touched turned to gold.

No one ever said no to Sulli Key. He could do whatever he wanted and most always have whatever or whomever he wanted. It wasn't that he particularly fancied the swarthy good looks of Joshua Krantz, but these people desperately wanted something else and he was curious to learn what it was. Money? Introductions? A part in a movie?

When he walked into his living room, Sulli found Joshua Krantz standing over that slimy detective who had worked for his ex-wife. It looked like he was about to pummel the guy.

Krantz was quick to speak up. "My friend here may have given you the wrong impression. There are issues of great importance that we wanted to speak to you about."

Sulli recognized the accent. He had performed in Israel many times. And the Israelis were always a good audience, always interesting.

"*Slikha*," I'm sorry, Sulli said in Hebrew, quickly breaking the ice and putting the Israeli at ease, "but you're just not my type. So tell me, what's so important?"

After more civil introductions, Joshua Krantz and Maggie Wagner did most of the talking. Sulli listened, fascinated by their story. It was like a movie, he thought, full of twists. There was the

murder of a Nobel Laureate, clandestine genetic research, military secrets, and kidnappings, all wrapped up with code words and ancient
myths. It didn't matter that some picayune LA private detective had
gained entrance to his home with titillating photos. He was being
invited to participate in a great adventure. How could he not go?

———————

It was a long flight—halfway around the world. They refueled
in Anchorage; again in Sapporo, Japan; Bangkok, Thailand; and
Mumbai, India. They departed Mumbai at dawn. From Mumbai,
it was a straight hop to Pretoria. It got earlier and darker as they
headed west. After two hours, they were over the middle of the
Indian Ocean with the Chagos Archipelago below them. Chagos
was made up of fifty-two tiny islands—the largest of which was
the seventeen-square-mile atoll called Diego Garcia in the British
Indian Ocean Territory called BIOT.

In the day before their departure, Krantz had driven up to a small
airport in Lompoc, just north of Santa Barbara. They advertised
a sky-diving experience there. For two hundred dollars, you could
jump in tandem, strapped to an instructor who, after a brief free fall,
pulled the rip cord. Krantz had done dozens of jumps as an Israeli
army officer, but none in a decade. But jumping was easy, like falling
out of an airplane. He had not driven to Lompoc for jump lessons;
he had gone to buy a used tandem chute.

"Why not new?" Maggie asked with some dismay. "Used means
worn, and isn't a parachute one thing you'd want to buy as brand new?"

"Used means tested," Krantz answered. "And if the owner is
alive, I know it worked."

———————

Sulli Key dialed 7700 into the Gulfstream's transponder, the code for an aircraft emergency. Then he radioed a "Mayday." The plane descended rapidly toward the airstrip on Diego Garcia. The runway lights that had been off, came on. At five thousand feet, the plane slowed to 180 knots and an aft door opened. The plane shuddered from the rush of air whipping through the cabin. Everyone was strapped into their seats except Krantz, who wore a parachute and had Maggie strapped tight to his torso like a kangaroo mother with child. Lockstep, they stepped out into the darkness. The Gulfstream continued on its final approach to DG with Sulli at the controls. He beamed proudly as he landed the jet "right on the numbers." They had not yet coasted to a stop when they were surrounded by emergency vehicles and a half-dozen Humvees with soldiers brandishing automatic weapons.

Maggie and Krantz descended safely, dropping in near a utility road at the south end of the island. He decided to make their way along the beach toward the major infrastructure in the middle of the island. It was second nature for a military man to avoid roads. He need not have worried. BIOT security staff were busy interrogating a celebrity and his guests and did not suspect they had other interlopers on the island. It took the air force mechanics only an hour to determine that nothing was seriously wrong with the Gulfstream. But it was decided that rather than chance sending an international movie star off in a plane that could crash, they would make a more detailed inspection of the plane in the morning. Sulli Key and company, however, would not see Diego Garcia in daylight. An hour after landing, they were guests aboard an Air Force C-130 en route to Cape Town.

At seven a.m. with the rush of folks going to work, Maggie and Krantz simply walked off the beach and into the largest building they saw. They were wearing army fatiques and seemed to fit right in. Maggie was astounded at the research facility. It surpassed any university or private facility she had ever seen. The equipment was all state of the art. And researchers, rather than sharing a quarter-million-dollar microscope, each had their own. She recognized a few faces from conferences she had attended in the past. These were the top scientists in their fields—microbiology, genetics, embryology, electronmicroscopy. They gave her curious looks for a moment but then paid her no attention. And then she saw two people she knew quite well—Sarah Zito, her father's old assistant from Stanford, and Professor Joshua Jaymes from Princeton.

In the first hour after Sulli Key's jet landed, Security on Diego Garcia was kept busy questioning the passengers of the "distressed" aircraft. Within the second hour, they were unceremoniously put aboard the C-130 and transported off the island.

While Security didn't expect anyone to be able to get on or off BIOT without their notice, they also wanted to keep track of every person—every living creature—on the island. No one wanted to misplace a great scientist or a living experimental product. Surveillance was accomplished by a drone airplane that circled DG at sixty-five thousand feet. The Aerovironment Global Observer was a high-altitude long endurance, or HALE, unmanned air vehicle. The airplane, with a wingspan as long as a football field, stayed up for a week at a time and traded missions with a twin aircraft to maintain constant real time and infrared views over the island. A ground computer counted those infrared signatures every hour. The official count of persons and animals on the island was 5,678. When Security got around to checking the computer analysis of the infrared signature, it indicated a population of 5,680. There were two creatures on the island that were not suppposed to be there.

Dr. Jaymes greeted Maggie Wagner warmly and was cordial to her Middle Eastern–accented companion. After all, she was the daughter of his mentor. But he also realized something was quite awry.

"How did you get here?" he asked.

"We just dropped in," Krantz replied curtly. "And we have a lot of questions."

"Of course." Jaymes turned to whisper something to a younger colleague. Two calls had to be made right away.

Krantz's first question: "Is an Egyptian woman, Fala al-Shohada, being held here?"

"Yes, but she is not a prisoner. She has free run of the island."

It was at that moment that four armed security guards entered. They pointed automatic weapons at the couple.

"Are you armed?" the lieutenant in charge asked.

"We're not," Krantz was quick to reply and raise his hands. Security quickly patted him down looking for weapons.

"We went to a lot of trouble to get here," Maggie countered and was less cooperative, pushing away the security guard who intended to search her.

"You've broken the law by coming here. This is a military installation."

"I don't give a damn."

Maggie turned to Professor Jaymes. "I don't believe my father was a murderer or a suicide."

"We think he was murdered," Krantz said, entering the verbal fray, "and I bet you know why."

"I deserve an answer," Maggie was yelling now, her voice cracking. "I deserve an answer."

"Yes, you do." The voice at the door was familiar. When Maggie turned, she was looking into the eyes of her father. Julius Wagner was still balding with that wild shock of hair at the back of his head—but he looked thinner, tanner, and more at ease than she had ever seen him in her life. He was wearing cargo shorts and a floral Hawaiian print shirt.

"Dad?"

"Flesh and blood." Wagner embraced his daughter.

He could feel her trembling with emotion. "It's all right," he said, caressing his little girl's hair. "It's all right," he said again, nodding toward Security for them to leave.

The lieutenant hesitated, but Dr. Wagner added a caveat. "Where are they going?"

"You're not dead," she said, her voice cracking.

"Honey, I do regret the charade. But it had to be done."

"They found your body," Maggie said, bewildered. "Shot and burnt."

"I myself still have unanswered questions. I did check into that motel with a woman, just so that everyone could identify that I was there. I was told that the intelligence services of nine countries spent months looking for look-alike murder victims to fake my death. But I know I work for the military, and I do not bemuse myself of the fact that they can be vicious in their tactics."

To change the topic, Wagner turned to Colonel Krantz. "You must be the private detective my daughter hired. You are very good."

"I am and I'm not. My name is Joshua Krantz. I did help your daughter, but I had other motives. I have come looking for the woman your people abducted—Fala al-Shohada. Where is she?"

"Oh, you're the Israeli spy."

"I am not a spy. I am an archaeologist, formerly of Israeli intelligence."

"Do the Israelis know about Lemuria?" Dr. Wagner queried.

"I think they know enough," Krantz conceded. "And Fala?"

"She's well," Dr. Wagner replied. "And you can see her. But tell me, would the moon have been far enough away to keep this a secret? No matter. Maggie, come. Everyone, come. We'll sit down and talk, and I'll tell you about my little miracles."

Dr. Wagner's office was on the top floor of the six-story research center. Other than from atop the airfield's control tower, his office had the best view on the island. A picture window overlooked a grove of palms, and beyond it McGraw's tent encampment and the sea. The old man sat at his desk in a leather swivel chair feeding a newborn chimpanzee from a baby bottle like a doting grandfather.

"This is my latest miracle. Every day a dozen more are born. And every day we refine our capabilities at breeding. By manipulating their genetic core, we have freed them of many common diseases, fine-tuned their senses so that they have better night vision and improved hearing. With alterations in hearing, they have developed some human speech capabilities and with that, more temporal lobe brain activity."

"You isolated and inserted the genes that create alpha-tectorin," Maggie said, eyeing Krantz with an "I told you so" gaze.

"Exactly." Dr. Wagner beamed like a proud father, pleased with his daughter who had chosen to follow in his footsteps. "And they have the capability of sensory substitution."

Now Maggie was surprised. "Your animals have synesthesia?"

"Most, but not all. We haven't been able to consistently merge the senses in every animal."

"What's synesthesia?" Krantz asked.

"They can see what they hear. Taste what they touch," Julius Wagner clarified.

"What?"

"I'll explain it to you later," Maggie said, anxious to hear more about her father's work.

"And we have enhanced all their own best attributes—more muscle strength per pound than natural-born chimps and far more than humans, a more sensitive olfactory sense, adaptable to greater temperature variations."

Dr. Wagner smiled, pleased with himself. He held up his infant chimp, letting it grasp tightly and dangle from his index fingers.

"We once calculated that the chimpanzee was 98.4 percent genetically identical to us. This animal is more than 99 percent identical—"

"And why," Maggie interrupted, "did all this require you to ruin your good name and put me through hell?"

"There are good reasons I didn't tell you about my leaving. The Lemuria Project was named for a mythological place. When the plan was first brought to me, it seemed just as much a fantasy. But then a general, Maximillian Shell, convinced me it could be made to happen. The military decided they needed a new weapon for a world gone mad after 9/11. We all know that the American public has no tolerance for casualties seen up close on the nightly news. And yet we must still overcome the never-ending needle pricks of terrorists and the genocidal and suicidal beliefs of barbaric warlords and rogue nations. Maggie, they offered me unlimited funding and an unrestricted, unfettered research environment for whomever I could recruit. The knowledge we've gained here will benefit humanity im-measurably. We can cure AIDS, regenerate organs, splice neurons together to reverse the effects of strokes and let a paraplegic walk—"

"But that's not what they hired you for?" Joshua Krantz interrupted.

"No," her father conceded. "No."

"What did they hire you for, Dad?"

"My job was to give them a division—ten thousand troops; in this case ten thousand non-human soldiers—chimpanzees especially bred and trained to fight America's wars. Genetic research has al-ways been about saving and bettering lives, Princess. I couldn't say no. And to succeed, it all had to be kept secret."

Maggie was unconvinced. "There are other ways to end wars be-sides making other creatures die for our insanity."

"You always spoke your own mind, insisted on taking your own path. I knew you would not have approved, and that is why I didn't let you in on it."

"You shouldn't have put me through this hell."

"I'm sorry."

"If you told me, I would have understood."

"Would you? I was chosen to bring this project to fruition. In the last year, I realized I couldn't playact as a department head at Stanford and successfully direct the greatest scientific endeavor of my generation by commuting halfway around the world every week. And I couldn't just disappear. People would ask questions. If they faked my murder, there would have been investigations. If it was a simple car accident, there would have still been reporters searching into my most recent work and questioning my most recent comings and goings. Just as you did. So, they conjured up my strange and shameful death. The lurid became more interesting than the truth, and I was quickly forgotten.

Had I told you all about Lemuria, you may have wanted to come along or visit and that would have aroused more suspicion. Or, you would have vocally disapproved. And not even government threats would have kept you quiet. My God—and I didn't have anything to do with it—but they drugged you, tried to take compromising pictures of you, and you still didn't give up. And, Maggie, I really didn't think you cared that much about me anymore."

"Well, you didn't win your Nobel Prize for affection. But you're my father. I do love you."

"There's one other thing. You'll find out eventually, and you would have disapproved of that, too, but—"

"What?"

"Well, the human DNA that I used to splice into chimp DNA came from many sources. Much of it came from the stored sperm cells of the greatest men of the last fifty years. It also came from my most elegant creation," Julius Wagner said.

Tears welled up in his eyes as the director of the Lemuria Project set the infant chimp onto Maggie's lap and handed her the baby's bottle. She was uncomfortable for a moment but then took to cradling the infant and feeding it. Julius Wagner smiled like a—grandfather.

"I used your DNA, cord blood I saved when you were born."

Maggie eyed the baby chimp more closely. "So what are you saying, Dad? We're like sisters?"

Krantz instantly perceived the relationship differently. "More like mother and daughter."

> *To believe is to be strong.*
> *Doubt cramps energy.*
> *Belief is power.*
> —F.W. Robertson

CHAPTER
THIRTY-SIX

Krantz found Fala later that afternoon. Squatting on a berm over-looking the beach, he watched her jog along the shore. From a distance he thought she was shadowed by two soldiers in black camouflage uniforms. As she got closer, he realized she was jogging with two chimpanzees. When she caught sight of him, she ran even faster and leapt into his arms, knocking him down. She kissed him hard and long.

"Holy cow, slow down. Slow down."

"You found me," she said ecstatically, breathing rapidly from exhaustion and excitement.

"Yeah, I found you. I don't know if I would have tried so hard if I knew you'd be cavorting with two guys with their dicks at full staff."

Fala looked up. Her chimp companions were standing over them with bright red erections.

"Home," she yelled at them. They lifted their right arms and touched the side of their flattened hands to their brows. Then they ran off.

"Was that a salute?"

"In a fashion."

"Who taught them to salute?"

"An American colonel. He has two companies of chimpanzees."

"I'd like to meet him."

"You will. He's lovely."

"Lovely, is he?"

"He's been nice, I meant. Gracious."

"A gracious jailer?"

"He's not my jailer. Colonel McGraw is the man who conceived of having his chimpanzee soldiers use Alexander's battle scythe. You see, it's a weapon perfectly suited to be used by his chimps. It allows them to run and climb without bulky equipment to hamper them. It's lethal but quiet. And the animals, they—they almost worship him. I've seen them train together. He's not just a commander. He's like a god to them."

"Like a god?"

"Well, you know what I mean. You'll never guess who he thinks he is."

"Who he thinks he is?"

"He believes in reincarnation."

"Oh? He thinks he's Alexander the Great," Krantz quickly concluded.

"No," Fala smiled. "But close. He believes he was Alexander's greatest general, Ptolemy, who eventually became one of my forbears, the pharaoh of Egypt."

"I don't know if I like you cavorting with reincarnated pharaohs."

Krantz smiled and rolled atop her on the sand.

She pushed him away and stood up. "One other thing, Joshua."

"What?" he said, somewhat disappointed.

"I have quite a nice hotel room on this island."

She held out her hand to help him up and hurry him away for some more intimate knowledge.

Moments later, they were in her room. Krantz had taken off his shirt and was slowly undressing her when a key unlocked the door. When it opened, Colonel McGraw stood there awkwardly.

"I'm terribly sorry."

"You don't know how to knock?" Fala rebuked.

"I didn't know I had to knock."

They were buttoning up when McGraw turned to leave.

"General Ptolemy?" Krantz asked.

McGraw turned back. "Are there no secrets?"

"Probably some still," Krantz said, eyeing Fala for a moment with jealous suspicion. "So," he went on, "you're Ptolemy the First—who began the Ptolemaic dynasty of ancient Egyptian pharaohs and created the great Library of Alexandria?"

"I was. Yes," McGraw answered.

Krantz smiled.

"Are you laughing at me?"

"Not at all, Colonel," Krantz replied. "I've been reborn, too."

"You don't have to be demeaning," Fala said, berating him.

"No. I'm serious," Krantz began again.

"Somebody famous, I'm sure," McGraw said, willing to deal with the teasing he anticipated.

"I didn't create a dynasty certainly, but—"

Joshua Krantz stood behind Fala, wrapped his arms around her, and nuzzled at her neck a moment. She did not retreat. Krantz was plainly indicating who was in possession of her.

"So, who were you?" McGraw inquired.

Krantz hesitated.

"Yes." Fala turned to face him. "Who were you?"

"I was once Rabbi Zalman of Liadi," Krantz replied.

Even Fala was taken aback. "Who?"

He kissed Fala's forehead and gently buttoned the top of her blouse. "You think you know all about someone. But people are complicated. You never do."

"I don't believe you," she said.

"You don't believe me?" Krantz pulled out his wallet. In the back, among some worn business cards, was a ratty black-and-white picture, perhaps a page from a magazine. It was an image from an old lithograph of a rabbi in eighteenth-century garb with a long white beard and bushy mustache." He handed it to Colonel McGraw.

"That's me. Rabbi Zalman of Liadi."

"You two are nuts," Fala said sarcastically.

"So, who was this rabbi?" McGraw asked, roped in.

"Unlike you, I cannot claim to have conquered countries or created dynasties."

"There was, of course, something great you did in your former life?"

"Of course," Krantz went on. "I was the first Rebbe of Chabad, a branch of Hasidic Judaism. It was during a time in Eastern Europe when the Jewish people were once again being persecuted. Always in times of persecution, Jews sought answers, or sought refuge perhaps, in the study of Torah. The Chabad Hasidim studied Torah, but they also believed that Jewish life should not just be an academic endeavor but a quest for spirituality and joy, as well. In those times, I was their greatest writer, and a philosopher and a mystic."

"A mystic? Meaning you dealt in the supernatural?" McGraw posed.

"Anytime you try to know God, you're delving into the supernatural. Rabbi Zalman's philosophy was simple, but unusual for his time. He—I believed that the best way to serve God was by serving man better."

"I believe in that."

Krantz smiled. "Then perhaps then you were once a follower of mine."

"Perhaps so." Link McGraw grinned and held out his hand to shake and put any awkwardness behind them.

Fala said nothing. What she thought was, *I am in love with madmen.*

> *Fear the tax that conscience pays to guilt.*
> —Sewell

CHAPTER THIRTY-SEVEN

General Shell was returning to Diego Garcia the same way he most often did—flying in the rear seat of an F-14 Tomcat. The jet, most famous as Tom Cruise's *Top Gun* plane, wasn't as comfortable as the Air Force's executive passenger jets, fitted out with first-class accommodations for the top brass. The F-14, however, was, after thirty years in service, still a very reliable airplane. It wasn't a front-line aircraft anymore, but there were plenty of them around the country belonging to Reserve and National Guard units. So, ordering one up was no problem for a three-star general and had the added benefit of giving a lot of pilots the extra flight time they needed. There were newer jets he could have flown, but Mack disliked taking any plane out of service if there was any chance it could be used in combat. The F-14, stripped of everything but extra fuel tanks, was also fast. The flight from Washington, DC, to DG in a C-141 transport took twenty-two hours with a refueling stopover.

The F-14 had him there in eight. There were also other advantages.

After nearly forty years in the military, although Shell had sent many men into battle, he himself had never shot at anyone and had never been shot at. He had seen the horrors of war, the up close of death, but his rank always kept him distanced from the risk. He had never confronted his mortality until a near-death experience a dozen years ago. He had a pulmonary embolism, a PE. It began with a deep vein thrombosis, a DVT the doctors called it, a blood clot that formed in his calf, the bizarre consequence of sitting still during an interminably long flight. The blood clot in his calf floated up into his lungs and almost killed him. He was in a coma, on a respirator for weeks before recovering. Flying now aboard an F-14, the duration of his flights were shorter, and he also wore a compression flight suit with air bladders in the legs and abdomen that actually protected him from forming clots in his legs and the life-threatening risks of DVTs and PEs.

It was Shell's near-death experience that led him on a spiritual quest. He studied the world's great religions and found substantial similarities in their creation tales. Despite being separated by vast lands and great oceans, the same basic elements existed in the creation stories of African Bushmen, ancient Greeks, Australian Aborigines, American Indians from the Iroquois to the Mayan, the Japanese, and Christians and Jews. In each story, Shell found a supreme being—a god or gods. The god always created an above and a below—a heaven and hell, a sky and earth, land and sea, or a symbol of an above and below. At first humans lived on earth peacefully. Later, the god or gods took away that paradise, usually because of a loss of innocence, sin, or a challenge to the gods. And finally, there was a momentous event, usually a flood, in which man was destroyed and either reborn again or rescued, sometimes in graphic fashion like in Eastern mythology where Vishnu took the form of a tortoise and rescued the world by carrying it on his back above the flood.

Mack Shell didn't buy into the facts of any of the "creation myths." He recognized that each religion gave its believers inner peace. There really wasn't any one "provable" truth. So, almost on a whim, he chose to focus his spiritual quest on Lemuria.

The concept of Lemuria was popularized in the late nineteenth century by a French archaeologist, Augustus le Plongeon. Le Plongeon was the first European to excavate the ruins of Chichen Itza and other sites of pre-Columbian Mayan civilization. Although most scholars say that no one had ever successfully translated Mayan hieroglyphics, Le Plongeon claimed he had. The Mayan writings, he wrote, indicated that they had founded ancient Egypt. And the Mayans, he claimed, originated from an even older civilization that once lived on a great lost continent called Mu, or Lemuria. Later, a friend of Le Plongeon, James Churchward, wrote a series of books describing that antediluvian world. The rest of the scientific world, however, viewed both men as eccentrics with bizarrely vivid imaginations.

Churchward's story of Lemuria was very much like the Bible. It included a creation story, a flood, and renewal. What was different about Lemuria was that its civilization was not a primitive one, as in the Bible, but rather advanced, even beyond our modern world. The world of the Bible was populated with stories of kingdoms and wars, sins followed by redemptions. Lemuria, on the other hand, had a benevolent government, superb technology, and a flowering culture. Lemurians were free of war and disease and lived in complete harmony with nature. They also had psychic powers. Telepathy, teleportation, and astral travel were all possible in Lemuria. While

Mack Shell felt that Churchward's Lemuria was just as implausible as the biblical stories of the miracles, rewards, and retributions of an unseen deity, he preferred Lemuria's utopian vision. It was a life on earth more to be sought after than any nebulous afterlife.

Each time the general flew back to his Lemuria, there was one other benefit to flying in an F-14. Wrapped in the silent cocoon of a jet traveling faster than the speed of sound, he meditated and entered a peaceful place where he could project his mind out of his body. It was like a deep relaxing sigh that never ended. And when he landed, he didn't just feel relaxed; he felt almost reborn.

On their approach, Shell caught sight of the Gulfstream parked just off the main runway. He had already heard about his new guests. Their presence was a nuisance that he was glad he would not have to cope with for very much longer. His adjutant, Major DeVita, anxiously awaited his descent as the plane's engines wound down. As the general stepped onto the tarmac, the major hurried him to his Jeep.

"We've had an accident, sir."

"One of our scientists?"

"No, sir. It's the Israeli. They attacked him."

"Who?"

"Our chimps. They almost pummeled him to death."

Shell slid into the front seat of the Jeep, and DeVita drove off. The weather was hot and dry, like a sauna. The breeze in the open Jeep was refreshing. The sky was cloudless.

"It's no accident," the general muttered.

"What, sir?"

"I said, it's no accident. A trip and fall is an accident. This is a warning. They know."

"Who knows what, sir?"

General Shell kept quiet. He felt a sudden brief tingling sensation, like a million ants crawling up from his feet to his scalp. Perhaps the senator from New York was right. They had created a chimera, a new creature. Not chimpanzee, not human, but an unusual melding of instinct and intellect in union with nature. Could his new soldiers sense what he was thinking? He would know soon enough.

Oh, that pang, where more than madness lies,
the worm that will not sleep, and never dies.
—Lord Byron

CHAPTER
THIRTY-EIGHT

Colonel McGraw had lain awake all night blaming himself for what had happened. These were troops he had trained and disciplined. They had independence in the methods used to carry out a task but they performed no task without his explicit command. Had he sent them an unconscious signal? What was the defect in breeding or training that had caused this?

He had invited Joshua Krantz to watch his troops during one of their usual training sessions. And, for no apparent reason at all, three of his best suddenly broke ranks and began pummeling and biting the Israeli colonel. Fala, who was sitting beside Krantz, began hitting at the chimps to distract them away. The animals, however, were undeterred and never for a moment turned their attention or aggression upon her. McGraw had repeatedly ordered them to "stand down." His orders had never been disobeyed before. They would have beaten Krantz to death had not one of his sergeants arrived and in quick succession dispatched each of the three renegade chimps with a pistol shot to the head.

There was a long weighty silence after the last shot rang out. Two of the animals were dead. A third still had a flicker of life in his eyes. To Fala the chimpanzees all looked alike. McGraw saw them all as individuals. He had given names to most of them.

McGraw gave a fleeting glance toward Krantz, who lay bloodied and unconscious. He felt neither enmity nor compassion for the man. Others would attend to him. He fixed his attention on his soldiers. A moment ago, they had been so filled with energy, and more than that, potential. And now they were so very still. He had never "petted" his boys. It seemed inappropriate for a commander to do. But now he caressed them. Their body fur was soft, still warm. Their faces felt like a man's coarse unshaven beard, but their skin underneath was soft and textured like human skin. Coarse and powerful yet soft and gentle creatures, that's how he would describe them as they lived.

McGraw was bewildered. "Why, Fish?" he asked the dying animal. Fish was one of his best. He learned quickly. He could teach others. He had special gifts. And he had a personality that radiated an exuberance for life. Fish's huge close-set eyes looked up at his god, and in the last flicker of his life, McGraw sensed he was asking for forgiveness.

McGraw turned to the rest of his troops. A company of chimp soldiers stood in an orderly phalanx on the beach. They had seen everything, but they had not moved an inch.

"Company atten-tion!" McGraw called out.

Two hundred chimpanzees stood upright, feet together, their long arms pressed to their hips.

"Hoo-rah," McGraw yelled.

"Hoo-hah!" his army replied.

"Dismissed."

And in a quick and orderly fashion, they rushed back to their tent encampment as if nothing of import had passed before them.

The base hospital was a modern facility in the basement of the main research building. Two navy surgeons spent three hours operating on Krantz—repairing a lacerated liver and ruptured spleen. His rib, arm, and leg fractures were minor considerations. Two veterinary pathologists spent about the same time dissecting the three mad chimpanzees. Had genetic manipulation created brain tumors or metabolic derangements? Did they succumb to a disease like encephalitis? But nothing seemed amiss. The animals were healthy.

After quickly looking in on the Israeli colonel in recovery and offering apologies to Fala, General Shell sought out Gordon Guffman, Lemuria's chief primatologist.

"I have never seen anything like it," Guffman began. "Or even heard of such behaviors."

"What are you talking about?" Shell responded, bewildered. "Chimpanzees have often attacked humans. And that's especially what we've trained these animals for."

"Yes, sir. Of course they have. But while these three animals apparently went on a mad frenzy, two hundred others stood nearby—perfectly quiet, still, and obedient. There were no screeches, no pounding of feet, no herd instinct to participate. That's what's remarkable."

"So, do you suggest I give the rest of my Lemurian army

medals?"

"Some reward would be appropriate. Yes, sir."

"Fine," the general replied. "But that still doesn't answer the main question. Why did those three go crazy?"

"Most behaviors that seem irrational actually have a rational adaptive significance. The behavior provides a benefit."

"What was the benefit of nearly beating a strange man to death?"

"I don't know, sir. Usually such dramatic and violent behaviors give the animal an edge—an edge for survival or reproduction. In this case, I don't know what kind of edge. I haven't figured it out."

"Then do that," the general said. "Figure it out." It was an order.

CHAPTER THIRTY-NINE

It was Father's Day—or at least it felt like it. Julius Wagner felt a sense of warmth and pride at having his daughter beside him. He was especially gratified that she had followed in his footsteps. She had nearly completed her PhD, and as she described her work, Wagner knew she was well on her way to becoming her own world-class geneticist.

Side by side, father and daughter peered through a dual laser scanning optical microscope at chromosomes from a Pan troglodyte—that is, the genus chimpanzee. There was a substitution on one of the strands of the eighteenth chromosome.

"You can see the exchange has occurred very close to the end of the 'ss' region at the gapped circle."

"And what happened past the 'ss' region at the duplex part of the gapped circle?" Maggie asked.

Dr. Wagner beamed. He had purposely passed over the most

significant success with this particular chromosomal link and she had seen it anyway.

"That's you," he said. "We made a four -strand exchange reaction and a Holliday junction fashioned from your ribosomal DNA. That resulted in an improvement in hemoglobin oxygen-carrying capacity, almost doubling endurance testing in the succeeding generation."

With a clearing of his throat, General Shell, shadowed by two aides, made his presence in the microscopy room known. He had been standing there a few moments listening to father and daughter chitchat.

"Don't be so impressed with your father," the general interrupted. "He won't tell you about his failures."

"General, have you met my daughter?"

"Not officially. But I know a lot about her already. She is quite the persistent young lady."

"Maggie, this is General Maximillian Shell, project director of Lemuria and its prime visionary. I wouldn't be here today if it wasn't for his insistence that the impossible was possible."

"I just had faith in talented people. And faith, along with time and plenty of money, makes all things possible."

"General, are you going to have me shot for disturbing your secrets here?"

"I can't say you have made my work easier, but no firing squad."

"Honey"—Dr. Wagner took his daughter's hand–"it may not be what you planned on, but you'll have to stay here on Diego Garcia for a while. But I'm looking forward to us working together."

"No," the general was quick to reply. "You'll be going home soon."

Julius Wagner was surprised. Just a few weeks earlier, Shell had informed him that Fala, the Egyptian archaeologist who had come too close to knowing the secrets of Lemuria, would be their guest for the "duration." That, he assumed, meant for another three years, until their project reached its culmination with the creation of an alternative non-human fighting force of at least division strength—ten thousand chimpanzees. They even had bantered about names for it—the First Troglodyte Division; the First New Army Division; the First Lemurian Division.

The word from the general that secrecy was no longer paramount was actually a disappointment. For the last several months, Dr. Wagner had worked hard to conceal his depression. He lived in a pleasant climate with superb intellectual stimulation and none of the stresses of academia, and yet he felt hollow. Something was missing. With Maggie's arrival, that feeling had immediately vanished. What he was missing was the need to care about someone and for someone to care about him. General Shell had done a superb job of catering to the needs of his scientific and military community. There were wonderful accommodations, good food, entertaining diversions, intellectual stimulation. However, there was one human need he could not supply—love.

"What about security?" Professor Wagner asked. "Do you expect my daughter to simply follow your orders and keep quiet about what she knows? She's not one of your soldiers."

"What your father didn't tell you," the general abruptly changed the subject, "was that this same technology, what he created for that chromosomal link that gives our chimps extraordinary endurance, can also be applied to curing sickle cell disease and hemophilia."

Mack put his arm around the old doctor.

"You did a great job, Julie. Extraordinary. But starting today, I want you to start organizing your findings so that you can begin disseminating the information to your colleagues worldwide. Your research is going to save lives and improve the quality of life for people all over the world. It was billions of dollars well spent."

"What about your First Troglodyte Division?"

Shell smiled. Dr. Wagner had always preferred using the species name for the chimpanzee to describe his new army. Mack Shell knew, though, he would call them the Lemurian Division, a link to his ancient utopia and his hopes for a new one. He took off his glasses and rubbed his eyes as if he was tired and strained. There was a wetness there, as if he had teared. But that couldn't be. Generals didn't cry. Particularly not this one.

"Our experiment with chimpanzees is over," Shell announced. "I have been ordered to close down Lemuria."

"But why?" Wagner asked, astounded. "You're on the verge of success. No. Except for a few missteps that are easily correctable, you have succeeded."

"America doesn't like the idea."

"What do you mean 'America doesn't like the idea'? The public knows nothing about it."

"They've done polls, Julius," the general answered. "Congress and the president do nothing without knowing how the American people will respond. When the questions involved experimenting on monkeys and saving the lives of American soldiers, nobody hesitated and the Lemuria Project was given the green light. The questions they're asking now are quite different."

"How can they be different? What kind of questions are they asking?"

"Let's ask your daughter. She probably represents a fair sampling of American opinion."

"Don't make me out to be the devil, General," Maggie retorted.

"I believe we should make human life better by genetic research. And experimenting on primates is ideal."

"Do you approve of animals killing humans?"

"No."

"Even if they're terrorists and murderers?" Mack countered.

"Well, what about capturing people? Or people who want to surrender? And what about trials—"

"You see," the general responded. "American opinion. But that wasn't the main reason people didn't like the idea of my chimpanzee army."

The general stood silent for a moment, looking for a way to explain something that he, too, still didn't quite understand. Then, he undid a ribbon from his jacket.

"Major," he ordered his adjutant, "step forward."

"Arnie, I couldn't have done this job without you. You put up with my temper, which was job enough. And when a bunch of egg-head scientists made impossible demands, you fulfilled them."

The general then pinned the ribbon to his aide's uniform shirt.

"I hereby award you this first Lemuria campaign ribbon for a job superbly performed."

Mack Shell then turned to Dr. Wagner and his daughter. "And that, my friend, is the reason Lemuria will be no more. The pollsters not only asked questions, they also rated how important the issues were to people. Sure, Americans abhor the deaths of young soldiers and want things done to prevent them. But the one thing they were not willing to give up in any scenario were their heroes. America is all about heroes. It just wouldn't be the same country without them. And no hairy chimpanzee is ever going to get an Independence Day ticker-tape parade down Main Street."

> *And God said to them, "Be fruitful and multiply, fill the earth and subdue it; and rule over the fish of the sea, the bird of the sky, and every living thing that moves on the earth."*
> —Genesis 1:28

CHAPTER FORTY

The night, as usual, was pitch-black with a trillion bright stars overhead. McGraw sat on the beach at the edge of the outgoing tide. Fala sat beside him. They were on a tiny dot of an island in a great sea on a tiny blue pebble planet, no more significant in the universe than the specks of sand on the bottom of their feet. After meeting with Julius Wagner, the general had gone on to break the news to Colonel McGraw. And, he gave him new orders. It was not an order that McGraw relished carrying out, and he made the most intelligent arguments he could to alter it. But the general made it clear. There would be no reprieves from this order. McGraw was a soldier who had received unpleasant commands before. He would carry out this one, as well. The general made one more thing clear. Link McGraw would not be returning to Leavenworth. He was too valuable an officer.

"Even if I can't get you reinstated, Colonel," the general promised, "you will continue to be my 'go to' man. You may have to pretend to be my Filipino houseboy—but you're not going back."

There was a chattering in the nearby chimp encampment. It was nothing unusual. His men were—*no*, McGraw suppressed that thought. He had caught himself thinking that time and again. They were his "troops" but not his "men." They were not human.

"Do you smell it?" Fala asked. "Do you think they do?"

More than eight hundred baby chimps had been euthanized during the day. Their bodies, along with a huge assortment of embryos and other genetic materials, were being disposed of in biomedical waste incinerators. Behind him, McGraw could still see the smoke curling into the starlit sky.

"Sure, they do," McGraw replied. "But do they know what it means? In World War II, the Jews walked passively into gas chambers past chimneys spewing the remains of their families and friends. And most didn't know. I don't think they know. I hope they don't."

"Link, in this last week I've been reading a lot about chimpanzees and this genetic research. If humans and chimps are over ninety-eight percent genetically identical to us, how come they have ten percent more DNA than us?"

"I don't know," McGraw replied, obviously distraught at was happening. "The science geeks have left a lot of unanswered questions. You know what's interesting, though," he went on, "every primate—chimps, orangutans, gorillas—doubles the birth weight of their brains from birth to adulthood. We humans—we triple ours."

"So?"

"Well, my chimps, they've been measuring them. Some have nearly tripled their brain weight, as well."

McGraw had mentioned those facts and more when he argued

with General Shell to save his troops.

"Their DNA is nearly identical to ours, and we've made them even more like us," McGraw pressed his argument before the general.

"They're not human, Link," Shell responded. "Just because their DNA is ninety-nine percent like ours doesn't make them ninety-nine percent human. Our DNA is about seventy-five percent similar to a worm's. And a worm is not seventy-five percent human. I can't save worms, and I can't save your chimps."

"Sir, would the cavalry have ever considered killing their horses? Or the dogs that sniff out bombs and our men lying under rubble, would we be so cavalier in doing away with them? These animals have served us well. They deserve better."

He had felt like Abraham pleading with God to save Sodom and Gomorrah—if but for ten righteous souls. But the general had orders, too. The decision was made. The "how to" was not.

"You know, I never told anyone this," McGraw continued with Fala, "but when we were in the field, just me and my troops, I used to read them children's bedtime stories to relax them."

"Did they understand?"

"I don't know, but they didn't like it when I read the same story a second time and changed the ending."

There was a collective sigh. McGraw gently stroked Fala's hair, but she abruptly pulled away.

"I can't be with you when we all leave here," she said. "I have to be with him."

"If you fall in love with somebody else, it's not your fault."

"No, you don't understand," she said remorsefully. "I still love him."

Fala stood and kissed McGraw gently on the cheek.

"*Astaghfir Allah*," she said in farewell. "God forgive me for lusting after you—my monkey man."

He took her hand and held it tight. While his heart told him not to let go, he knew when a battle was lost and it was time to retreat. He kissed her hand, one last time, and she departed.

> *Imagination is the beginning of creation.*
> *You imagine what you desire, you will what you*
> *imagine, and at last you create what you will.*
> —George Bernard Shaw

CHAPTER
FORTY-ONE

Withdrawals, Mack Shell thought. That had always been his specialty.

It would take only a few days to return Diego Garcia, BIOT—British Indian Ocean Territory—back into the sleepy military outpost it had been a decade earlier. Huge air force jumbo cargo jets landed with the frequency of a major airport for several days—ferrying personnel and equipment back to the United States. The advanced science buildings were gutted. In months ahead, universities throughout the country would be reaping the benefits as a great deal of very expensive scientific equipment was listed on the Internet for sale for pennies on the dollar.

Although the maps called it Diego Garcia, those who came to work and live on the island for years came to call it Lemuria. Many resented the end of their time in "paradise." And if anyone was looking to place blame, it was understandable they might exorcise their anger against those they viewed as interlopers on their island. General Shell had Fala, Krantz, and Maggie Wagner on the first plane out. It was a six-hour flight on a C-130 to Singapore and then on to the United States on a commercial flight.

From the air, Fala saw the base garbage barge. A tug was towing it out to sea. The barge was as big as a football field—ninety-one meters in overall length, twenty-seven meters wide. Its shell was six meters above the waterline. The barge was loaded with a mountain of garbage—the detritus of over five thousand military and scientific personnel on the island. Scampering atop the pile were several hundred brown figures, and Fala instantly knew the plan. These were the chimps of Lemuria, and McGraw was towing them out to sea to drown. She trembled. She felt nauseated. Trying to put the picture out of her mind, she walked back to the rear of the aircraft where Krantz was strapped to a gurney. He was conscious but sedated with several intravenous lines running in fluids and antibiotics. She took his hand and squeezed it hard.

"Some adventure, huh?"

Krantz exercised a weak smile.

She held up a small wooden object with a carved moon-shaped face at one end and fork prongs at the other.

"It's a barrette. I found it at an abandoned construction site on the north end of the island. You know, the original inhabitants of the island were not from Mauritania or the Seychelles. They were slaves from East Africa—judging from this piece, probably from Somalia or Mozambique."

Fala then held up some photographs. "And there were probably much older civilizations on the island. I found these petroglyphs."

Krantz studied the photos. Petroglyphs were drawings carved

into rock. They were prehistoric, usually Neolithic symbols, a form of pre-writing used in communication approximately ten to twelve thousand years ago by the classical cavemen. The drawings were either easy to decipher, like pictures of animals, or, after millenniums of cultural separation, near impossible to decipher. But through his drug-hazed eyes, Krantz clearly saw what these images represented. They were pictures of troops in formation, of airplanes, and dead humans. These were not petroglyphs carved by some ancient cavemen, but modern drawings made by chimpanzees who were recording their history. *Recorded history is the hallmark of human civilization,* Krantz thought. *These chimpanzees are not millions of years behind us in evolution. They're perhaps now just ten thousand years behind.*

Fala set the photos aside. Krantz had tried to speak, but his morphine pump weighed his lids shut and he fell asleep again. *That's best,* she thought. *When he wakes, he'll be feeling better and this horrid adventure will be our own ancient history.* She was anxious to resume their old life—archaeologists in search of the truth of the past. Other than being together, she wanted no more to do with the world of the present.

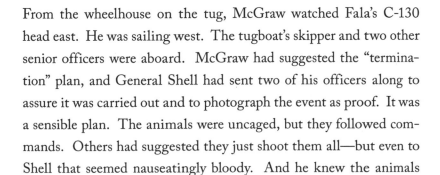

From the wheelhouse on the tug, McGraw watched Fala's C-130 head east. He was sailing west. The tugboat's skipper and two other senior officers were aboard. McGraw had suggested the "termination" plan, and General Shell had sent two of his officers along to assure it was carried out and to photograph the event as proof. It was a sensible plan. The animals were uncaged, but they followed commands. Others had suggested they just shoot them all—but even to Shell that seemed nauseatingly bloody. And he knew the animals

could be vicious. One or two could get away and maim or kill soldiers or civilians. And then there was the mess. No, McGraw's plan
was simple and clean. There would be no need to bury or incinerate
the bodies. They would simply disappear into the sea.

McGraw watched his former "command" frolicking on the
mounds of garbage on the barge. If they didn't find things worthy of
eating, they found plenty of things for play. The tug captain wanted
to turn back about twenty miles offshore, but McGraw insisted they
sail on for several more hours. When they were nearly fifty miles
from Diego Garcia with no land in sight, no other ships, McGraw
released the tow rope. The barge floated free. His two chaperones
prepared to video the event. McGraw had set explosive charges on
the hull of the barge. With a nod for the officers to begin filming,
he hit the switch on a remote and set them off, rupturing airtight
compartments in the hull. The barge filled with water and began
to quickly settle under the water. Soon, hundreds of monkeys were
swimming frantically amidst the garbage. McGraw knew from what
he read that chimpanzees did not like to swim. Their stocky bodies prevented them from being good swimmers. They had enjoyed
splashing in the surf, but he had never seen them swim and never
taught them to. Clearly several were already drowning.

"Semp fah, semp fah!" several of the animals began to yell.

"What are they yelling?" one of the captains asked.

"I don't know," the other replied, turning to McGraw for an answer.

"Words. I taught them some words."

"What?"

"Semper fi, semper fi," McGraw repeated. *Semper fidelis*, the
motto of the U.S. Marine Corps. It was Latin and meant "always
faithful."

"Do we need to see this out, Captain?" McGraw asked his escort and videographer. The officer knew the work that Colonel McGraw had accomplished with these animals. And seeing the colonel's chin tremble, the captain knew McGraw was drowning inside, as well.

"I've got enough."

McGraw moved to the helm of the tug, turned the boat east, and gunned the engine. He wanted to be far away very soon. Ten minutes later, the scene of the crime was well out of sight.

There were twelve watertight compartments on the shallow-keeled garbage barge. McGraw's explosives had ruptured four, enough to sink a ship holding two hundred tons of cargo. But empty, the ship could still stay afloat if only half those watertight compartments remained intact. McGraw had spent a long night doing the math and praying he was right. At a depth of two hundred feet, the sea had finally swept away the tons of garbage. The barge then ended its descent and slowly began to rise. More than half of his chimpanzees had already drowned when the great barge erupted to the surface. The survivors frantically clambered aboard.

McGraw had spent an informative afternoon the day before with the base meteorologist, an army lifer who didn't know the front end of a gun. McGraw chatted him up about some vague combat missions. That kind of talk made the weatherman feel more like one of the "warrior" class. In exchange, McGraw got a quick but useful education on air and ocean currents. Fifty miles offshore and south of the island of Diego Garcia, they would be at the edge of the Agulhas current. Except for the Gulf Stream, the Agulhas was the swiftest of all the world's ocean currents. The warm Agulhas ran west—and unfortunately south, as well. McGraw had taken a gamble. The current would either quickly carry the great barge west to the east coast of Africa—to Somalia, Kenya, Tanzania, Mozambique, or even the island of Madagascar, places with terrain and climate where his troops could survive—or the current could carry the barge south, to the freezing waters of Antarctica.

His orders were to sink a barge in the middle of the ocean and dispose of an experiment. Colonel Link McGraw had followed his orders. If his "experimental" animals survived, it would be because of a miracle—and the fortunate scientific pairing of physics and oceanography.

———————

Mack Shell had not been immune to the emotional and logical arguments posed by Link McGraw. But he, too, had orders—from a commander-in-chief. In the days preceding the "drowning," Mack trekked alone through the chimp compound. Despite the "accident," he wasn't afraid of these animals. He went looking for solace. He wanted to see animals and animal behaviors. Indeed, most of the chimps just lay about on the ground, some in their own filth, or just staring vacantly at nothing. And it pleased him.

"Am I a god?" he mused. "I have the power to create living beings and destroy them." At times he would stop and close his eyes. He wanted to listen, to hear. This was Lemuria, and if there was any place on earth where creatures could commune with their thoughts alone, this was it.

"Speak to me of your righteousness," he demanded, sprinkling his thoughts like seed in the air. But his mind remained silent of anything incoming and he walked on. Then, he stopped to watch two of the chimps groom each other. One stopped and stared back at him. The animal reached out and plucked some debris, a piece of a fallen leaf, from his hair and with a gentle fingertip tried to clean the birth-mark from Shell's cheek.

Shell smiled. "That's Sicily," he said. "It won't come off."

Shell began to walk away when the chimp called after him. He abruptly stopped to look back.

"What?" the general asked.

The animal tilted his head and proffered a chimpanzee's congen-itally amusing ear to ear toothy smile. "Sissy," the chimp murmured again. This time Shell heard him clearly.

Nothing happened on Lemuria of which Mack Shell was unaware. So, when Colonel McGraw delved into the design configuration of barges and chatted with the base meteorological officer, Shell knew. But he had given his orders and said no more. McGraw was a like a good son. He made him proud. But more important, Link McGraw understood the magic of Lemuria and his heart was pure.

Sissy, Shell thought. *Only my best friends ever called me that.*

> *God hangs the greatest weights upon the smallest wires.*
> —Sir Francis Bacon

CHAPTER FORTY-TWO

It was drizzling when Joshua Krantz exited the American Museum of Natural History on the Upper West Side of Manhattan. He had been doing research there in their basement archives for several weeks. He ran with a limp across the street to the corner of Eighty-first Street and Central Park West and tried to hail a taxi. He still had a limp. One of the animal bites he had sustained eight months earlier had become infected, and after they had debrided his wounds and pumped him full of antibiotics for weeks, he had recovered. But with scarring, he still favored the leg. He was in a hurry to get uptown. Fala was pregnant, and he had just gotten a cell phone call that there was a problem. She was being taken to Mount Sinai Hospital on One-hundredth Street between Madison and Fifth. It was a short cab ride to the medical center on the other side of Central Park and just a few blocks uptown. Getting a cab was impossible. It was a damn drizzle, Krantz grumbled inside—a petty sun shower. But as soon as a drop of water fell from the sky, no New Yorker would tolerate walking anymore. Too much suede and leather at risk, he thought. Everyone was hailing cabs. Damn the leg, Krantz thought, and he began his wobbly jog across the park, past the Jacqueline Kennedy Onassis Reservoir, and out the other side at Eighty-sixth Street. He had been in New York for sixth months now and was familiar with all the landmarks. He hobbled by the Guggenheim and the Jewish Museum. He was almost there.

Fala was due in another month. That was one of several reasons they had come to New York. Although she had wanted to be near her family in Cairo, Joshua didn't feel comfortable—as an ex-*Aman* agent—spending months in an Arab den. Krantz suggested they live in Jerusalem. But Fala, as much as she loved him, didn't want to give birth to a *sabra*—a native-born Israeli. The solution came easily after her first ultrasound. Her doctors felt there was some possibility of fetal abnormalities. The measurements they took of head circumference, head to rump length, and fetal age were abnormal. They suggested other studies such as amniocentesis to look for genetic abnormalities but Fala declined. It didn't matter what the tests showed. Abortion was not an option. Whatever gift Allah had decided to bestow upon her, she would accept.

Krantz arrived at Mount Sinai soaked. He didn't know if he was wet from the rain or sweat. He sighed heavily to catch his breath and calm his nerves. His wife was in premature labor. He was there to be her strength. But they had already taken her to surgery for an emergency caesarian section.

She had ruptured her membranes and there was some fetal irritability, a delivery room nurse explained. Krantz tried to remain calm. The baby was only one month premature. He knew babies that young survived all the time. And anyway, Mount Sinai had a neonatal intensive care unit, as well. Fala was in the hands of the best doctors in one of the best hospitals in the world. He walked over to the hospital chapel anyway.

In the operating room, everything was quick and routine. The doctors and nurses had performed a thousand similar "crash" C-sections. Anesthesia was rapid, the prep quick, and unhesitant incisions were made through skin and then the uterine wall. In a minute, they had the distressed newborn in hand and the umbilical cord cut. The infant did not cry out, but it did take a single breath—and that would be recalled as the most remarkable fact. Taking a breath on its own, the baby could not be declared stillborn. That single breath was the definition that it had lived. Despite the unusual appearance of the newborn, the OR crew worked frantically to resuscitate the dying child. They intubated, suctioned, performed cardiac compressions, infused drugs first through the endotracheal tube and then through an intravenous line established in the newborn's umbilical cord. The staff had seen unusual, horrid births before—conjoined twins, anencephalics, limbless infants. This baby was a new experience. The child had the puffy pink cheeks of a newborn but a small-sized head and high, overriding arched brows; most remarkably, it was covered in fine hair from head to foot. *A monkey child*, the doctor thought.

Joshua Krantz was shown his dead child and immediately he suspected what horrific and unusual events had occurred. He asked that the dead baby not be shown to Fala when she awoke. He would tell her it was stillborn and no more. That grief would be enough to handle. He asked that a pathology study be performed, including DNA sampling. And he particularly wanted a tissue sample sent to a geneticist at Stanford, Dr. Julius Wagner.

CHAPTER
FORTY-THREE

It had not been particularly difficult to rehabilitate Dr. Wagner's reputation. His disappearance to head the secret Lemuria Project was revealed. But when it made headlines, there was no mention of any army division of chimpanzees. Instead, Lemuria was advertised as the president's grand gamble to rid the world of cancer and AIDS and Alzheimer's.

"Just as Einstein forewarned Franklin Roosevelt of the potential of the atomic bomb," the president announced, "Dr. Wagner, one of our foremost scientists and winner of the Nobel Prize, informed me that we were on the verge of great discoveries in medicine and genetics. 'We are on the cusp,' he told me, 'of eliminating the great scourges of human life.' But this great leap forward, he warned me, would be endangered if left to competitive greed among multinational pharmaceutical companies anxious just to reap profits, or other nations who have a track record of stealing the intellectual property of others and calling it their own. I elected to invest not only in America's future, but in the future of all mankind."

For weeks after the president's announcement, Dr. Wagner announced one new scientific advance after another. The patents and copyrights were owned by the United States government and made freely available to anyone. It was a great humanitarian gesture applauded by every nation, every person in the world. And just as importantly for the president, it assured his reelection.

The one person who was initially most unhappy about Dr. Wagner's rebirth was Nathan Stumpf. No dead doctor. No life insurance money. Despite an interesting adventure, he was as broke as ever. But those doldrums quickly ended. Because he had taken such good care of his daughter, Dr. Wagner used his significant influence to get Stumpf the job as head of security for Stanford University. He also began to get quite a few government consulting jobs. Nate Stumpf was a man who usually had plenty of things to say, but he quickly came to learn how lucrative not saying them could be. There was one more significant reward.

"I don't know why I didn't find you handsome before," Maggie said, as she cuddled with him on her couch and played with his curly hair.

"You were distracted," he said. "You thought you're father had been murdered."

"I never paid you, either," she smiled.

"I've been paid," he said, kissing her neck and fondling her breasts.

Indeed, he had been well paid. Nate Stumpf had a newfound prestige, a new wardrobe, a sporty new car, straight and shiny new teeth, and perhaps best of all, he had the girl.

When Mack Shell heard about Fala al-Shohada's unfortunate childbirth experience, he felt some guilt but also perhaps relief that he had put an end to Lemuria. He had authorized the abductions of both Fala and Joshua Krantz. At the time, they had both been asking too many of the right questions. Shell had suggested the solution.

Colonel McGraw had trained several pairs of chimps to perform abductions. Four chimps had been easily transported into the Philippines as zoo animals and placed into a local chimpanzee sanctuary. Unfortunately, they had caused considerable disruption there when they escaped. However, they weren't prevented from completing their mission. They rendezvoused on schedule with their commander, McGraw, who secreted them in oversized luggage and brought them into the Manila hotel. From there, it was easy to get them into the right room, where they anticipated the arrival of the Israeli colonel and his Egyptian paramour. The manpower, or rather chimp-power, was relatively overwhelming. An adult chimp had the strength of seven grown men. When Krantz left so quickly, the teams dealt with Fala alone. While one chimpanzee restrained her, the other slapped a prepared syringe into her thigh, injecting a high dose of ketamine, an anesthetic agent chemically related to the hallucinogen PCP. The sedative-hypnotic drug would incapacitate her for sixty minutes. She would be amnesic of the event. The team was, of course, adept at climbing. They carried their victim along the outside of the building to the roof. There, they entered the hotel's elevator shaft and, holding their quarry, made their way down eight stories to a garage where McGraw waited with a recovery truck.

Once Fala and Krantz entered their hotel room, all the events were scheduled to unfold in exactly ten minutes. As long as there were no unexpected occurrences, McGraw knew his animals would perform exactly as rehearsed. But Krantz was not there, and there were four chimps to accomplish the task. They reached the bottom of the shaft in six minutes, not ten. There they would sit and wait for the exact time to exit. They had an infallible mental clock. Fala, however, had the misfortune to be in the middle of her menstrual cycle, that time when she was ovulating. She was secreting phero-mones, a virtually imperceptible sexually alluring scent that evolution had refined in mammals to attract a mate at exactly the appropriate time for conception. McGraw's chimps were not only chockful of new human genes and capabilities, but they still preserved their in-nate superior qualities, including a better olfactory sense. They were helpless in avoiding Fala's chemical lure.

Mack Shell was horrified when he imagined his animals rap-ing a woman. Thank God, he thought, she would never know. He also knew the encounter was brief. The primatologists had taught him a lot—an aroused chimp ejaculates in 4.3 seconds. If the deed was done, it was done fast. Fala's pregnancy also answered one other gnawing question. Why had McGraw's well-disciplined chimps at-tacked Joshua Krantz? The chimpanzees that attacked Joshua Krantz were the ones that had impregnated Fala. Joshua Krantz was attacked because he was a competing male. He put the future of their progeny at risk. It was a simple choice—survival of the species.

Julius Wagner also came to know what had happened. It was easy to surmise when he examined the dead infant's DNA. But it wasn't the terrible vision of bestiality that disturbed him. It was the fact that an interspecies breeding of man and monkey had survived. The child had taken a breath. Scientifically that should never have been possible. Humans and apes could not produce offspring because they each had a different number of chromosomes. Chimpanzees had forty-eight X, or forty-eight chromosomes. Humans had forty-six. Evolutionary theorists suspected that millions of years ago our chimp ancestors fused two chromosomes into one and that mutation resulted in the beginning of the new "human" species. Dr. Wagner's experiments had been designed to mutate the animal for the purpose of performing a particular function—becoming an animal warrior. Somehow, and he had no idea yet how, those alterations had also altered the ape's gametes, or sperm cells, so that it could successfully fertilize a human egg. Most hybrids were sterile—like a mule, a cross between a donkey and a horse. If this child had lived, would it have been sterile? He didn't know.

A hybrid had been born—a humanzee. Had a new species been created? Humanity, Dr. Wagner believed, was an evolutionary accident. He would not debate religion and would willingly concede that man could have been designed by God. But if God had designed man, he certainly made his creation seem like an accident nevertheless. If the world, however, discovered that Julius Wagner had played God and was responsible for creating a human-ape hybrid—a creature that spoke, that reasoned, that had emotions —he would be vilified by every scientist, politician, theologian . . . everyone. But far worse, the foundations of science, politics, and theology would crumble. All men are created equal, was the world's mantra. It was a noble thought that was still nigh impossible for men to live by. How would man ever accept another living creature being equal to them?

Lemuria was a myth that men had tried to make into a new reality. Julius Wagner was too much the scientist to bring himself to destroy a new species, so he placed the remaining DNA of the first humanzee in Stanford's cryogenic storage facility. For the time being, Lemuria would remain a myth.

> *Man that is born of a woman is of few days, and full of trouble. He cometh forth like a flower, and is cut down; he fleeth also as a shadow, and continueth not.*
> —Job 14:1–2

EPILOGUE

S even years later, Link McGraw had his star. He was a brigadier general assigned to direct another peacekeeping mission in Southern Somalia. For decades one warring clan after another fought for a dwindling piece of fertile land. And year after year, the United Nations or other benevolent states would send soldiers to try to stop the slaughter. But the land was clearly dying. A country that had always been principally desert was being enveloped by more desert with each passing year. When there weren't monsoons and floods, there were droughts or dust storms. It was almost always intolerably hot. And there was always famine. Unless the world poured its wealth into irrigating a desert and educating people to care for the land, this country would never see peace. Short of that, McGraw knew he was on a humanitarian mission that would never end.

His troops had retaken Kismayo Airport. Located ten kilometers northeast of the city, the airport had been a former Somali air force base. Over the years it seemed just a pawn traded back and forth between governments, warlords, and peacekeepers. This week it was McGraw's turn to control the derelict airfield. The roads in Southern Somalia were in terrible shape. Resupply along those routes was always dangerous and unreliable. With the airfield, he thought his men would be well supplied for a while.

The airfield bordered the ocean, and there was a strip of jungle to the south. He took a couple of Humvees and, with helicopter support, headed south to check his perimeter defenses. When he arrived, he found two platoons of his men well dug in and spaced. They had their backs to the airfield and the sea and were well prepared for any assault from a jungle area in front of them. But they were behaving strangely. They were tossing MREs, their ready-to-eat rations, into the tree line.

"Cavanaugh, what are you doing?"

A lieutenant popped to attention and saluted. "Sorry, sir. We were just trying to lure them out again."

Instinctively, McGraw pulled his M9 9mm Beretta pistol.

"There's no hostile contact, sir. They're monkeys."

And then he saw them—several chimpanzees, mothers with their white tail-tufted babies clinging to their backs. They grabbed the treats and darted back into the jungle. McGraw knew that the Pan troglodyte species of chimpanzee was native to eastern Africa. They were also rare and endangered. Feeding them would do no harm.

"All right, carry on." And McGraw turned to leave.

"You've got to see this one, sir."

The lieutenant retrieved one of his RLW (ration, lightweight) meals. Unlike MREs, these were precooked, dehydrated, and hermetically sealed packages. Unless the food was mixed with water, it tasted like and had the consistency of wood chips. And it took some doing to open them, as well. He tossed the RLW like a hand grenade into the woods. A moment later, a larger animal came out, a male, at least six feet tall. McGraw watched, entranced as were his men, as the chimp advanced to retrieve the packaged food. Chimps had arms longer than their legs, and stooped over, they traditionally "knuckle-walked." This one did not. It stood more upright, and when it did "knuckle-walk," it never let its right hand drag the ground. And then the animal did something even more remarkable; it picked up the RLW, tore open the package, and began spitting inside to "water" the contents. The chimp then mashed up the moistened contents and squeezed the contents into its mouth.

McGraw knew that chimps were smart. They often copied favorable behaviors. Was this something the animal had been taught? McGraw surprised his men when he began walking toward the animal.

"Sir," the lieutenant called after him. "Be careful. They might be dangerous."

"Don't worry, Lieutenant," McGraw replied facetiously. "I know my monkeys."

The general holstered his weapon and walked steadily forward, the animal eyeing him every step of the way. He stopped when he was but a chimp arm's length away. Was this one of his troops? No, this one was too young, maybe six or seven years old. The two creatures—man and ape—stared at each for a long moment. The chimp then turned and walked away. McGraw was about to depart as well when he had one more thought. He retrieved a candy bar from his pocket and threw it at the chimp. Although the animal had its back to him, it turned quickly, caught the treat in midair, and simply walked on. Was it just good timing, McGraw wondered, or was it synesthesia? No matter, he thought, that was a past life and he had to be back at his base camp before dusk. His covering choppers overhead nearly drowned out the call, but he was sure he had heard it and he turned again to peer into the jungle overgrowth.

"Semp fah," he heard the voice say again.

Hidden in the woods, behind myriad of shades of green, he glimpsed patches of gray. And then, for the briefest moment, he saw the eyes—an older chimpanzee was looking back at him.

"Semp fah," the general said and he raised his right hand slowly to his brow—a salute, a hello, and a farewell.

———————

After her miscarriage, Fala and Joshua settled in Cyprus. America, they both felt, was, well, too American—too arrogant, insular, and full of materialism. They also wanted to separate themselves from the turmoil of politics in the Middle East but yet be near to the heart of their interests, Mediterranean culture and archaeology. Cyprus was perfectly located for their work—an island cradled between the ancient cultures of Rome, Greece, Egypt, Israel, and the Islamic empires of the Middle East. They had a small home in the hills overlooking Nicosia, the capital. With the exception perhaps of Jerusalem, Nicosia was the only divided capital city in the world, the north controlled by Turkish Cypriots and the south by the Greeks, with the United Nations holding a demilitarized green zone between them.

Being neither Greek nor Turkish, they found themselves welcome in both worlds. Krantz also found himself welcome back into the world of Israeli intelligence and often flew home to consult.

Although there were no more antique weapons that required his expertise, *Aman* found his ability to think "out of the box" useful.

"What do you think?" General Echod asked, handing him a document with lots of blacked-out redactions, but whose language and source were clear. What he was reading came from American intelligence.

"Refugees fleeing small communities in the lower Juba region of southeastern Somalia are reporting the area as under the control of a new warlord. Contacts have been minimal . . . atrocities . . . casualties . . . their leader . . . a heavily bearded black man . . . stutters . . . wearing a camouflage garb . . . known as Colonel Maimun."

SPECIES	CHROMOSOME NUMBER
Fruit Fly	8
Dove	16
Snail	24
Earthworm	36
Cat	38
Human	46
Chimpanzee	48
Elephant	56
Cow	60
Horse	64
Chicken	78
Butterfly	380

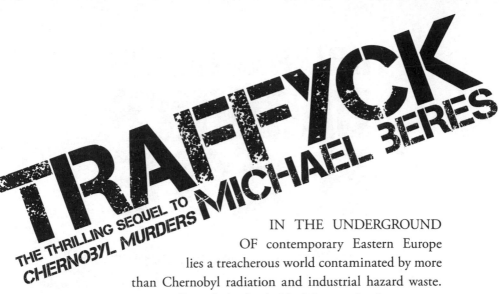

TRAFFYCK

THE THRILLING SEQUEL TO CHERNOBYL MURDERS
MICHAEL BERES

IN THE UNDERGROUND OF contemporary Eastern Europe lies a treacherous world contaminated by more than Chernobyl radiation and industrial hazard waste. As communism collapsed, the foothold of the social order gave way to a lurking subculture of child pornography and human trafficking in prostitution. *Traffyck*, as they say.

A former runaway and nightclub stripper, Mariya Nemeth was a discontented only child raised by her Hungarian mother in an Orthodox background. She pulled herself from the dredges of wretchedness to attend business school and marry Viktor Patolichev, a man she believed had abandoned his shady past. One day Mariya learned his past was present. Viktor had been murdered, a consequence of his sex trade operations.

When private investigator Janos Nagy, ex-militiaman, enters her life to probe the case in Kiev's Podil District, Mariya knows she has met the real passion of her life, a lover immersed in the romance of Gypsy culture. From Chicago's Humboldt Park to the Romanian Carpathian Mountains to the bleak abandonment of Ukraine, a frightening chain of events threatens to end Mariya's life as the truth unfolds. Together they must combat perversion and pleasure deemed unacceptable by educated society.

Savvy and perceptive, only Janos can protect her . . . if it isn't already too late.

ISBN# 978-160542105-6
Hardcover
US $24.95 / CDN $27.95
Thriller
Available Now
www.michaelberes.com

BRIAN ULLMANN
DARWIN'S RACE

No maps. No checkpoints. No support crews.

Darwin's Race is the most ambitious adventure race ever attempted, pitting twelve hardened racers against each other and the daunting elements of the world's deepest and unexplored gorge. The first to reach the top of the 22,000-foot Kuk Sur will claim a $2 million prize and the first summit of one of the last remaining unclimbed Himalayan peaks.

Conner Michaels, haunted by his brother's mysterious death on Kuk Sur six years earlier, decided to come out of seclusion to lead one of the teams and to once and for all determine what happened to his brother. On his team, Preston Child, the millionaire financier of the race, and his beautiful daughter, Malika, harbor their own dark reasons for descending into the gorge. And hotshot television producer Terrance Carlton, bent on a ratings bonanza, outfits each racer with a shoulder-mounted camera for live broadcasts around the world.

But as the racers plunge deeper into the legendary gorge, death follows. And as the carnage mounts in the treacherously remote mountains, the racers—and millions watching the tragedy unfold on television—realize the mist-shrouded gorge is not as uninhabited as they believed.

ISBN# 978-193475507-5
Mass Market Paperback
US $7.95 / CDN $8.95
Thriller
Available Now
www.myspace.com/BrianUllmann

THE JAKE HELMAN FILES
PERSONAL DEMONS

FROM THE AUTHOR OF *JOHNNY GRUESOME* GREGORY LAMBERSON

Jake Helman, an elite member of the New York Special Homicide Task Force, faces what every cop dreads—an elusive serial killer. While investigating a series of bloodletting sacrifice rituals executed by an ominous perpetrator known as The Cipher, Jake refuses to submit to a drug test and resigns from the police department. Tower International, a controversial genetic engineering company, employs him as their director of security.

While battling an addiction to cocaine, Jake enters his new high-pressure position in the private sector. What he encounters behind the closed doors of this sinister operation is beyond the realm of human imagination. Too horrible to contemplate, the experimentation is pure madness, the outcome a hell where only pain and terror reside. Nicholas Tower is not the hero flaunted on the cover of Time magazine. Beneath the polished exterior of this frontiersman on the cutting edge of science is a corporate executive surrounded by the creations of his deranged mind.

As Jake delves deeper into the hidden sphere of this frightening laboratory, his discoveries elicit more than stereotypical condemnation for unethical practices performed for the good of mankind. Sequestered in rooms veiled in secrecy is the worst crime the world will ever see—the theft of the human soul.

ISBN# 978-160542072-1

Mass Market Paperback

US $7.95 / CDN $8.95

Horror

Available Now

www.slimeguy.com

LEAPFROG

STEVE HENDRY

In a test to the human race, highly advanced aliens decide to offer free secrets that will enable universal space travel without time or distance constraints. Earth snaps at the challenge and collectively musters resources to develop the most advanced starship ever built on Earth, which is appropriately named, Leapfrog, for the technological jump over existing science. Unfortunately, corrupt secret services, greedy politicians, and overly wary generals condemn this mission from the start.

While in deep cryogenic sleep, the crew of Leapfrog encounters a disastrous meteor shower that destroys the main engines. Thousands of years pass while the stricken ship slowly meanders its way back to earth with two hundred and seventy five humans solidly frozen in deep suspended animation.

As the crew finally awakens, they find Earth is no longer the same. Seeking clues as to what has happened; the survivors attempt to re-colonize, only to discover that a new ultra-evolved creature now predominates and ruthlessly rules the top of the food chain. The explorers are forced to abandon their derelict starship and face a horrifying battle among cannibal Neanderthals and the ultra-evolved creatures, barely escaping with their lives.

ISBN# 978-193383650-8
Trade Paperback / Science Fiction
US $15.95 / CDN $17.95
Available Now
www.stevehendry.com

DAVIE HENDERSON
TUMORROW'S WORLD

A dozen years from now the world is at the tipping point of environmental catastrophe. Supercomputers have determined that much of what made the world wonderful is beyond saving, and life is only sustainable in logically administered communities where every resource is rationed, every action monitored to ensure it is in accordance with The Common Good. There are no more butterflies, no coral reefs, no rainbows. Only The Common Good.

Supercomputers have also formed a new global government, the EcoSystem, to cope with a new problem—division between Names (naturally born people) and Numbers (those who have been genetically engineered due to falling fertility rates).

The EcoSystem has become corrupted, however, a potentially fatal corruption which comes to light during the seemingly insignificant death of a plant prospector. The inquiry brings two detectives into conflict: Ben Travis, who can't match the intelligence of his Numbered partner, and "Perfect Paula," who can scarcely comprehend Ben's intuition and imagination. Then Ben discovers the randomly generated emotional flaw in Paula to make her seem more human: a belief in love.

Eventually, on the run in the ruins of a world in which people haven't been able to live for sixty years, Ben and Paula—and a handful of dazed survivors—must rediscover the lost reverence for nature, life, and love.

ISBN# 978-193383646-1
Trade Paperback
US $15.95 / CDN $17.95
Science Fiction
Available Now
www.daviehenderson.bravehost.com

CHASTISED FOR NOT COOPERATING WITH the oil company giant New World Petroleum, zoologist Cassidy Lowell is reassigned from the jungles of the Niger Delta to Yellowstone National Park, where wolves are disappearing. Jake Anderson, Special Forces operative, is working within the shadows of Cassidy's organization, Zoological Environmental Bio Research Agency. His mission? To determine the threatening connection between ZEBRA and NWP.

An alarming genetic mutation of the parvovirus is discovered: CPV-19: human parvovirus merged with canine. And the virus is loose in Yellowstone. Murder, execution, and deadly helicopter rides lead Jake and Cassidy down a road rife with double-crossing and an underlying plot that forces them back to the Niger Delta and into the heart of NWP.

This is the twenty-first-century gold rush—welcome to the dark side!

ISBN# 978-193475555-6
Hardcover
US $25.95 / CDN $28.95
Thriller
Available Now
www.juliekorzenko.com

Be in the know on the latest Medallion Press news by becoming a Medallion Press Insider!

<u>As an Insider you'll receive:</u>

• Our FREE expanded monthly newsletter, giving you more insight into Medallion Press

• Advanced press releases and breaking news

• Greater access to all of your favorite Medallion authors

Joining is easy, just visit our Web site at <u>www.medallionpress.com</u> and click on the Medallion Press Insider tab.

Want to know what's going on with
your favorite author or what new releases
are coming from Medallion Press?

Now you can receive breaking news,
updates, and more from Medallion Press
straight to your cell phone, e-mail, instant
messenger, or Facebook!

Sign up now at www.twitter.com/MedallionPress
to stay on top of all the happenings in and
around Medallion Press.

For more information
about other great titles from
Medallion Press, visit

 m e d a l l i o n p r e s s . c o m